THE THII
YEAR SCREAM

BOOK ONE

AFTER THE WAR......
IN THE SHADOWS OF PREJUDICE

By

FRANK THORLEY

Illustration by Chris

The Thirty Year Scream – Book 1
After the War......
In The Shadows of Prejudice

First paperback edition printed 2005 in the United Kingdom.

Third Revised Edition printed 2013 in the United Kingdom.

A catalogue record for this book is available from the British Library.

ISBN 978-0-9575021-0-9

Published by Thorley Publishing.
www.thirtyyearscream.com

For more copies of this book, please email:
info@thirtyyearscream.com

Printed in Great Britain.

To the Memory of my mother and father.

To the Memory of Doctor Maz.

and all the others lost along

the way.

INTRODUCTION

The Shadows of Prejudice lurk in the hearts of all men. Controlled by the strong, controllers of the weak, they have pervaded The Human Race since time immemorial. These instincts, basic to the survival of Individual, Family or Tribal Group, have been sublimated by the onset of Civilisation.

Once, our eye sought out the familiar and the unknown, the normal and the abnormal to trigger fight or flight, acceptance or ostracism.

Now, we live in an age when the Individual is governed by the constraints of Law and the morality of Creed. The weak and the infirm, those that are, or dare to be different; all share Society's protection.

These principles stem only from the mind; Father of Civilisation. But those base, primeval instincts remain. Locked away in our hearts, they show manifest in so many, different ways. Perverse reminders of our origins, they encompass everything from the eccentricities of Taste to The Hate of Man for his Fellow.

This account mirrors a post-war era; the story of parents, childhood, education and final passage into Manhood.

Now, in middle age, I write not to rail against the Shadows of Prejudice but to exorcise by revelation, the demons of my past. I write that the Scream be heard.

For; Maxine of the long, red hair, Bilbo; who said it could be done, and Howard; who showed it could be done.

The calendar so clearly defines the end of war.

For those untouched by its vile nature, war represents a mere ripple in the passage of time. For others, its victims, war brings pain unheralded, memory eternal to twist its poisoned dagger in the hearts and minds of their generations.

PART ONE

THE HAPPIEST DAYS OF YOUR

LIFE

"Do you ever find yourself talking with the dead?"

CHAPTER ONE: THE COUPLE

The Woman carefully closed the door behind her. She lowered the latch with slow deliberation, hands working to prevent the slightest noise. As if to frustrate her attempts at secrecy, yellow rays of light made their escape, piercing the cracks and chinks in the gnarled planks. Unhindered by their would-be captors, they darted out into the darkness, intent on betrayal.

On the grey flagstone in front of the House, she turned to face the Man. Even in the dim light, it was obvious that she was foreign to the region. Long, fine hair framed a face that, as yet unblemished by Fenland wind and winter, glowed smooth and white. Her hands, also, were like alabaster, delicate fingers more used to tapping at a keyboard than attending the chores of a country life. Taller than the Man, her height was exaggerated by the stone on which she stood. War and rationing had taken their toll on the slender figure, so the once-fashionable dress hung loosely about her. As she leaned forward to speak, a great gust of wind blew through the Yard, stealing her soft words.

"DO be careful", she repeated as loudly as she dared, mindful of the neighbours.

When she spoke, her accent was from the North, not of that desolate region.

The Man standing before her was short and squat. Even the bulk of the greatcoat that he wore could not hide his deep chest and powerful shoulders. Muscles, enlarged by years of farmwork, had been fine-hewn by his time at sea. Face, burnt by the sun, weathered by wind and salt air, was topped by a great mop of black curls. When he spoke, his country drawl and bass tones were in deep contrast to the Woman's voice.

"Get you on in, out of the cold, Joy. I've left a shilling on the mantelpiece. You'll have light. There's plenty of coal for the fire".

He moved towards the old bicycle that stood, propped in the entrance to the Shed.

"Be careful", the Woman pleaded.

"Don't worry. Everything will be fine".

He pushed the bicycle through the Yard and out into the roadway. As he turned the corner, the Woman moved back into the House. She gently closed the door, even though the wind now howled so loudly that she could have slammed it, unheard. Blankets across window and door trapped both heat and treacherous light. Safely inside, she gathered the money from above the bright fire then stooped to push the silver coin into the slot of the meter. It dropped through with a loud, metallic ring. The sound of the coin, spinning in the empty, metal box, echoed around the room.

She pulled the small chain that hung from the gas lamp in the ceiling. Now, light could not betray her husband's return. Besides, she would need the gas for cooking, should his foray be a successful one.

The Woman sat by the fire and waited. In the blue and yellow flames, her eyes reflected on better times, on times gone by, on times yet to come. She thought of her mother, sister and brother at home in the city. She dreamed of her husband, resplendent in blue and white, walking arm in arm through the great port. Kisses, as they lingered beneath the giant hulls of the grey warships. Her eyes moistened when she remembered; the brass bands at quayside as the destroyer glided into dock, her search for her Man among the sailors that lined its deck and her relief at his final, safe and victorious return. Now, her only dream for the future was that they should, one day soon, escape the misery of the House.

With the exception of the large, chalk dog that imperiously guarded the window, the Man's medals, with their bright ribbons, were the only objects of colour to grace the drab room. Pinned to the ancient wallpaper above the sideboard, they reflected twinkling stars of firelight into its darkest corners. Reminders; of oil-fuelled carnage in the North Atlantic, of Normandy's bloodied seas, of ice-laden convoys to Archangel. These were the Man's testaments to a world gone mad.

Still, the Woman sat and waited, waited for her husband's safe return.

CHAPTER TWO: THE HOUSE

The House was small. With its outbuildings and twin, next door, it formed a short terrace. These were the original buildings of the Yard.

The roof was made from grey slate and covered a single bedroom above the living room. Outside the bedroom was a small landing with staircase that led down to an alcove at the rear of the living-room. This alcove served as kitchen.

The living-room was poorly furnished. Two, dusty armchairs faced each other across the blue-tiled fireplace. One sat beneath the chalk dog. The other was pushed against the back wall of the 'kitchen'. Drop-leaf table with oilskin cloth, wooden chairs and sideboard crowded the room. Grey, 'Red Cross' blankets hung from nails over door and window; improvised reinforcement for the threadbare curtains. Even so, every gust of wind from the Yard billowed curtains and blankets into the room. Its cold breath flickered gaslight, sent shadows scurrying across the bare flagstones.

There was neither lighting nor plumbing in the makeshift kitchen. On a table, next to the gas cooker, stood a large, white, enamelled bucket. Apart from when it rained, this was the only source of fresh water inside the House. It was filled from a communal tap in the Yard. On a night such as this, if the

Woman needed more water, she would thaw the tap with boiling water from the kettle.

Very little daylight braved the shadows of the House. The Woman usually prepared food in the living-room, shelling peas and peeling vegetables by the fireside. The cupboard beneath the stairs served as larder when there was food enough to store.

Wardrobe, sagging bed and sea chest stood on the bare boards of the bedroom. Its window, also, was protected by the 'Red Cross'. On a table at the side of the bed, stood a large, battery-powered radio; the House's only concession to the Twentieth Century.

This place, she called 'Home'.

Here, with only hunger and the howling wind for company, the Woman waited and waited. Waited, because she loved a poor man.

CHAPTER THREE:

HOME IS THE SAILOR ....HOME FROM THE SEA

He lowered his head and pedalled into the wind. He ignored the cold. It did not bother him. It was the wind. It lashed at his face and hands, sucked the very air from his lungs. As he cleared the last of the Town's buildings, it gathered strength, making the wheels of the bicycle ever more difficult to turn. A thousand invisible fists beat at his chest, forcing him backwards.

He fought on. Standing on the pedals, he used all of his weight to turn them. He was determined that the wind would not be his master. It whistled and jeered when, breathless, he dismounted. But it had not won. He carried on, pushing the bicycle, head bent over the handlebars. He did not abandon it because it would be needed for the return journey.

He turned from the road to follow a track between the fields. Numbed fingers fumbled for the torch mounted on the handlebars. He turned it on. Although he had known this track since childhood, he still needed the bright eye of the torch to guide him. For he knew that the countryside holds hidden dangers. It remains the same to the town dweller. He sees only roads and buildings in his search for greenery. However, the country man knows that the land is ever changing in its minutiae, that every change has a significance or consequence. Especially in the dark, when a collapsed dyke or fallen gate spells disaster. Torch in hand, he abandoned the bicycle and made his way across the dark fields.

There were few trees, only hedgerows and drainage ditches to bar his path. He followed the lines of hawthorn to where he had affixed the first trap. His heart sank when he saw that it was still set; bait stolen. Using a stick cut from the hedgerow, he tapped until the wicked teeth snapped shut. He reset the trap, replacing the lost bait with stale bread from his pocket, prising back the steel jaws in readiness.

The thief had not foiled the second trap. Pinned by the neck, head almost severed from its body, lay a rat; the size of a small dog. He amputated its tail with a single cut from his sheath knife and left the body for the crows. He did not reset the trap. It would be useless until cleaned. At least, the bounty for the tail would go towards the price of a loaf of bread. But rats were not his chosen quarry.

His heart leaped when he came to the third trap. A buck rabbit, body stiff with death, stared back at him in the torchlight. Only the mangled leg in the trap bore witness to the violence of its death struggle.

Traps and torch in one hand, rabbit held by its ears in the other, he carried on, to the next trap. It, also, clutched a hapless victim. Two rabbits!!! He returned to the bicycle and hung both traps and rabbits from the handlebars.

Frozen fingers plucked at the thick bailing string that secured his short-handled fork to the crossbar. Armed with the fork and a Hessian sack from the basket of the bicycle, he made his way back into the fields.

He passed by the mounds of potatoes safe in their straw houses. He would not take what others had gathered nor by such a theft betray his passing. Instead, he moved into the first field. Walking between the rows, he took great care not to trample the crops. In the middle of the field, he halted. Bending from the waist, he plunged the fork through the white crust of frost and into the hard, black soil. The shock jarred wrist and elbow but nothing could prevail against his powerful arm.

He prised out three then four more handfuls of carrots. Shaking off the loose earth, he dropped them into his sack, leaving their green fronds intact. From the next field, he took potatoes. Next, parsnips and swedes disappeared into the bag. He even managed to salvage a few onions, rare survivors of the frost. Nowhere was there trace of his theft. Rats and rabbits would bear the blame for the occasional gaps in the long, green lines.

He sailed along, booty safe on board; his old enemy, the wind, now a slave at his back.

The smell from the stewpot drifted up the stairs. The Woman, belly swollen from the food, slept in his arms; long, brown hair cascading across the pillow and onto his chest.

In the darkness, teeth clenched, white in a bitter grimace. Tears welled and sparkled in his eyes. He had never before stolen. Not in his entire life.

Carefully, he slipped from beneath the bed-clothes and groped his way down the creaking staircase. In the light of the fire's dying embers, he plucked the medals from the wall. He folded the ribbons then stowed both ribbons and medals, safe in their little cardboard boxes, into the bottom drawer of the sideboard. He would leave them there … forever.

With sudden fury, he drove his fist into the wall. Over and over again, he punched the hard brickwork until finally, his tears escaped, streaming down to a mouth locked in a silent scream.

Awakened in the room above, the Woman shuddered her fear and misery.

CHAPTER FOUR: THE SHED

"Times are better, now", the Woman thought as she entered the Shed.

Her husband was working in one of the many 'gangs' that harvested crops in the area. She could now afford a few luxuries; perfumed soap and lipstick, even a few cigarettes bought on the 'Black' market. The radio broadcasts hinted that rationing might soon end.

Inside the Shed, at its far end, was the toilet. This was housed in its own brick cubicle with wooden roof and door.

By the entrance to the Shed stood a copper boiler, also set in bricks. Heated from a fire beneath, it vented through a stone chimney in the roof. There was no plumbing in the Shed, so toilet and boiler were serviced with buckets of water hauled in from the Yard. The rest of the building was filled by a large heap of coal in one corner and a jumble of bicycles and work tools in the other. From a nail above the coal heap, hung a long, galvanised bath.

On a Sunday, which was bath night, the Man would carry buckets of steaming water from Shed into House, buckets of cold from Yard into Shed. Thus, he would refill the boiler in readiness for the following day's laundry, while his wife bathed before the open fire. She loved him for this consideration.

What his strong arms could carry in minutes saved her slight frame a long and arduous task.

Although it was neither bath day nor laundry day, the Woman knelt to kindle a fire beneath the boiler. Then, bucketful by bucketful, she slowly filled it with water. Once the fire was blazing, she pulled the bath from its place on the wall. With great difficulty, she dragged it into the House.

CHAPTER FIVE: MRS. P.

The adjoining house of the terrace was occupied by Mr. and Mrs. Smith, an elderly couple. The terrace formed one side of the Yard.

Thirty feet away, across the Yard, stood a larger house and outbuildings. This fronted onto the main road. With its own fenced garden, it formed the opposite boundary of the Yard. In this house, Mrs. P. lived with her husband and father.

Mrs. P. was a large, plump woman in her middle years. Her face was care-worn and morose. Hair, prematurely white, contrasted with the dark clothes that she always wore. For this was a woman in constant mourning. If there ever was a victim of war, it was she.

Her father was crippled, legs lost to a land-mine on the Somme. She had given up her sons; both dead on the beaches of Normandy. Hers was a life that looked only backwards; an endless round of care for father and grief for her dead boys. Her husband had become little more than a drone, feelings eclipsed by his wife's apathy towards him. Each day, he returned home from the farm where he worked, only to eat and sleep.

Mrs. P. missed none of the comings and goings in the Yard. Several, unnecessary trips to her garden had allowed her to witness the struggle to fill, empty and return the bath to its place in the Shed. Peeking from behind the curtains of her front window, she had watched the Woman, dressed in her Sunday best clothes, pedal into the Town. She despised the Woman for her strange accent and 'fancy' clothes. She envied her youth and perceived happiness.

On the Woman's return, Mrs. P. had resumed her 'gardening'. Now, as she leaned over her fence to speak, she saw the 'glow' in the Woman. Her heart seethed with jealousy and bitterness at the thought.

"Good afternoon, Joyce", she said.

"Good afternoon, Mrs. P.", the Woman answered from her seat on the flagstone.

The low, autumn sun dazzled her, making her squint as she spoke. Hand shielded eyes as she smiled into the sunlight. This child-like pose served only to emphasize her youthfulness, make the 'glow' ever more obvious.

"I saw you, going out, earlier".

"Yes, I went into Town".

"Been to the doctor's, haven't you?"

"Whatever makes you say that, Mrs. P.?"

The smile was gone, the Woman's face hesitant, confused, like a child caught in a lie.

"Either you've been to the doctor's or you've got yourself a fancy man!! Going up Town on a Thursday, dressed to the nines!!! It being early closing day and all".

"Perhaps, I was just visiting a few friends?"
The Woman's face had flushed red at the implied insult. She had no friends in the Town, so her answer had seemed hollow. She could find no words with which to parry the incisive questions that followed, until;

"Besides, half the Town knows that you're expecting!"

"And what does the other half know, Mrs. P.?" The Woman replied angrily before running into the House and slamming the door.

Nobody else had guessed her secret. However, that evening, she did not wait for her husband's return. Instead, she walked down Canal Street to meet him.

That she should be the first with the joyous news.

CHAPTER SIX: THE GOOD NEWS.

The Man dropped down from the back of the 'Dodge' to where Herb, his friend and workmate, waited.

"O.K., Jack", he called, slapping his hand against the wooden planks of the tailgate.

"See you all, tomorrow, lads".

"See you".

"See you, Lefty".

"Certainly!"

The lorry moved off, towards the centre of the Town. Hessian sacks containing tools and vacuum flasks, over their shoulders, the two men began the short walk to their homes.

Beneath the mask of sweat and dust that covered his face, Herb could have been the Man's brother. He sported the same, dark curls and ruddy complexion. Although not barrel-chested like his companion, he had the same, broad shoulders and wide back from working in the fields.

The Man held his friend in great respect. Like many others, he had forsaken his 'protected' status as a landworker and enlisted to 'Fight the Hun'. Fate had sent him to Burma with the 'Forgotten' Army for six hundred days and nights of Hell.

The experience, it seemed, had not weakened his resolve. He hid scars from battle and torture beneath buttoned shirt, lest pride erode his will. Only sleep could steal its power. In truth, he had returned home to a lifetime of screaming nightmares. Sometimes, the Man would catch a look of despair in the soft eyes of his friend. A look that he had seen many times in the eyes of men after battle. But of such things, true men never spoke.

So, as the two walked along, they chatted about that day's work and the next day's weather.

"There's Joyce", Herb said, pointing down Canal Street.

"Looks like, you're in trouble! What have you been up to?" He joked.

The Woman came up to them. Throwing her arms around her husband, she kissed him, full on the lips.

"Yes, you're in trouble, for sure. Either that, or she's burned your dinner!"

Just then, they reached the entrance to the Yard. Arm in arm, the couple walked into the House. Herb carried on, to his own home, a little farther down the street. As he came to his front door, he heard the Man shout,

"Hey, Herb. I'm going to be a DAD!! And you, you're going to be a godfather!"

Herb did not answer. Slowly, he opened the door to where his own wife waited: - alone.

CHAPTER SEVEN: A SENSE OF PURPOSE

During his wife's confinement, the Man was busy in the fields. He took all the extra work that he could find. The backbreaking labour did not daunt him. He was still young and strong. Now, he worked with a sense of purpose that he had not felt since his time in the Royal Navy. He avoided the Town's many public houses where he once drank, played cards and dominoes. At first, he found it difficult not to enter. He missed the gossip and ribbing, the false bonhomie of the drunkards.

Instead, he cycled to the fields, tools tied to the crossbar of his bicycle. At first, he hoped that somebody would call him inside; later, that he would not be noticed. At weekends, he scoured the railway tracks and canal banks for coal fallen from train or barge, or shopped and performed the heavier household chores for his wife.

Before the child was born, he had been able to buy clothes, crib and perambulator. Of these achievements, he was proud.

After six months', the Woman rewarded him with a son and at the christening, Herb was godfather.

The next four years passed, lost in the humdrum routine of every-day life. The Man had money to spare. On Sundays, if the weather were fine, the couple would take the Boy to the seaside, riding on the steam train. The Man would swim in the cold waves while the Woman and child played in safety on the beach. They would make sandcastles and eat sandwiches, bread gritty from the same sand. They would then walk along the promenade, the child perched on the Man's shoulders.

When the travelling fair came to the Town, they would tour the rides and stalls. Then, the Man's strong arm and keen eye would be sure to win a goldfish or coconut. The Woman would buy herself some nougat, a toffee apple for the Boy.

Soon, the Boy would be old enough for school. Then, she would find work. She was not strong enough to work in the fields but was confident of securing a clerical position.

One day, they would leave the House. They would find a place with electricity, hot, running water and: - her very own bath.

Then, she would be truly happy.

CHAPTER EIGHT: A HUSBAND UNKNOWN.

The far end of the Yard was blocked by a large, detached, four-bedroomed house. Its former glory was now tainted by the same, peeling paint and cracked windows as the other buildings in the Yard. Its walled jungle of a garden was home to a pride of feral cats, habitual tormentors of the Smith's Labrador, chained to his kennel.

This gloomy house was occupied by Mr. and Mrs. Allen, from whom the Yard took its name. At one time, the Allens had owned all the houses in the Yard. However, Mr. Allen's drinking and gambling had slowly but surely eroded their fortune until, one by one, the houses had been sold. It was a tight-lipped woman who paid the landlord weekly rent for a home that she had once owned. This tall, gaunt woman would ride her bicycle through the Yard, head held high, eyes fixed straight ahead. She steadfastly refused to acknowledge the existence of any of the other residents. She considered their presence, a constant reminder of her own destitution.

Her husband was somewhat younger than she, of the same stature but wiry and even leaner. He wore a permanent stubble and always appeared unwashed, hair uncombed. The sight of him, walking through the Yard, would send the Boy running behind his mother's apron.

So that the Boy could play in safety, the Man had strung a length of chicken wire across the Yard. Secured by nails at either end, it could easily be hooked and unhooked by the Woman.

One day, she emerged from the Shed, washing basket under her arm, to find the improvised barrier was down, the child missing.

Mrs. Allen, her imperious ride obstructed, had dismounted and unhooked the wire. Without a second thought for the Boy playing in the Yard, she had carried on her way.

The Woman, seeing that her son had wandered onto the roadway, dropped the basket and ran, screaming, to snatch him from danger. As she regained the safety of the Yard, a lorry swept around the bend in the road. Ten seconds earlier, she calculated, it would have crushed the child. She seethed with anger but knew, only too well, the futility of an approach to Mrs. Allen. With a rare curse, she carried the child into the House then returned to gather her laundry from the mud in the Yard. On her husband's return from work, she told him of the day's events.

"I'll have a word with Hector", the Man said.

"I'm sure, it'll never happen again".

The Woman had long experienced the Allens' cutting arrogance. She was not so sure that this would be the case.

The Man waited until he saw Mr. Allen pass his window, destination; public house or bookmaker's office. The Woman followed her husband into the Yard, mindful that she might bear witness as to the day's events.

"Excuse me, Hector", the Man's tone was quiet and respectful, "could I have a word with you, please?"

"Come on. What is it? I haven't got all day. I have a very urgent business appointment".

The Man knew this to be a lie. However, he persisted in his attempt to explain his grievance with the other's wife. Yet the more he tried to reason with him, the more aggressive Mr. Allen became. There was contempt in his voice when he answered.

"It's a bloody right of way and if that painted whore of a wife......"

The Man's fists were like stone pistons. He pummelled the face before him until it fell. He continued the assault on the ground. Screaming like a lunatic, he punched and punched until his victim was left unconscious. When he stood, his eyes were dilated, black with anger. Small, white flecks covered his lips. Blood dripped from his knuckles.

This animal was unrecognisable as the husband that she loved. She had never before seen him like this. It filled her with terror. Even the voice was not that of her husband. It was hard and hoarse,

"Go inside, Joy".

Stepping over the outstretched body of his stricken neighbour, the Man followed his wife into the House.

After that, whenever Mrs. Allen left the Yard, she always replaced the wire barrier.

CHAPTER NINE: TOO MUCH PRESSURE

Shortly after the incident in the Yard, her headaches had begun. Twice, she had almost fainted, the migraines forcing her to her bed. The doctor told her that the birth of her son, allied to years of poor diet, had left her weakened and anaemic. The pills, he prescribed, had little effect. She had almost laughed when he asked if she had any major worries or problems in her life. What could he know?

But he was the Town doctor. He already knew about the fight in the Yard. He had set Mr. Allen's broken jaw, stitched his cuts and bathed his bruises. He knew of Sergeant Green's interest in the affair. How the wise Sergeant, on learning of the incident with the netting, had demanded reconciliation between the two families. The doctor, as a man hardened by three decades of epidemic and slaughter, could not understand the Woman's hysterical reaction to the incident. He had dismissed the headaches as 'nerves.' For these nervous headaches, he now prescribed aspirin and tranquillizers. These pills, also, had proved of little comfort to her.

The Woman sat in the old armchair by the glowing fire and waited for her husband's return from work. She could not clear the vision of his bloodied knuckles from her mind. For a time, she had not known her husband, even recognised his voice. She felt so lonely.

She longed for her friends in the city, for her comrades in the operations' room; orders and conversations shouted over the ever-present headphones. She missed the bright lights and parties with her Man when he was on leave. Above all, she missed the warmth and happiness of the family home.

She hated her adopted poverty, this wild land where the wind never ceased. She hated these coarse people who scorned her make-up and occasional cigarettes. She despised the superficial morality that precluded her; The Outsider. How much longer could her love for the Man survive this pressure? She could not tell. She must get away from there.

Her head thumped with the migraine as she watched over her son. He had clambered onto the armchair beneath the window, ignoring her warnings for caution. Shouting and screaming with excitement, he trampolined on the cushion, intent on grabbing the chalk dog from the windowsill. The higher that he bounced, the louder his screams became. Their noise pierced her skull, sending arrows of lightning pain stabbing into her brain. She could not endure for very much longer. She had to get away from there.

With a final shout of triumph, the Boy grabbed his prize. As he tumbled back, down into the armchair, he held the chalk figure aloft, in triumph. His smile now fixed in victory.

For his mother had gone.

CHAPTER TEN: THE PRISONER

The Boy was to spend the next years in the care of Mrs. P. Until he was old enough to attend school, he would pass his days in the House across the Yard.

Mrs. P. never took him to play with other children. She guarded him closely, as her own. After lunch, she would sit him in the basket of her bicycle and pedal to visit this or that friend. She made a point of avoiding households where there might be other children. Denied play-friends, the Boy would sit silently in the circle of Mrs. P.'s tea set, witness to their petty gossip and bitter jealousies. At every house, the women would be waiting with the same greeting;

"Oh! That's the little Boy whose mother left him, isn't it?"

And if they were to forget their lines, Mrs. P. would be sure to prompt them. Sure with the reminder that she, herself, was now the Boy's carer.

He could no longer remember his mother; her looks, her smell not even the sound of her voice. Her very mention would set his lips to trembling, bring tears welling up into his eyes. The women would feed him sweets and chocolate, soft drinks laced with sugar. As if, by such kindness, they could stem the tears caused by their unnecessary questions.

Mrs. P. seemed to find some satisfaction in his tears, always adding a few more words of her own. She would whisper, still loud enough for all to hear,

"Mind you, I've seen her with those cigarettes". Or,

"I didn't think it proper for a married woman to wear make-up like that. It made her look like a tramp!"

Even when the Boy's schooldays began, Mrs.P. strived to keep her hold over him. She would push him to and from the school, high on the seat of her bicycle like some invalid. High and away from the other children, who walked alongside their mothers. The lack of exercise and constant over-feeding made him fat and slow. Scorned, precluded from the sports and games on which other children thrived, he was thrust further and further into solitude. And if one of the mothers should ask;

"Oh, no," Mrs. P. would reply, "he's as good as gold. He's happy as Larry, playing on his own in my garden. He loves to play alone. Funny isn't it? He prefers the company of adults to that of other children."

So it was that the Boy became a prisoner in the House across the Yard. He came to dread school-time and holidays alike. In the summer, he would pray for rain, in the winter, for snow. Rather, a prisoner of the weather with his father, than confinement to the House across the Yard.

However, he was to find a friend and ally in a most unexpected quarter.

CHAPTER ELEVEN: UNCLE STUMPY

Mrs. P.'s father was the oldest person in the Boy's world.

Hair, white as snow, matched the stubble that permanently graced his toothless jaws. Blue eyes sparkled beneath the flat cap that he always wore, day or night, indoors or outdoors. His shirt was blue with white stripes, fixed at the collar with studs and whale-bone but without neck-tie. The trousers of his dark, three-piece suit were fastened by two, large safety-pins to accommodate the stumps of his missing legs. The smell of pipe tobacco followed him everywhere that he went.

Uncle Stumpy was a man of indomitable spirit. He had lost his only brother, killed on the Somme and his wife, dead in childbirth. Two years of trench warfare had left him with no fear of death, or of life. He knew only too well, the landmine that had stolen his legs probably saved his life. For it had delivered him from the Hell of the Front Lines.

This irony was not lost on the old soldier, yet he showed no bitterness. He would dispel any thought of sadness with a laugh that seemed to rattle the very windows of the House across the Yard. He greeted every day as it came; an opportunity for fun and games. If he were to annoy his daughter in any way, she would punish him by confiscating his wheelchair. Rather than be confined to his bedroom, the old fellow would swing himself along on knuckles and backside, down the stairs, through the kitchen and outside into the garden.

So, the Boy had found a fellow inmate in the House across the Yard, a fellow prisoner who turned out to be his willing and able play-mate. Together, they played hide-and-seek and tag, the Boy squealing as the old man swung along at his heels, or built castles with logs from the wood-shed.

When Uncle Stumpy was tired, he would adjourn to the shed and fill his pipe with tobacco from a leather pouch, thumbing the golden strands into the bowl. Sweet, aromatic smoke would fill the air as he carved wooden soldiers with a pearl-handled penknife from his waistcoat pocket. When the afternoons were too cold, they would sit by the log fire in the kitchen and the old soldier would tell stories of how he, single-handedly, had whipped the Kaiser.

Despite this playfulness, Uncle Stumpy was no fool. He had witnessed the end of his blood-line with pious resignation, assuring himself that it was God's will. Now, he found himself powerless to help his daughter. Her grief at the loss of her sons was and remained inconsolable. Her deterioration had seemed almost daily. Even her father's laughter had come to irk rather than to cheer her. This bitterness made her resent everyone and everything. So much so, that the old man feared for her very sanity.

He abhorred her domination of the Boy and the loneliness that she caused him. Now, Uncle Stumpy sought to thwart her, at every opportunity. Initiating races and play fights when it was time for the daily bike-ride, he would seek to delay the child's departure. At meal-times, he would slip food from the Boy's overloaded plate onto his own. Gums racing to destroy the evidence, he would wink the Boy into secrecy.

Try as he might, he could do nothing to break Mrs.P.'s hold over the Boy

CHAPTER TWELVE: A STRANGER CALLS.

There were very few books in the House; some from the Man's own childhood, now worm-eaten and dog-eared, the Woman's bible, abandoned forever within the sideboard.

He had left school, aged twelve, to work for his own father. The latter owned a farm and warehouse with barges on one of the canals that skirted the Town. But for his twelve children, he said, he could have been a rich man.

The youngest of these five brothers and seven sisters, the Man had initially worked, cleaning the stables. In the evenings, he would feed and groom the great shire horses that towed the barges of wheat to the railhead. As a child, he was forever black with dust from the coal, loaded for the return journey, that gathered in the horses' coats and manes. The family joked that this was how his hair and eyes had become so dark.

By the time he reached his early teenage years, he was already working with his brothers. Together, they loaded the giant sacks of grain and shovelled coal by the ton. When there were no barges to fill or empty, they worked in the fields, harvesting wheat or potatoes.

This work had endowed him with the great physical strength that now enabled him to earn his living. But it had left little time for any formal education. So, when the stranger knocked at his door, the Man bid him enter.

The salesman sat perched on the dusty armchair beneath the window. Behind him, ears now missing, the chalk dog kept guard on the window sill. The Boy had never seen anyone who looked like this. The salesman's hair was combed down flat, slick and shiny with brilliantine. Pin-striped suit hid spotless shirt adorned with gold cuff-links, golden tie-pin, also. There was a smell that the Boy did not recognize: Eau de Cologne. But, what he noticed most of all were the man's hands. They were unlike any that he had ever seen. The fingers and palms were clean with no cuts or calluses. The nails were manicured and highly polished. None of the women of the Town had such hands!!!

Engrossed in his observations, he had ignored the conversation between the salesman and his father. Without warning, the salesman had clicked open his suitcase, filling the small room with a smell like new shoes. Packed inside, there lay ten, identical, leather-bound tomes; - a set of encyclopaediae.

The following evening, by the glow of the gaslight, he began their reading. First, he read of Hansel and Gretel then, of Aesop's fables. Next came Arthur and Lancelot, stories of Don Quixote. He fought the battles of Nelson and Wellington, travelled the world with Cook and Drake. He studied their maps, resplendent in the dull room; mere shadows of the bright birds and butterflies that followed. All, overwhelmed by the wonders of Sun and Universe.

In the red tomes, he would eventually discover History's hidden truth; distorted by the Victor's pen, seen only by the sceptic. Therein, lay no words from Indian or African, only the Christian's tale. Little mattered his misdeeds. Time had diluted their barbarity. Who cared, his Victims' fate?

In the red tomes, all praised the martyrs of Burma and Pearl Harbour; justified only Hiroshima's vaporized souls, pictured only the beauty of the mushroom cloud.

In the red tomes, all praised the saviours of Jew from camp, neglected his many exiles; censored the tortured Boer; deleted the Palestinian.

And, in the red tomes, all cursed the blasphemy of Germany's Eagle, Hitler's Phoenix risen from the ashes of the Reichstag.

Yes, by the glow of the gaslight, the Boy began his education.

CHAPTER THIRTEEN: TWO FORMS OF ESCAPE

The House across the Yard had two bedrooms; one for Mrs. P. and husband, the other for Uncle Stumpy.

This was the one and only obstacle between Mrs. P. and her total possession of the Boy. It meant that every night, after the evening meal, he could spend a few hours, alone with his father before bed-time. The Man had carried a bed up to the small landing outside his own bedroom. On very cold nights, the Boy would jump into his father's bed to sleep while the Man listened to the radio.

Before bed-time, they would play dominoes or ludo, cards or darts. The Boy would stand on a chair to throw at the board, the Man encourage him to do the scoring, racing him with the answers. In this way, he had learned the basics of mental arithmetic. Competition with his father made his mind as sharp as the darts that they aimed. On nights when the Man was too tired to play, the Boy would take up his beloved encyclopaediae.

In winter, the Man would stoke the coals until the room glowed with heat. Then, the two would sup on chestnuts and potatoes roasted beneath the fire, on bread and gravy from the Man's stew-pot. Torpid from the food and heat, the Boy would fall asleep, safe on his father's lap, ear tuned to the strong, steady thump of his heartbeat.

In summer, the Man would cycle to the canal with the Boy seated on the cross-bar of his bicycle. Here, he taught the Boy to fish and swim. On Sundays, when the weather was fine, they would travel on the steam train to re-visit the coast.

But on Saturday nights, the Boy would be left with this friend or that aunt. For on Saturday nights, his father would seek oblivion and solace in the many public houses of the Town.

And the Boy? He would find his own sanctuary between the pages of the red tomes. Where he was safe. Safe from Mrs. P.

CHAPTER FOURTEEN: TOO SMART, BY HALF

School did nothing to dispel the Boy's misery. Each morning, he found himself delivered from one domineering presence to another.

The schoolmistress was Mrs. Carter, a small, hard-faced woman. Her love of discipline made her feared, not just by those in her charge, but by all the children in the school. Even the local gypsy children, on their rare appearances in the classroom, maintained a respectful silence in her presence. Small as she was, she seemed a giant to the children in her care, towering over them as they sat at their desks. She would deride her pupils for their slightest mistakes. But her sarcasm did not sting as sharply as her hand.

Unlike the other classes of the school, in Mrs. Carter's class one sat, not in alphabetical order, but in order of preference. Thus, the front rows of the class were occupied mainly by the children of the local bourgeoisie. The Boy, fat and slovenly, seemed no more than a dullard to the schoolmistress. It was no surprise that he found himself seated at the back of the class with the gypsy children.

This arrangement suited the Boy. He found the basic levels of study uninteresting. Ignored by the teacher, he would daydream away the hours, gazing out of the window at the grey mists that enveloped the forbidding Fenland, yawning his boredom until it was time for his prison transfer. Until the day, he betrayed himself.

The subject of the class was English. Mrs. Carter patrolled the classroom, walking between the rows of miniature furniture. As she passed, she demanded a word and its spelling from each of the seated eight-year-olds. She had already questioned her favourites, rewarding them with a,

"Well done, Roger",

"Brilliant, Jane".

Even a dry smile for some. By the time she reached the rear of the classroom, she had already exhausted more than half of the alphabet.

"Patrick, give me a word beginning with the letter 'P', please".

Patrick looked up, confused that the designated letter should begin the word 'Please', that it should be his own initial.

"P… Patrick", he stuttered.

"No, you stupid boy, not your own name!"

The unchastised laughter from the front of the room only served to compound the lad's humiliation.

"Eddy, give me a word beginning with the letter "P".

"Pony, Mrs. Carter", Eddy replied, eager to please, eager to avoid his neighbour's fate.

"Spell it".

Eddy sat for a few moments, in deep thought. Although he and Patrick could name every part of a pony's anatomy, fit saddle and bridle, even ride bareback, neither of them knew how to read or write.

"P.O.N.I.", came his desperate answer.

"You are a stupid boy, aren't you? Well, aren't you?" Mrs. Carter pressed.

"Yes, Mrs. Carter," the young gypsy replied, eyes filled with tears of shame.

This time, the laughter from the front of the room was deafening, forced in its falseness.

"You, Boy. Stop looking out of the window! Give me a word beginning with the letter 'P."

"Pendant, Mrs. Carter," the Boy replied, eyes lowered to the top of his desk.

The front rows had fallen silent, bemused by the unknown word. The teacher hesitated. She had been surprised by the speed and nonchalance of his reply, the relative complexity of his chosen word. A thin smile tugged at her lips.

"Spell "Pendant," she said.

Impassively, the Boy looked up. With studied voice, he slowly spelled the word;

"P.E.D.A.N.T."

The teacher's smile had disappeared. She again hesitated, unsure for the briefest of moments. Was this a genuine mistake? Surely, this dullard could not have intended such a play on words?

Her temper gave the answer. Wild anger surged through her body, sweeping away her self-control. Face contorted, she crashed her fist down into the side of the child's head. As one, child and chair crashed to the floor.

He had never before been struck by an adult. The force of the blow had been so great that it had numbed him to its pain. He did not cry immediately. Only when he felt the wet warmth spreading down his leg, running along the floor, did he cry...... tears of both humiliation and shame.

"Get up! Get out! Get out! You dirty, dirty boy," the teacher screamed.

There was no thought that she might have injured the child, no regret for her loss of control. Her only thoughts could be of justification for his punishment, camouflage for her vengeance.

Exiled to the draughty corridor, the Boy sat on the cold, wet tiles. The slow trickle of blood from his ear drip, dripped its stain onto the shoulder of his jacket. Inside the classroom, absolute silence now ruled.

In due course, his other jailor would arrive to parade him in silent and public shame through the streets of the Town. Back to the House across the Yard, where she could have him to herself for an extra few hours. With a great show of self-sacrifice, she cleaned his wound then washed him. He sat in silence, wrapped in a towel, while she rinsed his only pair of trousers in the kitchen sink. There was no sign of warmth or sympathy in her actions, only of self-concern and duty. Not only was she responsible for the Boy's welfare and cleanliness, she told him, it was SHE who would be obliged to give shopkeepers and housewives an explanation for his early return from school.

Despite Uncle Stumpy's protestations, she had accepted without question the teacher's version of events; how the Boy had attacked her without warning. Her cold memory now stored the tale for future use.

The Man sat quietly in his armchair and listened to his son's tearful account of the assault. His eyes did not move from the child as he spoke. He did not miss a single word or gesture.

The Boy could not lie to him. That evening, he cycled to Mrs. Carter's home.

The Boy now spent his time in the classroom, ignored yet unmolested, sitting by the window. In the playground, he was nick-named and taunted by the other children.

Except by the gypsies, who knew only too well the full force of an adult's anger.

CHAPTER FIFTEEN: CHANGES

The Boy did not know it but his life was about to undergo some harrowing yet welcome changes. That morning, it was his father who wakened him.

"I'm having a few days off work. Come on, get dressed and eat your toast. Time for school."

As they walked through the Yard, there was no sign of Mrs. P. For once, the Smiths' dog was strangely quiet. It cowered in its kennel, ears flattened to the sides of its head, ignoring its feline tormentors.

The Boy had no time for the dog. Because that day, head high, chest proud, he strutted to school, accompanied by his father. Two mornings later, as they left the House, a large, black car moved off, down Canal Street. Accompanied by two, smaller cars, it moved slowly and silently towards the centre of the Town.

Uncle Stumpy was dead.

The next day as normal, Mrs. P. woke the Boy and took him to the House across the Yard. Seated at the large, wooden table in the kitchen, he ate breakfast under her watchful eye. The house seemed strangely quiet.

She waited patiently until he had finished his meal. The question was as terrifying as it was unexpected.

"How would you like to come and live here with me, Boy?"

He panicked. He could not look at the woman. His eyes searched the table for an answer, an excuse, anything to avoid the question.

"Where would I sleep?"

"In Uncle Stumpy's room. You'll have it all to yourself," Mrs. P. smiled.

"What about Uncle Stumpy? Where will he sleep?"

"Don't worry about him. He's gone to live in a home. He has gone. He has gone so that you can come and live with me!"

"I want to live with my dad!"

"He doesn't want you, anymore. He's given you to me! Come, come to mother, my son. You're my Boy, now!"

She had unbuttoned the bodice of her black dress, baring her bosom. Grabbing the Boy by the hair, she tried to force him onto her nipple. The Boy screamed with fright. He pushed and kicked to be free.

"Your mother didn't love you. She left you, didn't she? Now, your father doesn't want you, either! You're mine!"

"You're not my mother," the Boy shouted, kicking free from her grasp.

Mrs. P., hair in wild disarray, grabbed him as he ran, slapping her free hand across his face.

"I AM YOUR MOTHER," she screamed.

The Boy again struggled free, wriggling to safety beneath the kitchen table. She came after him, on hands and knees, trying to pull him out by the ankle. Arms locked around the table-leg, he kicked and kicked to be free. Before she could grab him once more, he ran from the kitchen and out into the garden. Across the Yard, he sought refuge in the Shed. Hidden beneath a pile of sacks on the roof of the toilet, he shivered away the hours until the Man's return.

"Come on down, Son," his father called, "Mrs. P. says you've been a naughty Boy. You've kicked her and hurt her."

The Boy dropped down from his hiding place, sobbing his terror in his father's arms.

"She said you didn't want me, anymore, Dad. Don't make me go back, there!"

Jaw set, the Man carried his son into the safety of the House.

He did not ask his son, why had he kicked Mrs. P. and the Boy did not tell him. But, never again would he be confined to the House across the Yard.

CHAPTER SIXTEEN: A NEW FRIEND

The Man had found a new carer for his son.   Mrs. Blackwell lived some fifty yards away from the Yard, along Canal Street towards the Bridge. She was the wife of the local postmaster. A thin, frail woman in her late twenties, she had a son of her own.

Her husband was short with dark features and pallid skin. Disabled from birth, he would limp along on the ball of his right foot, shrivelled left hand usually hidden away in his jacket pocket. He was a strict disciplinarian and much feared by his son. His wife also lived in dread of him. But she was a fine mother. Many were the times that she had taken a beating in place of her son.

The Man secretly despised the postmaster. He did not think it manly or honourable to strike a woman, much less a child. Whenever possible, he would slip the woman a few shillings above the carer's fee demanded by her husband. The Man knew that she was kept in penury by the avaricious postmaster and was happy to show his gratitude with money for a few luxuries. For this payment, the woman would feed the Boy his breakfast and take him to school, along with her own son.

Jack was thin and frail like his mother. His pale, blue eyes and blonde curls were a stark contrast to the dark features of his parents. Before school, the two children would play tennis or football, hitting the ball with bare hands or feet. Despite his physical weakness, Jack's skill at ball games made him more than a match for the heavy clumsiness of the Boy. For a short time, the two would escape the misery of their respective lives. Assuming the identities of their sporting heroes, they scored goals in the Cup Final and served aces on Wimbledon's centre court.

The Blackwell's house seemed like a palace. It had a kitchen with inside tap and sink, an electricity supply for lights and appliances. It even had a cistern to flush the outside toilet. In the living room, for limited and controlled use only, was a small, black and white television set.

But, what the Boy liked best was to walk to school with his new friend alongside the other boys and girls.

CHAPTER SEVENTEEN: THE BRIDGE

Mrs. P.'s tongue had not remained idle. The bruise on her face was displayed as testament to the Boy's violent nature. Soon, all her friends and neighbours knew the story of how he had kicked her in the face as she bent to tend her garden. The assault on his teacher, the occasional bruises on Jack's legs and arms, all were now cited as proof of the Boy's bullying nature.

"He has the Devil in him," Mrs. P. would whisper.

"Do you know, every time that I took him to church, he would struggle and scream? If I took my eye off him for a single second, he would run to the doors and try to open them. You know, he kicked his teacher in the shin, don't you? And me, in the face. For no reason at all."

"Yes, I think, I heard something about that."

"He has the very Devil in him."

"He gets it from his father. You know, he broke Mr. Allen's jaw. He should have been locked up for that. He would have been, if the Sergeant had done his job."

"I don't know what Mrs. Blackwell thinks, she's doing, having that Boy in her home," Mrs. P. would remark bitterly.

"Anyway, about the Sergeant ......," and the same gossip would be repeated over and over again.

Until it became fact.

The result was, that when Mr. Blackwell was transferred to a post-office in the city, only a few relatives would volunteer to look after him. Ironically, this opened up a whole, new world for the Boy. He was now allowed to play outside the Yard during the evenings. Although the Man imposed a strict curfew, it was more often than not ignored, forgotten in play. Most nights, the Man would be seen walking down Canal Street, laughing at the struggling child draped over his shoulder.

When the weather was fine, the local girls and boys would gather on the Bridge. Here, the Boy would meet his two schoolmates; Young Patrick and Eddy. Eddy was one of the many sons of the Town's chimney sweep.

The two lads, even though they could not read or write, were no fools. They recognized that, in some way, the Boy had taken their side against the schoolmistress. On many occasions, they had seen him protect his weaker friend from the bullies in the school yard.

On the Bridge, bullies were not tolerated. On the Bridge, differences were settled one on one, in fair and open combat. On the Bridge, the word had been passed to friends and brothers. On the Bridge, the Boy was accepted without question.

The Bridge spanned what seemed, at first sight, to be an empty canal bed. Drained of water, it was clogged with a mixture of grass, thistles and stinging nettles. This 'canal' had once been an open sewer that serviced the Town. It ran half the length of Canal Street before turning to pass the gypsies' encampment.

The Town's sewage was now piped beneath this 'canal bed' to disgorge at 'Tunnel Head' where the 'canal' was reborn. From here, the waste was transferred to sewage farm via a new pumping station; guardian of the water level in the surrounding countryside. Clean water then passed into the local drainage system of canals and rivers. When the water was low in the pipe, only the bravest of the brave would walk into the entrance of 'Tunnel Head'.

But none had ever dared follow it to its end.

CHAPTER EIGHTEEN: THE TUNNEL

Eddy was thin to the point of emaciation. So thin that his thighs, protruding like matchsticks beneath his short trousers, lacked even the width of his bony knees. He was the middle of five brothers. With as many sisters to feed, food and money were scarce in the family's household.

His clothes were; short, grey trousers tied by a cord at the waist, jacket and grimy, string vest. His only footwear was an old pair of hand-me-down Wellington boots. Still too large for him, they made him slide his feet to walk.

Eddy's mother also was very thin, her gaunt face lined from too many children and too many cigarettes. Cigarettes that helped cough away her hunger and desperation.

His father was the local chimney sweep, firm in the belief that he could substitute alcohol and nicotine for food, that his family needed no food at all. The sacks that he piled around his door, even inside the house itself, meant that Eddy and his siblings were permanently covered in soot.

The Boy had never met another child so completely unafraid. Knocks from elder brothers and sisters, cuffs from mother and father, had left him fleet of foot and hard as nails. His constant need for escape had made him the best climber in the Town. So, it was no surprise when Eddy was the first to drop nimbly down from the parapet.

The Boy, heavier by stones, gingerly lowered himself to his friend's side. Carefully, the two edged their way along the concrete ledge that led to 'Tunnel Head,' safe above the stinking mud that choked its approaches. One final look of derring-do and the two boys breached the dark entrance.

There was no light at all, inside the Tunnel. They groped their way along, hands slipping on the slimy brickwork, rubber boots splashing in the narrow trickle of sewage. Their frightened whispers echoed down the Tunnel, sending an army of unseen rats squeaking and scurrying away in the darkness. The noise of the fleeing vermin unsettled the two boys, even more. With dry mouths and pounding hearts, they carried on, into the Tunnel. Soon, the entrance and safety were no more than a circle of light behind them in the distance. Then, it happened.

Directly in front of them, with ominous deliberation, the monster raised its head. Another surge of foul water and its jaws creaked slowly open, snapping shut as the sewage passed through the pipe.

Before the Boy could turn to run, Eddy had sprinted past him. Screaming at the top of their voices, the two children ran, splashing down the Tunnel.

"Is it coming?" Eddy shouted over his shoulder.

"Yes," the Boy called, too afraid to look backwards.

Eddy shinned up the parapet and ran along its top, laughing with fear and elation at his close brush with death. The rubber boots, wet with slime from the Tunnel, betrayed him. Before the Boy could grab him, he had slipped and fallen into the filthy mud!

The Boy reached down his arm and Eddy clambered back up, onto the concrete parapet. Forlornly, the two boys sat and watched as the stinking slime oozed over and into the newly-captured Wellington boots.

Eddy's voice was a whisper, "I'm dead."
A certain beating and a barefoot future seemed to be his only destiny. So, the Boy grasped Eddy's ankles as, head and shoulders immersed in the Town's waste, he desperately fished for his drowned boots.

In the Yard, the Man laughed as he washed Eddy with buckets of water from the tap. Mud and soot disappeared as one beneath the freezing torrents.

Inside the House, he dried the salvaged boots while Eddy's threadbare clothes steamed by the fire. Then, he fed the shivering child with chunks of bread and steaming hot stew.

"How do you get two pints of stew into that half-pint of a body?" The Man had joked, amazed by the little fellow's voracious appetite.

That night, for the first time in his life, Eddy slept with a clean body and a full belly. He never forgot the kindness shown him by the Man, and the Boy had a friend for life.

The following evening, none of the children on the Bridge would believe the story of the 'Monster.' None, however, volunteered to investigate the claim.

CHAPTER NINETEEN: YOUNG PATRICK

Patrick was short and stocky. His dark features and olive skin were topped by a mass of black curls that gleamed like polished metal. Although born and raised in the Town, he affected his father's Kentish brogue. In the family home, he was known as 'Young Patrick,' his father as plain 'Patrick' and his grandfather, 'Old Patrick.' The Boy suspected that, once upon a time, the grandfather also had been a 'Young Patrick.'

The family was proud of its gypsy heritage. Every Sunday, they would parade in splendour along the main street of the Town. Old Patrick, in best suit and trilby hat, would take the reins, guiding the immaculate pony with little flicks of the whip. In the polished wood and brass of the carriage, the women of the family graced the leather upholstery, festooned with every piece of jewellery that they owned. Paradoxically, an old bucket and shovel hung from the polished woodwork at the rear, lest the roadsweeper rob Old Patrick of his 'free' manure.

Theirs was the only gypsy family in the Town to own a house. Several years' before, Patrick had the good fortune to win the football pools. More from a desire to preserve a portion of their newly found wealth than from any yearning for bricks and mortar, his wife had persuaded him to buy a house. Patrick then set about the considerable task of investing the money that remained in his three great passions. These were; drinking, gambling and horse-trading. Soon, all that remained of his good fortune were a single pony and the house. Here, Patrick lived with his wife, Young Patrick and his five, younger children.

Even at that tender age, Young Patrick was a tireless runner and obdurate boxer. His resilience on land was matched only by his incompetence in the water. And this is how he and the Boy became firm friends:-

There were twenty or more children swimming, playing and relaxing in the shadows of the metal bridge. Bodies, white from the long winter, glistened in the green waters of the canal. As the children splashed around, diving for fresh-water mussels, others slid down the banks on an improvised slide of packed mud, shooting into the water like seals from an ice floe. Seated aboard the inflated inner-tube from a lorry's tyre, Young Patrick splashed about, careful to avoid the playful antics of his friends.

Alerted by the whistle of an oncoming train, many of the children swam to the waters beneath the bridge. The locomotive, passing overhead, would make the bridge rattle and shake. The scream of the steam engine would reverberate beneath the bridge, filling the swimmers with a mixture of fear and exhilaration.

But this time, as the train rumbled over the bridge, a rusty girder dislodged, plunging down onto the children in the water. Struck a glancing blow, one of them sank beneath the surface. A scene of chaos ensued.

Some dived to rescue their stricken friend while more ran for help. Others thrashed about in their panic, churning the water into foam. Voices screamed, adding to the pandemonium. Only the Boy noticed Young Patrick, dislodged from his improvised raft in the mayhem, sink beneath the water. Diving after him, he grabbed a handful of black curls and pulled the coughing and spluttering gypsy back into the air.

As they stood and watched the ambulance bounce its way along the towpath, Young Patrick whispered,

"Don't tell my mum. She won't let me come 'swimming' again."

But it did not matter. From that day forth, nobody was allowed to swim beneath the railway bridge.

CHAPTER TWENTY: UNCLE SIDNEY

The children quickly found another place where they could swim. Two miles from the railway, a new, concrete bridge crossed the canal. Here, the banks sloped gently down to the water; perfect for swimming and sunbathing.

The Boy pedalled along the road that led to the bridge, ignorant of the fields where his father had once scavenged for food. As he neared his goal, he spotted a man mounted on a bicycle, come to a halt on the pavement by the parapet. At first sight, he thought that it was his father's friend, Herb. The figure was identical, short and squat. From a distance, the features seemed the same.

As he drew closer, the Boy saw that the man's curls were flecked with white, chin covered in grey stubble. By the time he had reached the bridge, the other had already dismounted. He stood, leaning over the railings, gazing down into the waters of the canal.

"Wotcha!"

"Wotcha!" The man replied without looking up.

The Boy peered over at the children splashing in the water.

"Nice day for swimming," he said.

"Yes."

"I don't think it's going to rain, do you?"

"No."

As the conversation progressed, it became clear to the Boy that his uncle had not recognized him. His answers were distant, abstract. His eyes were blank, stare fixed on the waters of the canal.

In the canal, he saw reflected the waters of the Manzanares.* In his mind, he fought across the Campo Universitario.** Bullets, like angry hornets, buzzed past his ears. Their stings showered him with wood and stone. He was caught, trapped in battle; too proud to run, too afraid to yield.

In his mind, he saw the face of the first man that he had killed; cold steel in soft flesh.

In his mind, he fled across the mountains. Rifles abandoned by frozen fingers, hands and feet bound in rags, an Army of the Damned marched at his side.

And in his mind, he screamed for the return of his youth and innocence, stolen away by that bloody Spanish conflict; stinking nightmare where brother hunted brother.

Their defeat had been total and uncompromising. And his reward? Sleepless nights of screaming terror.

"I'll see you, then …..Uncle?"

"I'll see you," Uncle Sidney answered to a child on a bicycle.

His stare had not left the water.

That night, Uncle Sidney took to the waters of the
Manzanares ......forever.

* The Manzanares: River that skirts Madrid.

** 'Campo Universitario'; University Campus, the scene of a fierce and bloody battle to defend
   Madrid from capture by Franco's army during The Spanish Civil War.

CHAPTER TWENTY - ONE: 'E' FOR 'B'

The Man pushed the empty plate to one side. He watched as the Boy finished the customary meal of stew and potatoes. In mock ceremony, he tapped his spoon on the oilskin that served as a tablecloth.

"I call this meeting of the tea-time committee to order."

He told his son of the idea to buy some hens. There followed gleeful talk of newly-laid eggs and roast chicken for Sunday dinner. This would be luxury compared with the normal fare of rabbit or pike, harvested from field and canal.

Together, they built a pen at the rear of the Shed. They hammered nesting boxes from wood, originally gathered for kindling. Here, the new residents would roost and leave their breakfast bounty. The Boy pleaded that he might go to buy the chickens. He had already enlisted the help of Young Patrick in the quest. Young Patrick knew everything there was to know about horses. Therefore, the Boy had reasoned, he knew everything there was to know about ALL animals, chickens included.

Five-pound note folded neatly in his sock, the Boy cycled with his friend to the market. They had tied wicker baskets to the handlebars of their bicycles, ready to transport the birds.

Although ignorant of all things chicken, Young Patrick did not wish to disappoint. He had watched the local farmers at the market, on many occasions. Now, he mimicked their actions. Moving along the lines of cages, he reached in to squeeze the crops of the outraged birds. His young face set in a determined frown as each of his 'patients' rewarded his unsolicited examination with a dozen pecks. With reddened hand hidden away in the safety of his jacket pocket, Doctor Patrick delivered his diagnoses.

"This is a good layer ...."

"This one's no good ...."

The farmers gathered around, uniform in grey suits and black Wellington boots. They winked and nudged elbows, soliciting advice from the young expert. The bidding completed, the auctioneer paid, the two boys stowed the birds in the wicker baskets. Then, they returned to the circle of farmers to buy bran for roughage. This would guarantee strong shells and perfect eggs, the Man had told them. He had told the Boy the price to pay but the bidding came thick and fast. Soon, the price had reached more than twice the level predicted by his father. The Boy suspected complicity between the farmers.

The ride home was not as triumphant as he had expected.

"I thought you wanted me to do ALL the bidding."

"Why? I had the money," the Boy said.

"Then, why did I have to bid for the chickens?"

"Because you know about chickens. My dad told me how much to bid for the bran."

"Then, why didn't YOU tell ME?" Young Patrick blustered.

"I thought that you knew."

And so the two boys, accompanied by a chorus of cackling birds, bickered their way along Canal Street.

When they returned, the Man just smiled and shook his head. The next six weeks, he and the Boy ate capon for Sunday dinner. On the seventh Saturday, he made the visit to the market in person.

From THAT day onwards, he and the Boy ate eggs for breakfast.

CHAPTER TWENTY – TWO: A SIMPLE SOLUTION

The Man was now faced with a dilemma as to the care of his child.

He knew that the Boy would never have struck out at Mrs. P. without reason. He did not believe the story of a theft from her purse, that the bruise on his son's face was caused by a fall as he kicked out at the woman. The hard glint in her eyes had betrayed her lies.

He had found half-truth in his reasoning for her mistreatment of the Boy, that her actions were directed at himself as much as his son. He believed that in her twisted mind she blamed him for the loss of her own sons. Had he not cleared the mines that they reach, unhindered, their deaths on the beachheads of France? Had he not survived while they perished? Hate, revenge, he could understand.

He could never have imagined that a mind drowned in despair could be so depraved as to begrudge him the birth of his son. So depraved as to believe that the child was conceived to taunt her loss. That he owed her his son. That she believed, the Boy should be hers.

Mrs. P.'s vicious gossip held sway among the women of the Town. So, when Mrs. Blackwell and family left for the city, the Man could not find a replacement to look after his son.

The Boy was old enough to feed himself breakfast and walk unsupervised to school. The Man could be home before his return but during holiday times the Boy would be left to his own devices. The mothers of the Town now denied their children the company of his 'vicious' offspring. The answer was a simple one. During the school holidays, he would take the Boy to work with him.

There, he would be relatively safe.

CHAPTER TWENTY-THREE: 'ON THE LAND': WINTER

He heard his father's voice calling him, calling him from far, far away. It awoke him to the weight of the blankets that pinned and protected him. It summoned him from the warmth and safety of the bed on the landing. It called him to a cold, cold world.

"Wake up, Boy! Breakfast's ready."

Dim light filtered through the cobwebs of frost that patterned the inside of the window. He prised himself free from the blankets and stood upright on the bed to breathe away the ice from the glass.

Outside, dark buildings rose out of the fog that swirled to engulf them. Snow-covered roofs glowed brightly in the light of the waning moon, diminishing the lamps that guarded the roadway. Fading stars hailed the grey light of dawn.

The mist and clear skies meant there would be no snowfall, that day. It also meant that the gangs of men would be returning to the fields. He dressed, hurriedly pulling on the damp clothing.

Downstairs, it was too cold to wash. He sat quietly before the embers of the previous night's fire and chewed toasted 'soldiers' prepared by his father. He dipped each one into the yolk of the egg before he ate; savouring every mouthful, delaying the inevitable departure for as long as possible.

His father sat opposite him. While he waited for his son to finish breakfast, he worked his left hand then his right. Alternately slapping palm then fist into his thigh, he vainly tried to bring blood and feeling into arthritic hands. In the background, almost drowned by the slap, slap, slap of the Man's hands, the groomed voice of the broadcaster quietly confirmed his predictions of the weather, made the previous day.

Breakfast at an end, the Man and his miniature self trudged through the drifts of snow to where Herb waited. All three were protected by duffel coats, woollen hats and Wellington boots. Hessian sacks hung over their shoulders. Breathing steam, the trio trudged into the freezing fog.

The lorry stood by the bus stop, rear clad in timber and green canvas. Silhouetted in the yellow glow from the street lamp, it resembled some mythical beast. Diesel breath disgorged beneath crimson eyes as its body shuddered to the beat of the engine. Inside the cab, Jack, the driver and his eldest son, Derek, read yesterday's papers while they waited.

Two men were already seated within the confines of the canvas hood. They had taken their customary positions on the straw-filled sacks that covered the wooden benches. The two were; Johnny and his son Lefty. In the darkness, hand-rolled cigarettes glowed red beneath their flat caps. Obscured faces lit with every puff of smoke.

The Man had christened Lefty with a second nickname, 'Certainly;' the only word that he was ever heard to utter.

"Morning, Johnny."

"Morning."

"Morning, Lefty."

"Certainly!", came the inevitable reply.

"Sit up front, Boy. You'll be warmer, there," his father ordered.

The Boy did not know whether or not his father was joking. Through the choking mix of dust and tobacco smoke, he groped to find a seat.

Shortly afterwards, Big Louis and his three sons made their appearance. One by one, they climbed the wooden ladder at the tailgate to take their seats. Each was greeted by three 'Good mornings' and one 'Certainly!'

Finally, Billy, another of the driver's sons appeared, hair tousled, eyes reddened from the previous night's alcohol.

"Come on, Billy," the men chided in chorus.

"Certainly!", echoed Lefty.

A thump on the wooden boards, a crunch of gears and the Dodge moved off, down Canal Street. Through the bleak Town it bumped. Stopping at intervals, it gathered up the dark figures that clapped and stamped for warmth.

Stopping until it had its fill of hired slaves.

Next to him on the bench, 'Cock' endlessly fanned the wheel of his cigarette lighter. The flint sparked like a strobe in the darkness but could not ignite the dried wick. The Boy watched, spellbound, wondering why the man did not ask for a light from another .....or at least buy some fuel. As the flint sparked once more, the little man looked up, fixing his gaze in the flash of light. Then, from the darkness,

"Is You Am You Is? Or Is You Am You Isn't?" He riddled.

"I Is. I Am. I Is," the Boy answered, determined not to be ridiculed by the unanswerable question.

"Wrong! You Is. You am. You Isn't!" Cock' said and continued to fan the lighter.

Onward, through the desolate landscape, the lorry trundled, carrying the men to the fields and the Boy from his childhood.

A chill wind was blowing. It chased away the fog to reveal the watery orb of the sun. The harvester, now at the far end of the field, had already initiated its day's work. Headlights blazing, it turned to make another run. Lines of unearthed carrots, tops amputated, marked its deafening pass.

The men did not immediately begin to work. They waited, standing in small groups, smoking and talking until the machine had made two more passes, for, hidden in the wet fronds that rained down, were frozen lumps of soil, hard enough to crack a skull. When it was safe, they started to work. Bent over in pairs, they filled baskets then sacks from baskets with the bright vegetables; only source of colour in that grey day.

Baz, the middle of Big Louis' sons, had taken a liking for the Boy. He agreed to work in tandem with him, showing him the fastest way to pick, how to fill sack from basket.

Rubber gloves, worn to protect his hands, filled with sweat that chilled then froze his fingers. Rubber boots, worn to defend against the wet, sucked the heat from his feet until they, too, were numb with cold. Ice wind tugged at his shirt and trousers, freezing back and hamstrings. Soon, the Boy was crying from the cold.

"Keep going," Baz urged, "we'll get a fire going at 'Dokky time."

Up and down the field, the men worked, devouring the orange lines. Hundred-weight sacks stuffed with vegetables marked their wake. On parade, the Hessian guard. Then, the machine stopped.

"Dokky time," the foreman announced and aching backs were slowly straightened.

The men built a blazing fire with wooden pallets soaked in diesel from the lorry's fuel tank. Squatting around the fire, they ate with pen-knives, cutting from hunks * then sipping tea from vacuum flasks.

The Man had prepared soup and luncheon meat sandwiches for him but he felt too cold to eat. Seated next to the bonfire, the Boy prepared to take off his boots.

"Come away from there, Son. You'll get the 'hot aches," his father warned.

Away from the blaze, he rubbed the Boy's stockinged feet with bared hands. To no avail, the 'hot aches' would not be denied. With an unforgiving surge of pain, blood brought feeling to toes and fingers, tears to eyes. But there was no time for crying. The noise of the harvester's engine told them that 'Dokky time' was over.

Once again, up and down the field, the men followed the lines of carrots, leaving only the Hessian rearguard behind them. Finally, the machine stopped.

As they walked from the field, the Man proudly laid his hand on his son's shoulder. He had not thought that he would last the whole day.

Bumping along in the cold darkness of the canvas hood, the Boy shivered with cold. He prayed to be home.

* A whole loaf, cut in half and packed with sausages, eggs and bacon.

In the House, the heat from the crackling coals overwhelmed him. Too exhausted to eat, he dozed in the armchair. Already asleep, he was carried to bed by his father.

The next morning, he sat, back and hams as taut as bowstrings, stiffened from the work of the previous day. He watched as Cock' initiated the daily ritual of the cigarette lighter. Smiling in the strobe light, the little man looked up, catching the Boy's eye. Without a pause from his endeavours, he shouted above the noise of the lorry's engine,

"Now, You Is! You Am! You Is!"

CHAPTER TWENTY-FOUR: 'ON THE LAND'; SUMMER

The lorry stood by the bus stop, rear clad in timber and green canvas. Only the bright, red eyes betrayed its presence in the morning mist. The short, wooden ladder was in its place at the tailgate. In the cab, driver and son read yesterday's papers while they waited.

Two men were already seated in the gloom of the canvas hood, presence betrayed by the glow of their hand-rolled cigarettes.

"Morning, Johnny."

"Morning."

"Morning, Lefty."

"Certainly!"

The Boy made his way through the acrid smoke and dust to sit behind the cab. Shortly after, Big Louis and his three sons appeared, taking their seats to three 'Mornings' and one 'Certainly!'

Finally, hair ruffled, eyes bloodshot, the habitual latecomer arrived, climbing the ladder to the usual chorus;

"Come on, Billy."

"Certainly!"

As the lorry moved through the mist, collecting its complement of workers, the cigarette lighter sparked over and over, again.

The morning sun had already cleared the mist to waist height. Solitary trees rose, dark shadows on the horizon. Hedgerows dripped white above the crisp, cold blanket that covered the fields.

Solemnly, the workmen gathered around Ducky, the foreman. A first glance had been enough to tell the Boy how the man had come by his nickname. For this was a man with large, protruding belly atop short legs and large feet. Arthritic joints made him waddle as he walked. With peaked cap and thick-lensed spectacles, he gave every appearance of a cartoon duck. His father had warned him against the use of the nickname. None dared use it to the foreman's face, lest they lose their employment.

Ducky produced a small, cloth bag from the inside pocket of his jacket. One by one, the men drew lots. Thus, the good or bad fortune of their day's labour was decided.

With an exaggerated air of self-importance, Ducky walked the field, short legs stretching to pace the yards between markers. He paused at regular intervals and bent to wrench a handful of carrots from the ground. In this manner, the border of each man's land was determined.

The men waddled behind him, in Indian file like so many ducklings. Imitating the foreman's gait, they pressed chins into chests to stifle their laughter. At each stop, they straightened up, faces deadpan as the foreman made the mark. Then, the charade began anew, continued to the next plot of land.

Each man carried the short-handled fork, low-walled riddle and bunk* in one hand, a roll of empty sacks over his other arm. As he reached his allocated tract, he pushed bunk into empty sack. Then, with fork in one hand and riddle to his side, he bent to begin his daily toil.

The Man stopped when he reached 'his land.' Legs covered with an empty sack, he paced the boundary from the foreman's mark, trampling a line through the sodden carrot tops. Then, he bent to work so that the Boy might watch. With one hand, he plunged his fork through, into the soft, black soil.

"Not too close, mind. Don't spike the carrots," he warned over one shoulder without pausing from his work.
With his free hand, he grabbed as many fronds as he could hold, prising the roots with the fork. A sharp tap on his boot to release any loose earth, a swift move of his other hand (fork now released) and a dozen topless carrots rattled into the wire bottom of the riddle.

* A large, galvanized funnel that fitted the neck of a hundredweight sack.

With an easy sway of the hips, he now worked crab-like along the green lines. With every sidewards step, he repeated the process, dragging the riddle atop his trailing foot. The Boy bent to follow his father's lead.

Within minutes, all of the men had disappeared, bending into the mist. The only sign of their presence was a steady crunch, crunch, crunch as they began to fill the riddles.

Then the first figure rose up, waist deep in the mist. With a dull, metallic 'Thunk,' forty pounds of carrots found their way to the bottom of a sack, then another and another; carrots rat-a-tat-tatting through the metal funnels. The sudden noise sent a dozen rats scurrying for safety in the headlands* at the far end of the field.

Like so many insects on the edge of a green leaf, the men crunched their way through the carrot tops. Fat sacks and carpets of fronds again marked their passing.

As the Boy bent over to work, hot stomach acid surged mercilessly down into his chest as the toasted 'soldiers' made their bid for freedom. His arms and legs soaked with dew. As if to protect their fruit, the green fronds lashed at his face with their cold fingers. Rubber gloves squelched with sweat as he worked. Soon, his back and hamstrings were begging him to stop, screaming with that old, familiar pain.

* Headlands: (Slang) term referring to the outer perimeter of a field.

At last, the riddle was filled. With great effort, he lifted it, shaking off the soil that remained on the carrots. One more heave and he emptied riddle into bunk, almost following the vegetables as they went tumbling into the sack. For a few precious moments, he had found an excuse to rise out of the freezing mist, straighten aching back and relieve the fire that devoured his legs.

"Bend that back, Boy," laughed Cock' from the adjoining plot of land, before emptying his own riddle and ducking back into the mist.

Cock' was the Man's drinking partner. They would turn up, late on a Friday or Saturday night, breath laden with beer. The Boy would clear the table of his books and the three then eat fish and chips from their newspaper wrappings.

"Here you are. This is for the gas meter," Cock' would say with a wink, flipping the Boy a two shilling coin for the one shilling slot.

Cock' was a small, wiry man. His skin was brown and wrinkled with age, forehead crossed with a white line from the flat cap that he wore to work. In the fields, his old, pinstriped suit, frayed at cuffs and elbows, gave him the bizarre appearance of a destitute banker. The Boy suspected, the ever-present cigarette that dangled from the corner of his mouth would never be lit.

Many guessed at why the little fellow had left the imaginary comforts of the Capital for that harsh life. But nobody really knew. Even the Boy's father did not know the true reason for his migration. Especially as most people were now migrating to the Capital, not away from it. A criminal past was the general consensus among the Town's gossips.

One Friday night, speech slurred from too much alcohol, Cock' had confessed to the Boy.

"Better fog than smog," he had confided and the Boy had kept this, the simplest of explanations, as their secret.

With renewed determination, the Boy returned to his work. As he bent stiffly, Cock's laughter at his distress followed him down among the carrot tops.

The sun, now a white orb overhead, burned stronger and stronger until the mist was gone. Steam rose from land and men alike as the harsh rays beat down. The men now worked, stripped to the waist, brown torsos glistening with sweat; each in his own, personal cloud of flies.

"Keep your shirt on," his father warned, "or you'll burn. These little blighters will eat you alive!"

A Land Rover bumped across the field, weaving its way between the upright sacks in its path. A young, well-groomed man sat behind the wheel, dressed in starched shirt and summer slacks. His appearance was completely at odds with the band of ragamuffins that he passed. This was Francis; landowner's son and manager of the farm where the gang now worked.

Before he would step down from the vehicle, he carefully exchanged patent leather shoes for boots, tucking expensive slacks into the safety of calf-length rubber. Only then, would he venture into the carrot-field. The Man stopped work to greet him.

"Afternoon, Francis," he said, dripping sweat into their handshake.
Together with the foreman, they walked the field.

"Looks like a good crop," Francis said.

"There's more light than dark," the Man argued. "Rough work for most. Two-thirds of the land will give a poor yield."

"No. The crop's good," Ducky interrupted, eager to curry favour with his employer.

"AND THE 'MARKET' is low," Francis added.

"ALWAYS THE 'MARKET,'" the Man thought bitterly.

Because none of them had control over 'THE MARKET.' 'THE MARKET' was blamed for everything. He knew full well the futility of his arguments because the manager already had a price for the crop fixed in his mind. Although, ostensibly, the men worked at a 'piece' work rate, it did not matter. However hard they worked, their daily wage rarely changed.

If each man could only harvest one ton a day, 'THE MARKET' would be 'HIGH' and they would be paid four shillings per bag. If the crop were good and each man could gather two tons, 'THE MARKET' would be 'LOW.' Then, the manager would agree to pay only two shillings per bag. And of course, there was always the possibility, THE THREAT, of a bad crop and a 'LOW MARKET.'

The men's only satisfaction was to fill a few more bags, scrape a few more shillings than his neighbour. Thus, they remained over-worked; divided and weakened by petty greed. The manager knew this, as did the Man. Still, he continued his bargaining into 'Dokky' time while the rest of the men carried on working.

The Man argued from pride and the hope that one day the others might support him in his efforts for a better wage. But they never would.

Rent had to be paid, large families fed and clothed. Better they live this life of economic slavery than the alternative of penury in unemployment. Many were those only too willing to take their place in the gang of labourers. So, eyes lowered, they squatted in a circle, eating their hunks and swallowing tepid water from glass bottles; Silent Witnesses to their own shame and cowardice.

Still, the Man persisted in his arguments, now supported by Herb and the two bachelors of the work gang; Billy and Cock.' Still, the farm manager's resolve remained unshaken. Still, the price per bag remained the same. And when 'Dokky' time was over, they all returned to bake among the flies and stench of rotting carrot tops.

From the sanctuary of the canvas cover, the men wolf-whistled past the women of the villages. Ignoring their shouted compliments and indecent proposals, the women scurried indoors to escape the dust devils thrown up by the lorry's wheels. Squinting through the choking haze, the Boy saw it for the first time. Somebody had burned two, large, capital letters into the wooden beam above his head.

The message read; 'I.F.'

CHAPTER TWENTY-FIVE:
A MOST UNEXPECTED INVITATION

The Boy sat at the table. Light from the afternoon sun, filtering through the window, barely lit the room. So he read, head bent into the book, squinting to distinguish the small, black print.

On this day, he sailed with Captain Cook, imagination lost in adventures on the South Seas. He was so engrossed in his reading that he had not heard his father's return to the Yard. He looked up, startled, blinking in the flood of sunlight from the open door.

The Man stood, framed in the doorway, silhouette steaming sweat from the bicycle ride. In his hands, he carried two shopping bags bulging with the next weeks' provisions. Through the door, he carefully placed the bags onto the seat of the old armchair beneath the window. He was smiling when he turned towards the Boy.

"Seems like, you've got an admirer, Son," he said.
Reaching into one of the bags, he produced a large, white envelope. The Boy's name was printed on the front of it in bold, red letters.

"Go on, then, Boy. Open it!" The Man said.
Blushing beneath his father's grin, he tore open the envelope.

"You are cordially invited to the 11th BIRTHDAY PARTY of MISS. JANE…," it read.

"Told you!!" His father said, reading over his shoulder. The Boy had turned away the card. But his father had been too fast for him.

"I, I'm not going," he stammered, confused.

Why would the gangly redhead from the front of the class, "cordially invite" him to her party? She had barely spoken to him throughout their days at the school. She was usually surrounded by her gaggle of friends, over whom she towered; unapproachable.

Such red hair and freckles were rarely seen amongst the swarthy children of the Fens. Yet, dark eyes seemed to deny her Viking ancestry.

The Boy sensed some trap.

"Why not?" His father asked.

"I…. I won't know anybody. There won't be anyone from this side of Town."

"Of course, you will. Jane's in your class at school, isn't she? You know her brother and most of her friends."

"Yes, but they're HER friends, not mine. They'll make fun of me."

"Don't you be so daft. Just think of all that cake and ice-cream."

Even the thought of a birthday beano could not allay the Boy's suspicions. He tried one, last excuse.

"I haven't a present to give her. I spent all my money at the sea-side."

"You'll think of something, Boy, Come on, it'll give me the afternoon off. I won't have to cook your dinner or tea."

With heavy heart, the Boy yielded to his father's arguments.

CHAPTER TWENTY-SIX: THE BIRTHDAY PARTY.

Clothes newly washed and ironed; hands, fingernails and ears scrubbed and double-scrubbed, he pedalled to the other side of Town.

He left the old bicycle hidden in the hedgerow and walked up the gravelled drive to the large, detached house. Inside the porch, he groomed brillantined hair with fingers, shaping it to the contours of his head with little pats from his open palms. He rang the door-bell.

Jane's mother answered the door. Without a smile, not even a single word of welcome, the woman ushered him, inside.

As he had suspected, the other guests were all girls. The only other males present in the house were Peter, Jane's twin brother, safely hidden away in his bedroom, and their father. The latter was the local bank manager, whose stentorian tones could be heard from time to time drifting from some far corner of the house.

Three, vigilant mothers lurked around the long dinner-table while two others put the finishing touches to the birthday spread.

The party had begun with games; 'Pass the orange,' 'Blind man's buff' and 'Pin the donkey's tail.' Much to the delight of the other guests, the Boy proved too large and clumsy for such skilful manoeuvres, failing in his every effort. At long last, the food was served.

He found himself seated opposite Jane at the far end of the table. All chatter ceased as sandwiches and sausage rolls, trifles and jellies, all disappeared from view, consumed by the voracious 'young ladies.' Candles extinguished with one breath from the hostess, the cake and its icing quickly followed. When all the food had been devoured, careful mothers cleared the table. Then, with great ceremony, the birthday presents were paraded into the room.

One by one, Jane opened letters and packages from the pile heaped on the table in front of her. Book tokens and postal orders, clothes and jewellery emerged: a watch from her parents. Each gift was greeted with 'ooh's' and 'aah's' from the guests and their mothers, sometimes even a round of applause.

As the cards and presents were revealed, the Boy felt more and more uneasy.

"How would his own gift be received?"

"Would the girl like it?"

It was his most valued treasure in the whole world.

"I've saved the best until last. I wonder, what is it?" Jane asked, prodding at the package with her forefinger.

"It's not a P.E.N.D.A.N.T., is it?"

The Boy, startled, sat rigid in his chair at the memory evoked by the word, at this reminder of his humiliation. The girl had understood! She had really understood. For, although the smile bespoke mischief, sympathy and warmth glowed in her eyes.

Fortunately, the joke was lost on friends and mothers alike. All the same, it had served to draw more attention to the Boy than was comfortable. Only the rustle of wrapping paper could turn their stares back to the head of the table. As Jane stripped away paper and cardboard, her jaw sagged, eyes grew wide with wonder.

On the table in front of her, stood a wooden solider. Some six inches tall, it was the exact replica of a Grenadier Guardsman. Fashioned from a single block, the figure stood to 'attention,' bayonette fixed.

The bearskin was of coney fur, dyed black with boot polish. Face, beneath, was intricately carved to match hands that clutched the small, metal pipe of a rifle barrel. Belts and pouches were of fine, white linen; their intricate stitching equal to any seamstress's embroidered perfection. Red lipstick stained tunic and face, with more black polish for eyes and moustache, trousers and boots.

Here stood the Boy's one remaining souvenir of Uncle Stumpy.

Jane seemed the only person in the room to appreciate the detailed beauty of the carved figure. Friends and friends' mothers saw only a toy soldier; a Boy's toy, most inappropriate gift for a young lady. She looked up, to thank him for his fabulous gift. Before she could speak, one of the attendant women burst into laughter.

"Whatever on earth, IS IT?" She chortled.

Within seconds, the rest of the girls were all screaming with exaggerated laughter, as ever, happy for an excuse to make loud noise, ignorant of the true reason for the woman's outburst.

As the Boy fled to his bicycle and escape, Jane remained seated at the table, the wooden soldier clutched in her trembling fingers.

That night, alone in her room, she once more cried for the Boy's unjust treatment and again, for her failure to win his trust.

Her attempts at reconciliation and friendship had only served to compound his misery and humiliation.

CHAPTER TWENTY-SEVEN: THE PHOTOGRAPH

It had been a good day, the visit to the bank a successful one.   The manager had sanctioned a loan to buy the old Blackwell house.   Electricity for himself and the Boy meant life would become more tolerable.   He had worked hard to save the deposit and there was enough money remaining to have bathroom and toilet fitted in the third bedroom of their new home.   The Boy would have a room of his own, a place to study.

The Yard was a desolate place.   The other residents had either died or moved away from the primitive dwellings.   One by one, the houses had been demolished, leaving only the small terrace.   The council workmen had pinned a notice to the Smiths' door.   In big, red letters it announced;

"CONDEMNED   NOT   FIT   FOR   HUMAN HABITATION."

The Man had laughed because the notice had not appeared until the Smiths' departure, because none would appear on his own door until it was time to leave.   This, he would do with no regrets.   The House held few, fond memories, only reminders of misery, deprivation and shattered dreams.

He was proud that he would soon be a householder, that his son would receive the education that he, himself, had been denied.   One day, the Boy would make his escape from the

Town.   The twin yolk of poverty and physical labour would never be his to shoulder.   He would leave behind all the petty jealousies and bitter secrets.

He peered down into the top of the box camera. Reflected in the small lens, the Boy squinted into the sun.   He had been dressed especially for the occasion.   Striped tie matched the new uniform; black with red braid at the lapels. Black shoes shined in gleaming contrast to the starched brilliance of his new shirt.   Gold shields adorned cap and jacket at the breast pocket.   Arms, flattened to pointed fingers, compressed the empty, leather satchel at his side.

"Smile, Son."

As the shutter clicked shut, his squint became even more pronounced.

He felt uncomfortable and ridiculous in the new clothes.

PART TWO

"ALL FOR AN EDUCATION"

"He who judges by appearance,

ignores the Essence of Man."

CHAPTER ONE: THE FIRST DAY.

On that day, the Boy walked alone to the 'bus stop. Robbed of the loosely fitting workclothes, his body chafed in the grip of the new uniform. The tie urged him to rip and tear at the starched collar of his new shirt. Shiny, black shoes pinched at his feet. Empty satchel hung from his shoulder.

Four figures in identical uniforms were waiting at the 'bus stop. Each boy greeted him before lapsing back into sultry silence. Gone, the long, summer days and their temporary illusion of freedom, none relished a return to the world of discipline and learning.

As for the Boy, nothing, he reasoned, could be worse than his last six weeks of back-breaking toil in the fields.

He was mistaken.

After a few minutes' time, a red, single-decker 'bus came into view. It was crowded with girls en route to the local "high school;" green-clad Harpies that crowded and pressed against the glass sides of the vehicle. As it passed the 'bus stop and slowed for the bend in the road, a cacophony of shouted insults and sexual taunts streamed through its opened windows. To the Boy's surprise, his companions replied in kind; screamed profanities accompanied by the rudest of hand and facial gestures.

Seated at the front among the 'new' girls, Jane smiled balefully out at him.

A few minutes' more and the double-decker 'bus appeared. One by one, the five joined the silent ranks of seated boys

The 'bus meandered out of the Town and into the countryside. Cleared of its crops, the land lay desolate to the far horizon. The few trees that braved this wilderness stood braced in naked readiness for the winter winds. Great flocks of swallows rose as the 'bus passed. They circled in a dark cloud before returning to line the telephone wires. Soon, they would flee, leaving only seagulls to scavenge the deserted fields.

The 'bus chugged onwards, through the Fenland villages. It stopped from time to time, stripping more, uniformed victims of their temporary freedom. Finally, laden with the dreams and aspirations of forty families, it reached its destination.

The school would prove more daunting than the Boy could ever have imagined. It was housed in a group of imposing Victorian buildings that formed a large, inner quadrangle.

At one end of this square were the classrooms and gymnasium which doubled as an assembly hall. This main building was flanked by workshops and the prefects' common room on one side, courts for 'fives' and outside toilet-block on the other. Facing the classrooms, dominating the playground, were the headmaster's house and office.

This configuration provided a very effective method for control of the schoolchildren. Within its confines, over-zealous prefects, conscious that they also might be the targets of surveillance, would cuff and cajole 'discipline' into their juniors. In fact, there existed at the school, a system of institutionalized terror whereby violence was considered 'discipline'. Only when it was meted from above. Over a hierarchy of prefects and teachers, the headmaster ruled with heart of stone and cane of birch.

This was a tall, hard-faced man whose standards and prejudices had been forged in a bygone era. To his shame, his was a 'grammar' not a 'public' school. To his great annoyance, there arrived at the beginning of each year, not only the sons of the middle classes but also the children of labourers and farm hands. He hated these boys for their bland faces and imperfect drawls. Even the homogeneous uniforms did nothing to disguise their heavy limbs and oafish appearance.

Appearances were paramount to the headmaster. The appearance of grooming, of dress, even the affectation of learning; these were his prime concerns. The fact that entrance to the school was regulated by ability alone was of secondary import to him. He believed, education could only be instilled by discipline and fear. The threat of discipline brought obedience. Learning would then, surely, follow. He could not understand that only a love, a thirst for knowledge, promotes genius. Fear brings only outward compliance and token achievement. Inevitably, it leads to resentment, mediocrity and failure.

It was here in this 'seat of learning' that the Boy would taste true prejudice for the first time; unjustified in its presence, violent and bitter in its reality. It was here that the seeds of rebellion would be so firmly planted in his heart.

The 'bus stopped in the market square at the centre of the town. Ignored by eagle-eyed shopkeepers and housewives intent on their daily forage, the schoolchildren filed from the 'bus. Formed up in pairs, they marched the short distance to the school. At their backs, prefects snapped like collies at the heels of so many sheep.

In the quadrangle, boys local to the school already waited. From the front of their ranks, a teacher shouted the roll call;

"Abbs, 4a, Room Two."

"Abrahim, 2 alpha, Room Six."

"Hurry, Boy. Step Lively! Don't Run. Walk!"

Behind the net curtains of his office, the headmaster secretly appraised each boy. Fists clenched at the sight of loose ties and sloping shoulders. Names etched into his cold mind.

The children entered his domain, ready marked and prejudged.

CHAPTER TWO: A POSITIVE INFLUENCE.

The class sat crowded into the rows of one-piece desks. Nervous voices answered the master's roll call. Red curls sprang beneath the mortar board as he read. Behind gold-rimmed spectacles, clear, blue eyes scrutinized each child, fixing names to faces. The boys little knew that behind the impassive stare lurked a bright and playful mind. Already, it planned the nicknames with which he would dub his charges. The red-headed boy would become 'Poil De Carotte;' the short boy, 'Monsieur Le Trec;' the fat Boy, 'La Pomme.' As the names droned on, the Boy's attention wandered to his surroundings.

High ceiling and giant windows ensured the futility of the cast iron radiators spaced beneath them. The master's seat and table, a blackboard and cupboard for books faced the rows of battered desks at which the boys sat. The floor was parquet, the interlaced blocks darkened and aged from too much polishing.

Before he realised it, the master was upon him, ruffling his hair and tugging at his ears. Then, they were away, the teacher at the rear of the bench skilfully manoeuvring Boy and desk through the ranks of children; like a bobsleigh in a slalom. Around and around they went, the desk rebounding from wall to radiator, from radiator to blackboard.

The teacher was wide-eyed, a madman. His gown flew behind him like bat wings, mortar board tipped to the side of his head. The Boy recoiled in terror as the giant eyes, large as saucers behind the lenses of the spectacles, appeared inches from his face.

"Attention, ma petite pomme!"

Then, the master laughed.

Little did the Boy realise, the influence that this man was to exert over his future education.

He would recoil from the endless repetition of facts and figures already known by heart. But French and Spanish figured hardly anywhere in his beloved encyclopaediae. Fate had cast as his form-master, a man whose enthusiasm would catalyse his thirst for subjects new, discover and fuel a talent that had, thus far, laid hidden.

A desire to impress this teacher would see the Boy's every, spare moment spent in the study of his new languages.

CHAPTER THREE: A GLIMPSE OF THE CLASSICS

The Latin master, like the wild French teacher, was a man in his late twenties. That is where the similarity ended.

Just as the modern language teacher was short and squat, flamboyant in attitude; so the Latin master was tall and athletic, introverted. The pate of his prematurely balding head was tanned, surrounded by a laurel of fine, blond hair. Blue eyes and chiselled features would have been more at home in a sun-drenched arena than the dimly lit corridors of the school.

Due to this appearance, the headmaster had appointed him as sports master. The truth was, he knew very little about sport. Instead, he preferred the company of a rusty bicycle; his only form of transport. Long, solitary rides across the Fens kept him in excellent shape and gave him time for meditation of the Classics.

Unfortunately, his command of Latin was not equalled by his control over the pupils in his classroom. They would seize upon the slightest excuse to run amok. His desk or seat would be booby-trapped, insults scrawled on the blackboard before his arrival. His classes often veered towards anarchy. Speechless with exasperation, mouth working like a goldfish in a bowl, he would shout voiceless commands at his unheeding charges.

The children considered this lack of resolve as weakness. Only his promise of a trip to the headmaster's study could bring order to the chaos but this sensitive and erudite man would have endured almost anything rather than subject his tormentors to such an ordeal.

A temporary armistice established, he would drill the class with an endless repetition of declensions and conjugations; his only cornerstone in an uncertain world.

So, the Boy was presented with yet another opportunity to explore fresh fields, discover the challenge of the Latin conundrum. He now divided his time between the three languages.

Soon, he discovered the inextricable link between old and new, between past and present.

CHAPTER FOUR: GAMES' DAY

The playing fields were at a three-mile walk from the school. These consisted of a large expanse of grass surrounding a run-down pavilion. The latter served as changing-rooms. Access to the grounds was gained through two, high, wooden gates. Their slats were covered with the same, peeling, green paint as the pavilion. The perimeter was a mix of thick hedgerow and metal railings. Giant, horse-chestnut trees were scattered around the edges of the pitches, jealous guardians of every ball that they could catch.

Studs clattered as the two teams; one dressed in blue, one dressed in white, trotted out of the pavilion. To a fanfare of silent trumpets, the games' master, in new track-suit and freshly dubbined boots, led the procession. He ran onto the pitch, knees pumping, leather ball held high on his chest. Symbol of authority; a bright silver whistle was hung proudly from a ribbon about his neck.

The boys gathered around the teacher, hands hidden in armpits. Biting wind reddened legs and faces. Teeth chattered to the sound of the master's voice as he explained the rules of rugby union.

What he explained had very little resemblance to the game as we know it. What he explained was a mixture of soccer, Gaelic and American football. What ensued bore no resemblance, at all, to the game as explained by the master. What followed was an all-in-wrestling match with the ball, more often than not, a forgotten spectator on the touchline.

To enthuse the boys, the master joined in the game, adding his physical prowess to the cause of the weaker team. The very first time that he caught the ball, friend and foe alike assailed him from all sides. Within seconds, he was flattened beneath a scrimmage of screaming, jostling children. Seeing the master so helplessly pinned, the Boy snatched the ball from his hands and headed towards the try-line.

Beneath the crush of bodies, the master struggled to bring the whistle to his lips. Only minutes before, it had been bright in shiny silver. Now, crushed by boots and clogged with mud, it could produce only a plaintive rattle.

"Foul," the master gasped, "bring back the ball."

The Boy dutifully trotted back to the blue and white mountain of bodies and handed the ball through the mêlée of thrashing limbs. There came the faintest of whistles from the centre of the scrimmage. With one lumbering dive, he added his bulk to the mass of bodies. There was a loud gasp as the last breath of air was crushed from the teacher's lungs. For a second time, he grabbed the ball and headed for the try-line.

This time, the whistle remained silent.

As he walked from the pavilion, Mr. Bailey felt a certain, inner satisfaction at his afternoon's work. The boys had been allowed to let off steam, deplete their youthful energy. He had definitely made progress with the class. At the entrance to the playing fields, he looked up. Two, old, bicycle wheels now adorned the tops of the gateposts. A rusty frame balanced precariously from one of the gates.

With a deep sigh, he lifted it down.

CHAPTER FIVE: RETRIBUTION

The last notes from the piano sounded around the gymnasium. Shuffling feet prepared to exit the assembly.

"School, stand still."

The voice was loud and menacing. All movement in the hall ceased. On the apron of the stage, the headmaster faced the school. Gold pince-nez glinted on the hooked nose. Hidden behind the terror reflected in their lenses, unblinking eyes stared out. Bald pate and lined face flushed red with anger. With wattled neck emerging from the black folds of his gown, he had every appearance of a great vulture. Behind him on the stage, his subordinates perched, ready for the feast.

"School, sit."

As one, the three hundred occupants of the hall crouched before crossing legs to sit on the floor. At the rear of the hall, the prefects remained standing. The cane in the headmaster's hand thrashed down against the table behind him. A shiver, like grass in the wind, spread its wave across the seated children. Strongest at the front where the younger children sat, it weakened and dissipated as it reached the line of prefects. At that moment in time, even the purest felt guilt.

"I will not tolerate thieves in MY school," the headmaster's voice rose to a shout.

"Jenks, 4a, come forward, boy."

On legs like rubber, a figure arose from the seated files. Very slowly, he made his way to the front of the stage.

"Come up here, boy."

The teenager climbed the steps at the side of the stage.

"You're a thief! What are you, boy?"

The answer was inaudible.

"Speak up, boy! What are you?"

"A, a thief, sir," the voice trembled.

The headmaster grabbed the boy by the arm and threw him, face down, across the table.

"Mr. Carter."

Mr. Carter stood from his seat at the back of the stage.

"Take a grip, sir."

His form-master pinned the boy's arms across the table. With an ungainly run, the great vulture lashed his cane across the youth's buttocks. By the fourth stroke, the lad was crying; victim of both his pain and this, most public humiliation. When the punishment was over, he stood stiffly to thank the headmaster.

"Stop snivelling. Get out! Go to your form-room."

The delinquent schoolboy limped past the seated rows of his peers. His stifled sobs echoed back from the corridor into the silent hall.

"Leonard, 3a. Come, boy."

The next victim came to the table.

"Mr. Bailey."

There was no movement in the line of teachers. The Latin master remained seated, arms crossed in defiance, ears deaf to the headmaster's summons.

"Mr. Bailey! Sir?"

Mr. Bailey's jaw clenched in a tight ball. His eyes fixed firmly on the back of the hall.

His silent protest had done nothing to save Leonard from his fate. He was duly flogged. Then, one by one, his four, other accomplices in crime made the long walk to the stage and the headmaster's retribution.

After that day, there was no more tumult in the Latin class. Even so, at the end of the school term, Mr. Bailey left the school. And the next term?

The same thieves were again flogged ... for stealing from the same shops in the town.

CHAPTER SIX: BIG JAKE (HERO)

His given name was John.   Everyone; teachers, schoolchildren, even his own family called him 'Big Jake.' Everyone, that is, except his father from whom he had inherited his massive size.   The latter was a vicious and vindictive drunk who would vent his anger and frustrations on his son.   In alcoholic rage, he would beat the lad to the floor, pounding him with stone fists and hurtful kicks, just as he would beat any man in a bar-room brawl.

Big Jake clung to his nickname.   He basked in its implied notoriety, as he believed that it evoked his heroes of the cinema screen; the American cowboys.   So, he wore his old scars and new bruises with pride; false testimonies to a secret and hectic lifestyle outside of school hours.

Big Jake did not like the school, its staff or the rules that they enforced.   He would use his size to intimidating effect when dealing with the bullying prefects in the quadrangle. Should one ever order Big Jake to 'write lines,' he would find the scribbled pages crumpled and stuffed into his breast pocket, his ear tweaked by a massive paw.   Big Jake despised them all. Even as a group, they dared not confront him.   At school, on the rugby pitch, he would crush them with bone-breaking tackles. And out of school?   Everybody treasured their weekly visit to the local youth club; focal point of the region's social life. Where Big Jake held court!

Expulsion from the school would have been the headmaster's admission of defeat, serve only to enhance Big Jake's iconic status among the younger boys. Expulsion? Never! So, Big Jake remained at the school; thorn in the side of authority, the pupils' hero.

On the top deck of the school 'bus, Big Jake would lounge across the front seats, tie loosened, Cuban-heeled boots crossed on the window ledge. School cap was worn pushed to the back of his head in deference to his 'Tony Curtis' hairstyle; a hairstyle that, every fifteen minutes or so, needed the attentions of Big Jake's steel comb. Although a non-smoker, the corked tip of a cigarette was ever barely visible above the braid of his breast pocket. When he walked, the rattle of a matchbox punctuated the 'click-clack' of his boots; sound of the gunslinger's spurs on the streets of Dodge City.

Despite his dubious status among the hierarchy of the school, Big Jake steadfastly refused to bully the younger pupils. Their whispered tales of his escapades only served to enhance his reputation, encourage him to further outrages.

Finished the Boy's second year, Big Jake left the school.

CHAPTER SEVEN: BIG JAKE (VILLAIN)

The news of his application to join the police force came as a great shock to Big Jake's army of supporters. Pupils gasped in disbelief as the word was passed from classroom to classroom. Denials and excuses were made in defence of their idol. Teachers seized upon the chance to defame the legend that was Big Jake, affirming the rumour at every opportunity. They even cited him as a success, testimony to the school's 'advanced' teaching levels. The headmaster, himself, had written a glowing reference for the reformed rebel. Despite Big Jake's appalling disciplinary record and mediocre academic standards, the headmaster had leaped at this chance to improve the school's success ratings.

Thus, Big Jake's reputation in the classroom became blackened and besmirched. Tales of his heroic exploits and invulnerability were no longer repeated to new arrivals. His legend, it seemed, was doomed.

When the police car passed the school 'bus, the boys hissed and booed at the uniformed driver. Officer Jake, hair and sideburns now trimmed short, carried on his way, oblivious to the insults that followed him. Betrayed and deserted by their hero, now silenced by the gloating prefects, the children sat in dazed anticipation of another year's servitude at the school.

Big Jake had become 'Traitor Jake.'

During the next twelve months, Traitor Jake, "You will address me as, officer," set about his new profession with uncharacteristic diligence. Working from a mental list of his former persecutors, he systematically harassed teachers, former prefects and bullies. The headmaster and his deputy were particular suspects. The new recruit stopped them at every opportunity. Spilling ashtrays onto carpets and upholstery, he zealously searched their cars for illicit substances. The suspicion of alcohol on breath meant that white lines had to be walked, alphabets recited backwards. Familiar names were taken, time and time again, by the smiling representative of law and order. After his first 'investigation,' the inexperienced officer was compelled to buy new shoes. In his enthusiasm to test the rear lights of the headmaster's car, he had used feet instead of truncheon!

Officer Jake remained in the area for the next few years. Then, he was gone, never to be seen again. Slowly, his legend faded into the folklore of the school.

Tradition has it; that he transferred to the Bahamas for a life of sun, sea and sand, that he carried on to the United States where he made his fortune as an undertaker before marrying the rich widow of one of his clients.

That he now spends his time on the verandah of his Kentucky mansion; shooting wild turkeys by day, drinking Wild Turkey by night.

CHAPTER EIGHT: BIG JAKE'S LEGACY

The Boy had managed to pass, unnoticed, his first years at the school.

His father reminded him at every opportunity, of the great chance in life his education would afford him. He encouraged his son's every effort to learn. Although the Boy seemed interested only in his new languages, sporadic study and limited application proved adequate in all other subjects. The Man refused to let him leave the house during the evening until he had completed all of his schoolwork. After a time, his gypsy friends stopped calling for fear of disturbing his studies. His expeditions to the Bridge became less and less frequent. Finally, they ceased. The Boy found himself pushed into his former solitude.

In school, seated at the back of the classroom, he strived to maintain his anonymity. He avoided teachers and prefects, dodged away from the cowardly bullies in the quadrangle. The violence of the institution did more than frighten him. The thought that the teaching body, the intellectual élite of the whole region, could stoop to such barbarism as to flog a child, sickened and reviled him.

The laboratories were situated in a cluster of prefabricated buildings pretentiously known as the 'Science

Block.' This annexe was a steady ten minutes' walk from the main school. The pupils were allowed five, unsupervised minutes to make this journey. On the way, through an alley that led from the school, was Blind Bob's sweet shop.

The Boy struggled to stay apace of the rest of the class as they half ran, half jogged, to the first chemistry lesson of the year. One of the joggers stopped in the shop doorway. After a quick glance in either direction, he ducked inside the shop. Breathless and inquisitive, the Boy stopped by the window and watched as the drama inside unfolded.

Alerted by the bell on the door, the shopkeeper, in dark suit and white apron, manned the counter. His young customer spoke and he turned sightless eyes to the lines of glass jars displayed on the shelves behind him. In an instant, two, young hands darted forwards, clutching at the bars of chocolate arranged on the counter. Alerted by the rustle of paper wrappers, the blind man whirled. With one practised move, the white cane in his hand flashed through the air, arcing down across the knuckles of one of the outstretched hands. The erstwhile thief let out a cry, clutching at his wounded fingers. With chocolate bars flying in every direction, he ran from the shop, the blind man close on his heels. Out in the alley, the Boy ran too, ducking the flailing stick.

"I know, who you are!" The shopkeeper shouted, impotent in the chase.

The thief laughed aloud. Confident of his invisibility, he insulted and goaded the old man as he made his escape.

The two fugitives arrived at the laboratory, barely in time to answer the roll call. The Boy took his place behind a bench at the back of the room, seated among the 'T's.' The deputy headmaster read from the register. When he reached the Boy's name, he paused.

"That's not any relation to Big Jake?" He asked.

Nobody, not even the headmaster himself, had ever imagined the connection. As for Big Jake, he would never have admitted to the association. Who would ever have thought that the immaculately groomed misfit could in some way be related to this fat adolescent in his ill-fitting uniform and grubby shirt?

"Yes, Sir. Cousin, Sir."

The class turned as one. Four rows of shocked faces looked back at him. A weak smile crossed his lips. His anonymity, now lost forever, had been transformed into unwanted and unwarranted notoriety. The rag, thrown with unerring aim, caught him, flush in the face. Chemicals, soaked in the muslin, stung at his eyes and forced tears streaming down his cheeks.

"Get to the front of the class! Change places with Abbott."

Looming over him, the deputy headmaster began his interrogation.

"I'm only a second cousin," the Boy explained, anxious to escape the unwanted limelight. His feeble attempt at salvation brought only laughter from the room.

"It's not funny. And you will address me as 'Sir!'"
The slap had silenced class and Boy as one.

The next day, the sweetshop thief was identified from the welt across his knuckles and duly punished. Despite all protestations, his accomplice and 'look-out' was also caned. He was given an extra two strokes; one for lying and another for not crying at his punishment.

"How dare he question the word of the shopkeeper and the deputy headmaster?"

So, finally, the headmaster was able to take his revenge on Big Jake.

CHAPTER NINE: THE CASE FOR RESTRAINT

He had never, physically punished his son. He knew only too well the futile harvest of violence. So, when he heard of the injustice at the school, his teeth clenched in anger.

He knew that his son had money of his own, saved from his toil in the fields, that he was no thief. The Man remained silent for a long time. The scars on his gnarled hands grew livid as fingers crushed into the armchair where he sat. When his grip finally relaxed, he spoke. Voice stifled with rage, his were the words of a wise father.

"You know that I would not see you hurt, Son? You must tough it out. Once you've finished school, you'll be able to get away from here, forever. We've both worked hard to get this far. Don't let them spoil it because that's what they want. You don't want to work on the land like me, for the rest of your life, do you? Get what you can from them. Just try to keep out of their way."

He felt a liar to both himself and his son. He longed to hit the man who had harmed his child. Yet he feared the harm he would cause, not only to the headmaster but to his son's prospects for a better life. His only ambition, the drive that took him from his warm bed, every morning, to work like an animal in the fields, was that his son should be free from that place.

Education would be his passport to a decent life; the Boy's fulfilment of a father's promise.

And the Boy? He would have traded a thousand schools and a thousand futures just to work in the fields with his father. His young mind had already diminished the rigours of that dour life, memory clouded by his fear and hatred of the headmaster. All the same, he gave his word that he would continue his studies.

And so he did, his every transgression, real or imaginary, pounced upon by his persecutors.

During the holiday times, he would go to the land with his father. In the evenings, they also worked, heads and bodies steaming in the floodlit barns where they prepared potatoes by the ton. The heavy work made the Boy grow bigger and bigger, stronger and stronger. When not in the fields or barns, he would spend his time in study. He was now too old to play. At the school, he controlled his anger against the headmaster and pupils who taunted him, ignorant of his bear-like strength.

Nothing, he found, would ever appease the brutish cowardice of the bullies or the bigoted snobbery of the headmaster.

CHAPTER TEN: THE FINAL STRAW.

This would be his last year at the school.

The following day would be 'Speech Day,' the annual prize-giving. Successful students would be paraded on stage before proud parents and school governors. To applause from the captive school audience, an 'Old Boy' would present prizes for athletic and academic achievements.

To the headmaster's exasperation, the teaching staff had insisted that the Boy be rewarded for his progress. The Man's chest had swollen with pride when his son told him the good news. He was to receive not one, but two prizes for his linguistic skills.

As the Boy walked towards the school entrance, the headmaster was waiting.

"Into my office. Sit."

So, the interrogation began. The headmaster berated him for his unkempt appearance, finding every fault possible with his attire. But this was only a taste of what was yet to come.

"You were seen, putting a note in the absentee box, yesterday morning."

"Yes, Sir."

"Not only was that note filthy and disgusting, it was placed there in the full knowledge that the secretaries would read it."

The headmaster's face had contorted with anger.

"No, Sir. It wasn't me, Sir. I'm the absentee monitor. I put a list of absentees in the box."

The headmaster had him now, caught in a lie. Warren was monitor for the Arts' form. In his anger, he had forgotten the Boy's banishment to the laboratories; linguist exiled amongst scientists and mathematicians. The form master, mindful that the Boy was the only one of his charges to return to the main buildings for lessons, had appointed him as 'absentee monitor.'

"You lie, Boy! Warren is the monitor."

"No, Sir. I'm not in Warren's form. Why don't you ask Mr. Smith? He's my form master."

The headmaster fumbled with the telephone on his desk. As he dialled the number, his eyes transfixed the Boy's, like some viper intent on a strike. He drummed his fingers against the desk before slamming down the receiver. Time for a change of attack.

"You do know about these other notes, don't you?"

"Yes, Sir."

"Tell me. Tell me, how? How do you know about them?"

Now the headmaster was sure of his quarry. Only schoolmasters and prefects in secret session had been told of the profane notes.

"How do you know?" The headmaster pressed.

The Boy, only non-prefect in a classroom full of prefects, had heard the gossip from the loose lips of his fellow students.

"Either you did it yourself or you know who did."

"I didn't do it, Sir."

"Then, who did? Tell me, who told you about it. Give me a name, Boy. NOW!!"

The headmaster was shouting at the top of his voice. His words resounded across the quadrangle, through the empty corridors and into the silenced classrooms. Here, beneath the vigilance of their masters, children feigned deafness, ears yet tuned to the slightest word or sound. While they waited, they read pages that never turned; heads low, eyes close to the print. It was as if the whole school cowered beneath every shouted accusation.

Inside the office, the interrogation continued; a storm unabated.

"Who told you?"

As if to demonstrate his intentions, the headmaster brought his cane down, smashing it across the wooden desk.

The Boy sat in silence. He could not have given the name, even if he had remembered it. His pride would not have permitted it. Besides, he had no idea from whose conversation he had gleaned such an irrelevant piece of information. At the time, he had been too engrossed in his studies to take notice of his 'informant.' Now, he racked his brains to avoid the question. His mind whirled at the injustice of the whole situation.

"Well? I'm waiting."

Once again, the birch slashed down across the desk in front of him.

"I can't remember, Sir."

His innocence had so far protected him. Now, he was lost for an answer. The cane sent pens and paper clips flying as it again cracked down on the desk.

His reaction was unintended, uncontrolled. In a flash, he was on his feet, rearing like a baited bear. Shoulders and arms strained in the tight jacket. Neck and eyes bulged with anger; his Father's Son.

For an instant, the headmaster lost all composure. His jaw sagged wide open as a shudder of fear raced through his body. The Boy's eyes had dilated; black as tar, hard as steel. With hand half-raised, defence against a blow that never came, the headmaster had recoiled from the desk. Frozen to the spot, for that moment in time, his face had drained of blood. He knew that the Boy had seen his fear. He struggled to speak, jaw working against his words.

"S, sit down," he stuttered, but the words lacked conviction.

Without waiting for compliance to his command, he stormed out of the office, leaving the Boy alone in front of an empty desk.

Anger abated, he sat and waited in the headmaster's study. His foe had retreated from the field of battle but he felt no sense of victory. All he felt was isolation. His body felt numb, like a sleepwalker in a dream.

He heard the school come to life as the bell rang. Feet scuffled and furniture scraped. Doors banged. An occasional voice raised in command. Shortly afterwards, the piano played and the school began to sing. The refrain of 'Onward Christian Soldiers' echoed across the quadrangle, bringing those same, old tears welling into his eyes. He felt the need to run, to escape from there.

He could hear the secretaries' whispered conversation in the adjoining office.

"You know, it's not him, Mrs. Bell."

"Of course not. You saw the spelling and handwriting. It's the work of a junior."

"You know, why this is happening, don't you?"

"It's pretty obvious. Such a shame. Poor lad."

The Boy felt hurt and indignant that now at an age of manhood, he should be accused of such a crime against these women. Their unsolicited pity made him feel weak and even more lonely. Teeth bit into trembling lips as he fought back his tears at this latest injustice. To compound his misery, the 'Christian Soldiers' carried relentlessly onwards .....

Thus, the headmaster had his way.

The next evening at the prize-giving, there were two, empty seats.

CHAPTER ELEVEN: A BITTER PILL

He had spent the remainder of the day, fighting back his tears. His head throbbed so he thought it must burst. Friends, in the mistaken belief that he had been flogged, offered whispered solace and advice on treatment for his non-existant wounds. Thieves and rebels winked in smiling conspiracy, convinced he was one of their own.

None could guess the murderous hate that burned within him. His only thought was to march back into the office and hurt that man, that bastard of a bully, that coward who thought to break him by intimidation and humiliation.

He did not kick open his door and throw the headmaster to the floor. Instead, he sat impotently at his desk, chained to the seat by the promise that he had made to his father.

At home that night, he swore that he would never return to the school. He would rather work in the fields. His ambitions lay in ruins, destroyed by the headmaster's bigotry. Without his support, he knew that his place at university was merely a dream. His mind had clouded to all reason, so that only his father's threat to fight him could make him return to the school, keep his promise.

The Man was saddened that their moment of 'Speech Day' glory had been snatched away from them, just as he regretted the argument with his son. But he had to keep his promise. He was determined that the Boy should leave for a better life in the City. His son had accepted the prospect of eight more months at the school with final resignation. He understood the Boy's anger because its fire had burned in his own heart when he heard the account of the headmaster's 'investigation'. He had thought to attend the prize giving and confront him but he realised, he could not promise to match his son's self-control. So, that Friday night, he did not go to the prize giving or the public house. He sat with his son and played cards until daybreak, losing as many games as he could.

To allay the Boy's disappointment, he decided on a very special birthday present.

CHAPTER TWELVE: BORN TO BE WILD?

The little motorcycle stood in front of the house, new and proud. Gleaming, black paintwork and bright chromium reflected the sun. Shiny wheels sparkled their promises of freedom.

He no longer passed any of his evenings in study. The red, leather tomes and foreign dictionaries remained unopened. These, his prizes, had been casually handed to him by his form master, the week after "Speech Day." Now, they lay ignored on the sideboard. Ironical symbols of success, their unopened covers signalled only failure. His studies were now perfunctory, written work hurried and unresearched. He would rather spend his time polishing and tinkering with the machine.

At weekends, he toured the backroads of the Fens. The little engine would chatter through the countryside, straining beneath its heavy load. Past the remote villages, it would race, until it reached the hostelries that dotted the flat and featureless horizon. Here, in moribund isolation, the Boy would drink warm beer from tall glasses, iced whiskey from small.

He would weave his way homewards, headlight bobbing through the darkness. Through the darkness where Officer Jake patrolled. Big Jake, whose only interest was how fast the motorcycle could travel. Cousin Jake, who wanted to race him in his panda car.

Soon, the Boy was to find that alcohol can have unexpected and calamitous effects; effects far beyond its promises of oblivion.

He was, already, quite drunk by the time he reached the 'King's Arms.' Inside, teenagers, flecked in white and purple light, danced or listened to music from the jukebox. Hands and faces glowed, ghostly in the ultra-violet rays. Motorcycle safely parked, the Boy entered the building.

A group of French workers, from the fruit farms to the East of the Town, was sitting by the door. Feigning to smash fists against table edges, they duped the unsuspecting locals into bruised knuckles and empty pockets. The Boy walked past them to the bar.

"Regardez, le grand salaud!"*
Ignoring the insult, he took his drink from the barmaid and went to sit next to the jukebox. The face leered over him, olive features lost in the darkness, eyes and teeth bright in the strange light.

"Would you like to play? Two shillings, the bet."
"What?"

---

* "Look at the great bastard!"

"To hit the table. The strong one wins."

"O.K."

His protagonist did not know it, the Boy had lost his pocket money, a decade earlier, playing Young Patrick at the very same game.

"Come to our table. Let her be the arbitrary."

He beckoned to Jane, as one of the local belles, come witness his machismo. The Boy clicked a two-shilling piece onto the table among the half-emptied beer glasses.

"You, go first," he said.

To all appearances, the French teenager's knuckles smashed down against the edge of the table. Beer leaped, frothing and overflowing down the outside of the glasses.

"I am karate expert," he smiled at the judge.

"Now, is your turn."

Jeering and leering, the rest of the French contingent gathered around the table. The Boy brought his knuckles crashing down against the table's edge. His hand, hardened by years of work in the fields, numbed by alcohol, felt nothing. Only bloody knuckles betrayed the 'morrow's pain, testimony to his own 'machismo.' Bottles danced before falling to the floor. Glasses toppled and shattered under the force of the blow, spilling their foaming contents across the legs of the spectators. His adversary leaped to his feet, cursing at his beer-soaked trousers, cursing the Boy.

"Now, listen to me. C'est toi, le grand salaud, n'est – ce pas?"* The Boy shouted above the music.

The punch had the effect of a bee sting on a badger. The anger that it caused, mixed with the alcohol that he had already consumed, was fire to gunpowder. A lifetime of frustration exploded. He grabbed his attacker and threw him across the room. He crashed into the jukebox before falling, winded, to the floor. Metal scratched into vinyl as the music came to an abrupt halt.

French and English united in flight from his screaming charge. The bar-room had emptied in a matter of seconds.

In vain, he pleaded with the barmaid to serve just one more drink. When he turned away from the bar, the white-haired Sergeant was there.

* "It's you who's the great bastard, isn't it?"

CHAPTER THIRTEEN: JUSTICE.

The Sergeant knew all of the Town's youths by name. He knew their fathers and their fathers' fathers. If a local shop were burglarized, he would know at which house to call. If a car were stolen, game poached or pony 'rustled,' he would be at the culprit's door within the week to demand retribution. Thieves spent weekends cleaning Panda cars. They groomed the horses that they had once stolen and dug the allotments they had plundered. It was a matter for the newspaper if criminal charges were ever instigated so the Sergeant rarely charged anybody. In this way, he maintained the delicate balance between the Law and Natural Justice.

The one thing that the Sergeant would not tolerate was violence. Violence, he reasoned, could never be adequately recompensed. To punish violence by violence only resulted in further injustice. His only answer was the courtroom but he knew that this rarely broke the cycle.

He had heard of the Boy's long-standing reputation as a bully. But in eighteen years, he had never seen cause to investigate the claims. Thirty-five years as a policeman had taught him to differentiate between fact and fiction. It had been his own daughter, witness among the fleeing teenagers, who had raised the alarm. She had told of the provocation that led to the

Boy's violent outburst. Further investigation had given him a very mixed profile of the miscreant.

Very few of the pupils at the school worked during their spare time. He knew of none that worked the fields with their father. The Boy's jealous protection of Jack in the school playground had often been reported to him by his daughter. This was at odds with the devastation that the Sergeant had found in the public house. He was perturbed that the teenagers should return to France, victims of violence in HIS Town. But, although he would never admit the fact, he preferred that they return with their cuts and bruises rather than with tales of the stupidity of his daughter and her friends. The Sergeant had finally come to his decision.

The Boy stood at the desk in the police station, eye bloodshot and blackened. The Sergeant, tunic buttoned to the collar, sat opposite him.

"This is an official warning ...", he began to read aloud from the sheet of paper on the table.
When he had finished reading, he unbuttoned the tight collar. Leaning back in his chair, he pulled cigarettes and matches from a drawer in the desk. He lit a cigarette and inhaled deeply. Blue smoke rose in the harsh light as he exhaled.

"Do you want one?" He asked, pushing the packet across the desk towards the Boy.

"No, thank you, Sergeant. I don't smoke."

"I suppose, you've got enough problems with your drinking?"

The Boy did not answer.

"I want you to listen very carefully. If you get into any more trouble, you'll be in the courtroom. You'll pay for the damage that you've caused. I know, you have the money because you go to work. Just think of what you had to do to earn that money and maybe, in future, you'll hold your temper. Either that or learn to duck!"

There was no hint of humour in his voice.

"I'm banning you from every public house in the Town until you finish your studies. Do you understand?"

"Yes, Sergeant."

"Boy, you have a great chance to better yourself. Don't throw it away!"

"No, Sergeant"

"Shake."

Rising from the chair, he offered his hand to the Boy.

"And don't let me see you, back here."

The rest of the school year passed without major incident. The Boy half-heartedly returned to his studies. He had burned the application forms, useless without the headmaster's endorsement, because he knew what even the wise Sergeant ignored. He knew that prejudice had won the day.

The headmaster then found easier prey to hound. That year, there arrived at the school, a new and even more unwilling beneficiary of Big Jake's legacy; his brother, Josh.

The sun reflected a thousand mirrors on the waters of the canal. As the 'bus crossed 'Uncle Sidney's Bridge,' a dozen school caps sailed down, sending as many moorhens flapping for safety in the reeds. The Boy sat on the top deck of the 'bus. His mind was numb. He felt no elation that the ordeal was at an end.

The future seemed as bleak as the landscape that surrounded him.

CHAPTER FOURTEEN: ONLY A COUPLE OF BEERS.

The four teenagers fought for space in the small car. Struggling elbows paused only for the bottle that passed from hand to hand and mouth to mouth. They had already stopped several times for further 'refreshments.'

"This is it," the driver slurred as the car turned into the drive that led to the large, detached house.

Tall, neatly trimmed hedges now guarded its approaches.

"Quiet, you lot. There's his dad! At the window."

Hands brushed back tousled hair, straightened ties and collars as a fifth lad emerged from the front door of the house.

"Pity, his sister's not coming," said one of the drunks, half in jest.

"Watch your mouth," the Boy said, twisting around in the front seat.

"Now, we know you!" the two goaded.

"It's not that. It's his sister. You didn't ought to talk about her like that,"

"Like what? Why have you gone so red? Bet, you fancy her!"

"Pack it in. Here he comes," the driver said.

"Good evening, Peter," the four chorused in mock sobriety.

Peter was dressed in new suit and tie, shoes polished to mirror-like perfection. His red hair was plastered with shiny brilliantine.

"Keep it down, will you? We're meant to be going to the end-of-term play," he said.

A quick look towards the house and he squeezed onto the back seat of the car.

The car swung around, reversing across the driveway. As it turned to pull away, it came to a sudden halt, bumper snared in the hedge. Spinning wheels sent gravel flying at the front of the house, peppering door and windows. Stumbling out, the passengers lifted it free before diving for their seats. As the front door of the house opened, wheels still spinning, the car gained the roadway. Just in time, they escaped the irate bank manager, leaving only a choking cloud of dust and gravel in answer to his shouted reprimands.

It was dark when they returned. This time, the car did not attempt to negotiate the driveway. Instead, it paused in the road by the entrance, engine running. The red-haired lad, crumpled, buttonless shirt hanging over his trousers, fell from the passenger seat onto the pavement. He hauled himself upright. Then, with his one, remaining shoe clutched to his chest for safe-keeping, he tiptoed unsteadily along the driveway. As the lights of the house blazed on, freezing him in dazzled silhouette, the car sped away into the darkness. It stopped on the outskirts of the Town.

"It's another three miles," the Boy complained.

"I'm too drunk. I daren't go any farther. I'll maybe see you, next year," the driver said.

Cursing, the Boy hauled himself from the car. This time, glass shattered as the car hurtled backwards into a road sign. He watched blankly as the single, red light disappeared into the darkness.

At first, he staggered along the white line that bisected the deserted road, guided by its incandescent glow. Then, fear took him to the grass verge, mind wary of non-existant traffic. Before long, he had stumbled into one of the many ditches that drained the tarmac. Wedged in the narrow trough, he struggled to free himself. Only drunken stupor could bring an escape from the trap.

The morning sun awakened him. Still half-drunken, he hauled himself from the ditch. Face, hands and clothes spattered with mud, he began the long walk home.

He found himself still dressed when he awoke. His clothes, face and hands were caked in dried mud. The afternoon sun flooded through the window of his bedroom, pounding pain into his forehead with its brightness. The rat-a-tat that had roused him was unmistakeable. Head throbbing, he made his way down the stairs to open the front door. On the doorstep, stood the grim-faced Sergeant.

"Some people, they never learn," he said.

"What do you mean?"

"Did you have a good time, last night, Boy?"

"What do you mean?"

"I want to know your whereabouts, last night?"

"I was out on the town. We all leave, next week."

"I've had a complaint about you!"

"About me?!"

"Yes, you. You beat up the weighing machine and punched out all the windows in the public toilets!"

"It wasn't me! I wasn't even in Town, last night."

"Don't lie! I've followed the blood-trail to your front door. Show me your hands."

Puzzled, the Sergeant examined the Boy's mud-stained palms then knuckles, free of cuts or blood.

"I think, it's me, you're looking for, Jim," the Man's voice came from inside the house.

Hands bandaged, wallet at the ready, the embarrassed father settled the damages, promising future good behaviour.

The stern-faced Sergeant climbed back into the police car. The uncharacteristic mistake had made him look foolish. At the wheel, Officer Jake smirked the length of Canal Street.

The Man made his way back into the house.

"Time to go, Son," he said.

CHAPTER FIFTEEN: YESTERDAY'S HERO

The canvas glowed, pure in the arc lights. In the centre of the boxing ring, the black-suited figure raised the microphone in his hand. Crushed into the small hall, the men of the Town fell silent.

"Good evening, gentlemen. Welcome to an evening of schoolboy boxing. Before we begin the night's proceedings, I would like to introduce our very special guest. Gentlemen, I give you our very own; former British, European and Empire champion, former World contender, the one and only …….
The words were lost in a tumult of cheers and applause as, arms aloft, the 'Champ' bounced into the ring. Jewellery flashed on wrists and fingers as he circled, hooking and jabbing at an imaginary opponent.   Beneath scarred brows and cheeks, porcelain teeth reflected white into the crowd.

From the front rows of tables, banknotes showered into the ring. From the rear of the hall, copper and silver came raining down. Seated with his son, the Man slowly clapped his hands. The gleam of paste had not fooled his sharp eyes. Shine on suit and scuffs on shoes told all. It was only too obvious why the 'Champ' had returned.

Gone were the purses; a fortune leeched by brothel and casino. Gone was the athletic body, ruined by alcohol and cigarettes. Last stop for yesterday's hero … home.

The lights dimmed and a slight figure trotted past the tables at ringside. Ignored by the chattering crowd, tomorrow's hero entered the ring.

On the walk home, the Boy enthused about the night's entertainment and the return of the 'Champ'. As they turned the corner onto Canal Street, the Man spoke.

"You'll see, Son. Come tomorrow, they'll have forgotten him!"

It was the last time that he would walk through the Town with his son. The next morning, the Boy departed for the City.

The Man had kept his promise.

PART THREE

THE STUDENT LIFE

"Too proud, he who seeks to shape the destiny of his fellow man."

CHAPTER ONE: THE CITY

He gazed from the carriage window as the train rumbled its way across the reclaimed marshland. He wore combat jacket, blue jeans and baseball boots, his hair, long; symbol of the times. Above his head on the netted rack, his rucksack danced to the rhythm of the train.

He found himself in that same, strange state of limbo. He had not wanted to leave the Town nor had he wanted to stay there. Where now, would he call 'Home'?

The fallow blanket finally yielded to green pastures. Here, beneath the golden leaves of oak and chestnut, swollen cattle browsed. This panoply of light and colour eclipsed all thoughts of the dark Fens, now left far behind by the iron wheels of the train. Animated by the beautiful landscape, he felt his spirits rise.

Alas, it was nought but temporary illusion. The train now entered the industrial heartland. What he saw made the Fens seem like paradise.

Canals, gorged with rusting corpses, reflected their oily rainbows. Factories loomed, dark with soot and grime. Chimney stacks like giant, smoking cannon, discharged into the sky, stealing its very colour. Above, the watery eye of the sun peered down, blind witness to this, mankind's latest barbarism.

As he walked from the railway station, a steady rain began to fall, raising stench from gutters and drains. It stung at his unprotected scalp so that he ran to the taxi rank. Here, he took refuge in the nearest vehicle. Safe within, he watched the bustling crowd. Eyes lowered, the pedestrians hurried to destinations unknown within the concrete maze. No-one paused to say 'Hello', not even for a passing handshake. Only the voice of the newspaper vendor challenged the roar of the traffic. The Boy had never before seen so many vehicles. Nor had he seen so many strangers together in one place.

The taxi left the City centre and stopped, a short time later, in a street of large, semi-detached houses.

"This is it, number 'noyne.' That'll be half a crown," the driver demanded.

He paid the fare. As the taxi pulled away from the kerb, he walked to the front door of number 'noyne.'

The doorbell was answered by Ira, the landlord, who led the Boy into the front room of the house. Here, two beds, two chairs and two small tables faced each other. The boundary of these two mirror worlds was marked by a large wardrobe that faced the chimney breast and electric fire.

"Strictly no girls in the room. Sheets are changed every week. The fire has a meter. It takes shillings. Breakfast is at

eight o'clock, dinner at six. Baths at off-peak time only ....,"
The list continued; a dirge repeated and ignored for the thousandth time. When the landlord had left, he threw his bag onto the nearest bed and flopped down next to it.

He was awakened by a loud voice as the door opened. Squeezing through the doorway behind a pile of suitcases, laden with bats and racquets of every description, an angular figure emerged. Still half asleep, the Boy gasped in amazement. Framed in the doorway, stood the ugliest person that he had ever seen in his entire life!

The accent was heavy, from the north,

"Er, um, which is my er, um, bed?"

The question seemed absurd.

CHAPTER TWO: THE STUDENT BAR.

The new arrival was dressed in a grey suit with leather patches at the elbows. White shirt was secured by black tie resplendent in gold shields. He began to unpack. From the suitcase, he produced a series of tracksuits and sports strips of every description.

Sitting up on the edge of his bed, the Boy watched, bemused. Cricket bat and tennis racquet seemed incongruous, piled in with rugby and soccer kit. He glanced out of the window.

"Yes, it is," the grey skies confirmed, "it's October!"
The wardrobe was filled, mobile sports shop safely stowed away.

"What's your name, mate?"

"It's um, er, Mick."

"What course are you on?"

"Er, um, modern languages."

There was no attempt to extend the conversation or to reciprocate the Boy's interest.

"Are you going to the student bar, this evening? There's free beer!"

"O.K."

Following the landlord's directions, the two walked to the City centre. At first, the Boy tried to engage his companion in conversation but the other's clipped, single-word answers stifled his questions. They arrived at the bar, in silence.

The party was in full swing. Teenagers, only hours before, total strangers, talked and danced to music from the jukebox, their inhibitions swept aside by the free alcohol. At the bar, competing with music and shouted conversations, raised voices called for more.

He carefully worked his way through the crowd. Beneath the lines of poster heroes that guarded the optics, members of the Federation served. Under the critical eye of Chairman Mao, the Boy ordered two pints of beer. The noble gaze of Ché Guevara followed him to the table where Mick sat waiting. The first drinks were quickly consumed. Thirst from the long march quenched, the Boy returned to the bar for a fourth round.

"Free beer's off," the bearded attendant told him.

"That'll be five bob."

Balancing the foaming glasses above the heads of the crowd, he returned to the table. Only then did he realise how much his companion was out of place. Seated bolt upright, dressed in his grey suit, he stared straight ahead, ignoring music and party-goers alike; an accountant at Woodstock.

"Now, that's one ugly mother," he heard somebody remark as he squeezed through the crowd.

One of the girls turned her head to where Mick was sitting. Her whispered remark brought loud laughter from her new friends.

"Free beer's off," the Boy announced as he passed the dripping glass.

"Is it?"

The two drank. Glasses empty, the Boy waited patiently.

"Fancy another?" He finally asked.

"Yes."

Thus, the Boy paid for every drink.

The music came to a stop and the lights of the bar blazed brightly. The pub' began to empty, students stumbling out into the night. Couples exchanged first kisses. Shouted goodbyes echoed down the deserted streets. Among the last to leave, the Boy realised; all night, he had hardly spoken to a soul.

In the doorway, stood a youth with long hair and mutton-chop whiskers. A black beret was pulled to one side of his head. Fixing him with an intense stare, the 'Leader' pushed a wad of pamphlets into the Boy's hand.

"Read and learn, Brother," he said.

"Join us! Soon!"

As they made their unsteady way back to the boarding house, Mick unexpectedly spoke. For the second time that day, the Boy gasped in amazement.

"Do you, um, er, know. I could have, um, er, HAD any of those BIRDS in there!

Inside the house, the Boy slipped into a deep, drunken stupor, the forgotten pamphlets clutched in his hand. He would never again socialize with his room-mate. Expense, he reasoned, was excuse enough to avoid this social pariah. Personally, he was sick of being ostracized.

He would seek out new friends among the other occupants of the boarding house.

CHAPTER THREE: 'HIGH JINKS'

He sat on the edge of the bed, engrossed in his reading. The light glowed so faintly in the high ceiling that he squinted to see the small, black and red print of the pamphlets. For the third time that evening, the coin-box clicked. Starved of energy, the fire quickly faded. Chill air seized its chance to enter the room, pinching at feet and ankles. Across the room, Mick remained hidden behind the Boy's Sunday newspaper.

This time, he did not feed the greedy, metal box. Money was tight enough without subsidizing his room-mate. Instead, he continued to read the pamphlets as if ignorant of the mounting cold.

"I think that I'll um, er, get an early night. It's the, um, er, BIG DAY, tomorrow."

Mick changed quickly into striped pyjamas and climbed into bed to escape the, now icy, draught. His feet were stopped, half-way down, by the top sheet folded into an 'apple-pie.' Without a word, he doubled up knees to chest and squeezed into the top half of the bed.

The Boy clandestinely watched his struggle. Glancing down, he could see the extra thickness in the blankets at the head of his own bed was all too obvious. Pamphlets read for a second time, he stripped sheet and blankets from his bed.

Straightening the top sheet, he disarmed this most basic of traps. In 'T'-shirt and underpants, he sought the warmth of the newly-made bed.

He was awoken by a flood of light, loud voices, cold beer in his face. With a speed that belied his size, he was upright. Standing on the bed, he grappled with the closest assailant. One foot on the drunkard's chest, he wrenched the bottle free from his hand. Shouting and laughing, he sprayed the remainder of the beer, shaking a foaming arc into the faces of his attackers.

Deterred by such unexpected and spirited resistance, the drunkards turned their attentions to the other side of the room. Over the bed, they burst bags of potato crisps, poured beer from bottles. Curled in the cramped sheet, Mick remained motionless.

"Wake up, little B'um,er. Wake up!!" The drunks slurred in uneven chorus.
One took a kick at the bed, almost falling backwards with the effort, foot flailing in the air. Yet, the figure in the bed did not move.

"Alright, that's enough, you bastards." The laughter had gone from his voice.

"O.K., O.K. Just messing about. Keep your hair on, big fellow!"

There had been instant sobriety in the room.

"No sweat."

The moment had passed, the anger abated.

"Just get out, will you?" Just get out!"

The quartet staggered from the room. Bursting into song, they mounted the stairs, heavy feet stamping rhythm on the bare boards.

"Wake up, little B'um,er. Wake up!!"

The noise sounded across the landing and through the rest of the house. Head throbbing, the Boy stripped soaked blanket and pillowcase from his bed.

When he finally fell asleep, the figure across the room had not moved.

CHAPTER FOUR:
NEW FRIENDS AND A NEW BEGINNING

A bell was ringing. Its harsh tones shattered his slumber. He reached out into the cold room, groping for his alarm clock. He pressed down on the button to stifle the din but the noise persisted. Its metallic sound was like a drill in his brain. It was coming from the room above him.!

Further sleep would be impossible in such a din. Cursing, the Boy pulled on his clothes. As he left the room to climb the stairs, still feigning sleep, the 'filling' remained in the 'apple pie.'

An electric fire-bell, rigged to an alarm clock by an elaborate pattern of white string, was sounding reveille. In the twin beds, the Boy found two more, immobile bodies. Bottles and cans littered the floor between them. Bell now disarmed and silent, he retrieved two of the bottles. With great delight, he emptied their sticky dregs over the two beds.

"Bastard," groaned one of the bodies.

"What comes around, goes around; or up!!" He joked.

From both beds came faint, weak laughter.

"Ha! Ha! Bog off! We're dying."

"No more bed baths?"

"No more bed baths. We promise!"

On the table, four, uneaten breakfasts had betrayed the midnight revellers. But the landlord did not need to inspect plates to discover the culprits. He already knew their identities.

"Any more messing about and you'll be out on your ears," he had threatened.

As the Boy and his two, new friends began the walk to the college, they decided that, at the first opportunity, they would move out of the boarding house. The Boy declared, he would never again speak to his room-mate.

On turning the corner of the street, his nostrils caught the heady smell. Drifting on the wind, it pervaded the entire district. At his side, his friends gagged and choked; stomachs churned by the windborne hops. As they walked along, he completed his revenge and compounded their discomfort by extolling the virtues of the missed breakfast. Detailed descriptions of runny eggs and greasy sausages carried them past the brewery, all the way to the college.

The first of his companions was a true son of David, athletic and heavily muscled. Jet black hair and moustache only emphasized the clear blue of his eyes. Apart from the rugby kit that lay ready and waiting in his wardrobe, the only clothes that he owned, he wore; denim jacket, shirt and jeans. His lifestyle owed nothing to such niceties as socks or underwear. Money was for three things and three things only; rugby football, beer and food. Fortunately, his talent for the former had so far transcended his capacity for the latter. Due to his insatiable appetites, his friends had nicknamed him 'Gross.' In turn, he had soon christened the Boy; 'Large.'

The second Welshman, although gifted with the same, dark features as his friend, was small and slight. He dressed in hat, coat and gloves; all of the same, ghastly, synthetic fur. Gross, his friend since childhood, had nicknamed him; 'THE YETI' for his love of the purple material. But today, the name could not have been more inappropriate. Today, he looked more like a child's toy than a mythical beast as he walked along between the two giants.

The college buildings were as blackened as the rest of the City. But progress was in hand. Red-brick extensions promised relief for the prefabricated blocks that lurked behind the stone façade. Joining the animated throng of students, the three friends climbed the stone steps.

Through the high, glass doors, they disappeared into the corridors of their new lives.

CHAPTER FIVE: A FRESH INFLUENCE.

The continued political exile of Iberia plus the economic miracle of a Germany reborn meant that Spanish had become much less fashionable for the career-conscious. The Boy found himself alone in the Spanish lectures. Privy to a one-on-one relationship with the tutor, he would receive a standard of instruction far beyond his wildest expectations.

His tutor's name was Alan, a man whose enthusiasm for teaching was matched only by his command of the subject that he taught. Happy in vocation and life, he was a moderate in every sense of the word. Every problem that he encountered, he approached from a broad base of knowledge, striving for wisdom and impartiality in all his arguments and conclusions. Explanation and solution were always justified in his quest for truth. Soon, he would be at odds with the Boy for the radical naïvety of his newfound ideology.

The two would argue like a pair of Spanish fish-wives; teacher urging pragmatism, student obdurate in his calls for the Freedom and Equality of Man. The flawless logic of Alan's arguments would do more than force the Boy deep into dogmatic defence.

It rekindled his thirst for knowledge and learning.

CHAPTER SIX: POWER TO THE PEOPLE!

The hall was crammed to bursting point. The balcony, manned by members of the 'Federation,' was festooned with flags and banners. Other 'Brothers' had arrived early to monopolize the seats at the front of the hall. Despite the cold weather outside, the air inside was hot and clammy from the crowd.

As the Principal spoke into the microphone, an expectant hush descended on the 'audience.' Leather-soled shoes echoed across the stage as the Politician* approached.

He was dressed in under-stated style. White shirt contrasted with black suit and tie. Grey hair and moustache were trimmed in military fashion, giving him every appearance of an undertaker. Eyes, grey ice, pierced the dim light in the silent hall. Lips parted to speak... but his words would never be heard.

Shouts and 'BOOS' erupted from the front rows of seats; deafening after the silence. As one, the members of the Federation were on their feet, shouting obscenities. They rallied the crowd to their 'Cause,' urged that others add to the cacophony of sound that engulfed the lone voice.

"OUT! OUT! OUT! RACIST OUT! OUT! OUT!" They chanted.

Within seconds, the entire hall was echoing with the words.

OUT! OUT! ENOCH, OUT!"

As the mob surged forwards, a hundred chairs clattered in its wake. A hundred clenched fists punched the air. The Leader was on his feet. Arms aloft, he faced the crowd, screaming his encouragement.

A phalanx of blue uniforms emerged from the wings of the stage. Surrounding their ward, the police officers unceremoniously hustled him from view as a barrage of eggs and tomatoes rained down upon them.

On the 'liberated' stage, the Leader turned to face his audience. Clenched fist raised, head in majestic Guevaran pose, he shouted into the microphone,

"Power to the People."

The Federation and Intolerance had won the day.

*The Politician; The Late Enoch Powell.

CHAPTER SEVEN: THE LEADER.

His name was Godsby but the members of the Federation jokingly called him 'the Leader' or 'Gods Bodeen'* Although in principle, the Federation recognized no hierarchy, his energy in pursuit of the 'Cause' and attention to every detail of its organization had earned him the title of 'General Secretary.'

In debate, his passion and logic were both feared and unassailable. Often, in the heat of the moment, he would forget the non-executive aspect of his position and create policy by his own personal action. If he aspired to leadership, it was ever by example, never by coercion.

Lecture hall, street or bar, the black beret was ever-present. As were combat jacket and jeans; the unofficial uniform of the Federation. It was rumoured by some that he even wore the cherished beret to bed! Beneath the famed beret hung a straggling mat of shoulder-length hair. Gold-rimmed spectacles and large, mutton-chop whiskers completed the image of the dissident.

The Leader's revolutionary fervour was marked only by his love for association football. At weekends, when not

*'Godsbodeen;' A corruption of the Russian word 'Gospodeen;' – 'Mister'

fighting for the 'Cause', he would continue his quest for anarchy on the terraces of the City's football ground.

As he passed the Boy in the corridors of the college, he handed him a piece of paper.

"Buses leave at 9.00am sharp," it read.

"Don't be late, Brother," he whispered.

CHAPTER EIGHT: THE FLAT

The flat occupied the ground floor of one of the many, ancient houses that crowded at the edges of the City. Access was gained through the back door of the house. The front door led only to the staircase and the first floor.

This had been converted into three bedrooms, lounge, kitchenette and bathroom. Central heating had been installed along with fitted carpets and new furniture. Each bedroom had a desk and chair for individual study. Fresh paint and new wallpaper completed the effect for this, most modern of student flats.

Its   occupants   reflected   the   prosperity   of   the accommodation. All three were trainees from the largest and most expensive department store in the City. The leader of this trio was Tristan. Black curls topped a bland face that ever promised politeness and good humour; a humour that at first sight seemed born of stupidity. He was famous throughout the college for the width of lapel of his checked sports jackets and his, seemingly endless, supply of floral ties. He bore the wisecracks and taunts that they caused with his usual, facile smile.   Few suspected the sharp intelligence that lay safely protected behind his foppish looks. Already risen to prominence within the students' union, his was the voice of conservatism.

As such, the members of the Federation duly despised him. However, none but the truly radical within its ranks could bring themselves to personally dislike him.

The house in its unfinished state represented a strange parody.

The ground-floor flat had received none of the lavish attention paid to its counterpart. It retained the original kitchen and bathroom of the house, complete with ancient gas oven, grimy bath and toilet stained from sixty years of use. A small electric fire in the 'lounge' provided the only source of heat for the whole apartment. In what had once been the reception room, there were three, single beds. Curtains were nailed permanently across the wide bay-window, ensuring that no stray beam of light should ever penetrate this dark refuge.

On the three beds, three slept, oblivious to the frosty sunlight that danced in the street outside. Two slept in sleeping-bags like giant cocoons; massive larvae that wriggled in sleep. The third bed was more lavishly fitted.

Its occupant slept beneath a quilt of dark, synthetic fur, his head resting on matching pillow. Dressing gown of the same material hung above the furry slippers at bedside; lone sentinel against the army of empty cans and bottles that cluttered the floor.

From the lounge, on automatic replay, Hendrix screamed Along the Watchtower for the hundredth, consecutive time. In the bedroom, the electric bell, triggered by its string bonds, rang its unending, unheeded alert.

Finally, the Yeti, eyes glued together by sleep, stumbled from his bed. Fur-covered, hot water bottle bounced down among the cans as he stood upright. Carefully groping his way through the debris, like a drunken sapper in a minefield, he disarmed the bell. Clattering through the beer cans, he returned to his bed.

"No need to get excited...", the voice boomed from the next room.

The advice was unnecessary......... and unheard!

CHAPTER NINE: THE FIGHT FOR PEACE.

They crowded onto the coaches that lined the car park, like eager children on a school outing. Fresh faces contorted against window glass to taunt friends still to board. Striped scarves, duffel coats, combat jackets and berets jumbled in mock scrimmage around the doors of the buses. Kit bags, held on high lest eggs and tomatoes be crushed prematurely, bobbed above the mêlée. Eventually, the anarchy melted into seated order.

In proud Indian file, the coaches left the City to find the motorway. The miles melted away in a concert of chanted slogans and left-wing anthems. Naïve in their convictions, they travelled safely and without hindrance to 'Protest for Peace;' most futile of exercises.

The motorway led them to another, wet and grimy city. Here, the police waited. Infantry and cavalry held ranks, black marias and ambulances at the rear, like troops on a battlefield. As the crowd marched, banners flying, they answered insults from the blue lines with chants and songs. Chants and songs were answered by kicks and punches, long hair pulled from its roots. Hurled eggs and tomatoes provoked a storm of unyielding mahogany lashing out from behind the lines of riot shields.

The noisy crowd pushed in its panic; part to escape the bone-breaking truncheons, part to retaliate against the blue violence. Without warning, the police lines crumbled. Police, protestors, women and children; all were swept away in the human tide.

Then, the horses charged. Dispersing the terrified crowd, they herded its ever-decreasing numbers into the small gardens that lined the streets of terraced houses. Long truncheons lashed down, blind to age or gender. They cracked the skulls and flailed the defenceless backs of fugitives and spectators alike. The rout was complete and uncompromising.

The Boy painfully climbed the steps into the coach. The Leader was already on board.

"Welcome to the Revolution," he grinned, dabbing at bloodied lips and teeth with his handkerchief. His eyes had already blackened.

The Boy tried to laugh but his body was too sore.

The return journey was quiet and sullen. Even the Leader's jokes seemed flat and found only silence in the darkness of the 'bus. On the car park, the students dispersed in small groups, shocked, bitter and demoralized by the day's events.

How could they have ever hoped to end the War with only slogans, eggs and tomatoes?

CHAPTER TEN: REACTION TO REACTION

Only two 'buses travelled southward on the motorway. The first carried the college's 'ice hockey' teams; grim foot soldiers of the Revolution.   In the second, the darts' and marbles' teams sat in impassive rows.

In the Great Square, black banners flew above a sea of red books. The union of the Left was complete. From the stage, the amplified voice vainly called for an end to War. Incongruously, below there raged a bloody and uncompromising battle. Flags and placards proclaiming 'Peace' lowered like lances against the blue infantry. Police fell back in confusion as masked insurgents breached their lines to rescue captured comrades.   Windows of 'black marias' exploded as prisoners kicked their way to freedom. Snatch squads were driven off, blue helmets flying in escape. Even the dreaded cavalry was thwarted, driven backwards in disorder by a hail of darts. Hooves slid desperately on rivers of ball-bearings. A horse reared and fell sidewards. Crushing down on a car trapped in the chaos, it neighed its terror above the pandemonium of sirens, screams and curses.

Time and time again, the police lines came under attack. Vastly outnumbered, they tried vainly to clear the marauding mob from the Square. For five, long hours, England's Glory stared down in granite disbelief at the insanity that raged below him; impotent, the stone lions that guarded his monument.

The storm was spent. Police reinforcements swept through the Square, chasing off the few, small groups that lingered.

As the 'buses sped northward, the Leader proclaimed a great victory for the Revolution.

How could they have hoped to end the War by such violence? They had not grasped the most basic of facts:-

War ends only in victory or capitulation.

CHAPTER ELEVEN: BIG DAVE (DAI)

His real name was Dave but he insisted that it was 'DAI.' Most people called him 'Big Dave.' Big Dave was the fittest man in the college. He could do push-ups and sit-ups by the hundred. He would run for miles, wearing heavy boots, through the country lanes that surrounded the 'Halls of Residence' where he lived. Here, in the converted barracks of an old army base, he was guaranteed warmth, shelter and as much food as he could eat.

Big Dave's hero, he would inform the unwary, was Jack Dempsey.

"He was thirteen and a half-stone. See? Just like me. See?"

As if to prove his point, he would drop down, albeit in lecture hall, bar or street, to do a dozen push-ups. Informing his victim that,

"You gotta be fit. See?"

Big Dave had two admitted faults. Practise as he would and try as he did, he could not catch. On the rugby pitch, he would grab the ball and gallop to the try-line. Defenders would hang from waist and shoulders, as incapable of halting his charge as ticks on a buffalo. But should a pass ever come his way, his great hands would betray him, sending the ball spinning out of control.

The second 'fault' was the accidental location of his birth. Although of Welsh parentage, he had been born prematurely, while his mother was visiting friends on the 'wrong' side of the border. One night in drunken confidence, Big Dave had confessed to the darkest of his secret sins. Sobriety had brought a need for explanation.

"It was only for a couple of days. See? And I was baptized in Wales and have lived there all of my life. See?"
But the secret was out, the Achilles' heel exposed.

On the occasion of one particularly drunken session in the union bar, things had finally come to a head. The Boy listened as Big Dave gave a blow-by-blow account of Jack Dempsey's career. Fortunately, the alcohol, consumed that evening, acted as euphoric anaesthetic against Big Dave's detailed description.

"Hey, English," Gross's drunken voice bellowed across the packed bar, accent emphasized by the immediate silence.
Big Dave turned towards the voice, fire in his eyes. He knew that he was the victim of the jibe.

"Catch!"

The melon described a perfect arc as it crossed the bar. It seemed to slow, to hover, as it cleared the heads of the gawping students. A moment fixed in time before it eluded Big Dave's thrashing palms and smashed into his groin.

With an outraged bellow, he sprang to his feet. Revellers scattered as the bull charged. Like many a full-back before him, the Boy clung vainly to the wide shoulders in his attempt to halt the wild rush. Bulldozed furniture and stumbling students had given Gross the few seconds that he needed to make his escape. Laughing over his shoulder, he sprinted out of the bar and into the darkness, his shouted taunts lost in the maze of terraces.

Big Dave stood, panting for breath beneath the light of the public house's sign. Fists clenched tight.

"I'll get you for this, Jones," he raged at the empty streets.

Then, the pain took him to his knees.

CHAPTER TWELVE: HAVE AND HAVE NOT.

The Boy dressed quickly to avoid the cold in the dark bedroom. He pulled on frayed clothes, baseball boots over bare feet. His supply of socks had long been exhausted. The high rent of the flat plus his drunken affiliation to brothers of the Federation and friends in the rugby club had left him a pittance with which to survive. There was barely enough of his grant remaining to buy food, as testified by the loose fit of jumper and jeans.

Leaving his flatmates to their slumbers, he picked his way through the debris into the next room. Here, he switched off the record player and disconnected the alarm bell. In the dingy bathroom he splashed ice-cold water onto hands and face. The liquid blasted sleep from his eyes, shocked feeling into mind and body. From the mirror, face framed by a mass of long hair, a gaunt stranger stared back.

"Forget it," he said, "breakfast's off."

Out in the street, he crunched through the snow, cold biting through the thin rubber soles of his baseball boots. Combat jacket and long hair conserved some of his body heat but fast as he might walk, his feet still ached with the numbing cold.

"Could be worse. Could be in the carrot fields," he muttered to himself.

A car had stopped at the corner of the street, exhaust sputtering in the fog. As he came level with the passenger door, the window rolled down slowly to reveal the fixed and infuriating smile of the occupant.

"I say, old chap, could I have a word?"

The Boy stood, stamping his feet in the wet snow.

"What do you want?"

"It's about the noise. You know, your music was playing again, all night? And it's too loud!"

"So what?"

"Well, the other chaps and I couldn't get a wink of sleep, last night. It's simply too bad. Isn't it, Jeremy?" Tristan said, turning to the driver.

"Yes. It's too bad," Jeremy echoed.

"I'm sorry but I shall have to make a complaint to the landlord."

"So what?" The Boy said, resuming his walk.

Tristan still had not realized, the record player had been playing all night for that express reason: to stop him from sleeping!

"Bet you know the words, by now!"

The car sped off, around the corner of the street, spraying him with a mix of snow and dirty water from the gutter.

"Capitalist pig!" The Boy shouted, shaking his fist.

Safe inside the warm vehicle, Tristan smiled blandly ahead.

CHAPTER THIRTEEN: A NIGHT TO REMEMBER?

The three friends had agreed that they could no longer afford to maintain the flat or support its hardships. Besides, Tristan's constant whingeing to the landlord meant that eviction was inevitable. The Boy had found a bed-sitting room for rent in one of the adjoining streets. Gross and the Yeti had been taken in by the 'Boss', who rented a small, terraced house, some distance from the centre of the City. The Boss shared the same biology course as his two, new tenants.

The Boss was short and stocky. Dark ringlets adorned his head and chin, lending him every appearance of a young gnome. The Boss was an organiser, meticulous in his every word and action: stark contrast to his two, new recruits. The Boss's lifestyle reflected the strict order of his mind. He knew the price of everything from a tin of beans to a second-hand washing-machine. He had used his avaricious talents to such effect that he was one of the few fellows of the college to own and finance the running of his own car: an ancient Hillman Imp.

The Boss had earned the nickname because, in his every household, he had held sway. Prop forwards subserviently washed dishes and swept floors. 'Sons of the Revolution' shopped and polished his car with painstaking attention. Why? Not from fear of the little dictator's caustic wit, which was daunting enough. They tolerated his tyranny for one reason and one reason only. The Boss knew how to cook. Not only did he know how to cook but he knew how to cook the most delicious of meals. Thus, he held his tenants to ransom;

"Clean up that mess, you great buffoon!"

"Yes, Boss."

"Don't put that down there, you fool!"

"No, Boss."

"Fetch some more coal, you stupid oaf!"

"Yes, Boss."

He who did not comply, walked hungry to college. He who did, rode like a king in the passenger seat of the Hillman, belly swollen with food.

The horn sounded for a fifth time, loud and impatiently.

"Come along, Large, you hopeless dullard," the Boss demanded, banging his fist on the steering wheel.

The Boy ran from the house into the snowbound street, pulling on his jacket. He dropped down into the passenger seat. Gross and the Yeti were already on board, crushed together on the back seat.

An atmosphere of anxiety pervaded the car. They were late. The Boss disliked unpunctuality because it interfered with his life's strict timetable. This evening, his three passengers were of the same accord. Because this evening, the beer was free!!

Headlights lost in the darkness, windscreen wipers struggling against the swirls of snowflakes, the Hillman slithered its way to the 'Halls of Residence.'

The beer was indeed free and they drank their fill. The Boss, conscious of the return journey, sipped conservatively from his glass. His passengers, free of any such responsibilities, were soon so drunk that they could hardly stand. Heavy in body, light in spirit, Gross struck up a rugby anthem, roaring at the top of his voice,

"SOSPAN GOCH…,"

The entire bar rang with the words as others joined in the chorus. Beer tipped from glasses as arms swung and mimed the lyrics of 'Sweet Chariot.' It was obvious to the Boss that it would be impossible, even for him, to herd his drunken charges back into the car. Besides, he feared for his upholstery.

"I've booked three rooms for you in 'C' block," he shouted above the din.

"I'm off, you stupid, drunken buffoons!"

Unheeding, Gross led the impromptu choir in ever greater efforts.

The last thing that the Boy remembered was; sitting on the tea trolley, Gross and the Yeti propelling him down the corridor, like two pit ponies at the gallop. Lights flashed past like an underground train speeding through a station. There was a sudden burst of light then…. nothing.

He awoke in the strange room. The bright light pierced his closed eyelids, thudding into his temples. Everything was spinning. There was no doubt about it. He was going to be sick. His whole body was stiff and aching. He felt as if he had fallen from a tree.

Slowly and painfully, he pulled a chair beneath the window. The noise of its wooden legs, scraping, on the floor, only worsened his discomfort. He clambered onto it. The cold air from the open window made him gag. He vomited; hot, acid stream gushing up from his churning stomach.

From his right-hand side, two Welsh voices seconded his pleas to the Lord as they reaped the rewards of the night's over-indulgence. Eyes filled with tears, the Boy watched as the last of the hops were returned to Nature.

"Good morning," he groaned.

"Good morning, Large," the two protruding heads replied without turning; eyes and nostrils streaming.

"Must have been a good night!"

"Must have been!"

The hole in the plasterboard wall at the end of the corridor was proof enough of that, as was the tea-trolley; battered chariot upturned, outside in the snow.

Despite their protestations of innocence, the three drunks were no longer made welcome in the Halls of Residence.

CHAPTER FOURTEEN: A BRUSH WITH REALITY.

On this day, the lecture was conducted exclusively in English as Alan berated the Boy for his falling attendance at the college. He was well aware of the Boy's participation in the nefarious activities of the Federation.

"….but that does not excuse you for cutting lectures. Let me tell you something. Time and again, we have argued over my Faith. The Opium of the people, you call it. I think that the Federation has its very own 'Opium.' Every man Jack of you is a drunken yobbo!"

The criticism stung the Boy. He had argued in defence of his 'comrades' but very few were the Brothers who had never staggered from the union bar on a Saturday night. He left the room convinced of one thing. He would never again drink alcohol. He would prove his resolve and dedication to the Cause by dispelling all such luxuries from his diet, all pleasures from his life.

Study and the Cause would now become the mainstays of his existence.

CHAPTER FIFTEEN: A DRIVING LESSON

Impressed by the independence afforded the Boss by the Hillman, the Yeti decided to invest his grandmother's legacy in four wheels. He was to be seen, touring the streets of the City in his new sports car; upholstery and steering-wheel suitably decked in the inevitable, purple fur. By way of convention, two, large dice of the same ghastly material hung from the rear-view mirror.

He and Gross now went back to the Welsh valleys at weekends. Time was divided between support of his fleet-footed friend on a Saturday afternoon at the rugby match and courting his girlfriend on a Saturday evening;- at the rugby club. The drive home was long and tiring. One Friday night, exhausted by a particularly arduous week of studying and drinking, he finally succumbed to Gross's relentless demands to 'have a go' behind the wheel. As if by magic, a set of "L." plates had appeared.

"I can drive on your insurance. See?" The enthusiastic learner had explained.

"You just relax."

Careful not to exceed the speed limit, Gross steered the car out of the City into the countryside. Through the borderlands he cruised, the needle of the speedometer never reaching the 30m.p.h. mark. The steady rocking of the car, compounded by the warmth of fur coat, hat and gloves before the heater, lulled the Yeti. He was soon in a deep sleep.

He woke to squealing tyres and racing engine as the car weaved at breakneck speed through the mountain pass. Hands, knuckles white, gripped the fur-lined steering wheel as Gross stared ahead in hypnotised ecstasy. The Yeti glanced down at the speedometer to see the needle nudge the 90 m.p.h. mark. Legs and arms locked in terror, he pushed away from the stone walls and trees that flashed past, only inches from his door.

"I think, I'm getting the hang of it!" Gross shouted above the roar of the engine.

"Stop, you crazy bastard," the Yeti screamed.

"Slow down! Stop or I'll kill you!"

Needless to say, Gross was never again allowed behind the wheel of the car.

Unfortunately, this first, 'driving lesson' had awoken in him an undreamed of …..desire.

CHAPTER SIXTEEN: A LIFT

A trio of drivers was completed when Big Dave purchased a Morris 1000.

One morning, a 'toot-toot' on the horn announced the Boy's lift to college.

"Good morning, Large." Big Dave announced as he proudly opened the car door, chauffeur-fashion, for the Boy to enter. The interior smelt heavily of wax polish.

Big Dave slipped behind the steering wheel. Looking up, he made a small adjustment to the rear-view mirror. A glance in the wing mirror convinced him to wind down the window and make another, minute adjustment. He rewound the window with great deliberation before making a final adjustment to the rear-view mirror. Now, he checked the gear lever for neutral, pushing it from side to side with exaggerated finesse. Another check proved the need for more mirror adjustment. Window rewound, he again checked for neutral. At last, Big Dave turned the ignition key and the engine rattled into life.

After several backward glances, he wrestled the complaining gearbox into first gear. Three more, careful looks over his shoulder and the car kangarooed away from the kerb; handbrake still engaged!

The car weaved its way through the back streets, maintaining a steady 15 m.p.h. between jumps. It stopped at every junction, driver engaging the newly discovered handbrake before crunching the gearbox into neutral. Intense stares to left, right, left, right and left again, before the car crossed to the next junction. Here, the complete 'systems check' was repeated.

In the car park, the Boy watched while the car pulled backwards and forwards until Big Dave was sure, it was perfectly parked. Handbrake and gear lever checked, double-checked and triple-checked, Big Dave emerged from the car. He shut the door, pulling so hard on the handle to check that it was locked, the car rocked from side to side. At long last, the two friends walked out of the car park.

"Did you lock your door, Large?"

"Yes, Dai."

"Are you sure?"

"Yes, Dai."

All reassurances were in vain. Big Dave walked back to the car and found that the door was indeed locked.

As they resumed their walk, "Hold on, a minute!" Big Dave jogged back to check that the boot was locked.

"Come on, Dai, we're going to be late," the Boy shouted.

In the distance, Big Dave polished an imaginary blemish from the tired, grey paintwork of the car. As the Boy walked up the steps to the college, he tackled a fingerprint on the windscreen; white handkerchief a blur of movement on the glass.

It was easier to tell Alan that he had missed the 'bus than give the true explanation for his late arrival.

Big Dave's diligence had turned a twenty-minute walk into a forty-minute drive!

CHAPTER SEVENTEEN:
CRIME (HEAVY ON THE PETROL)

His turn at the wheel had inflamed Gross's brain with a need for speed, for the power and independence afforded by the internal combustion engine.

He resolved to save the 'expenses' for his weekend appearances on the rugby pitch, to buy his own car. However, a demanding social life added to the actual costs of his weekend excursions meant that the 'car fund' was ever depleted. So,

"If you can't afford to buy, you find yourself forced to rent," the wild Welshman had reasoned.

"And if you can't afford to rent, you find yourself forced to borrow."

The train of thought had come to it's 'logical' conclusion.

Unfortunately, the legend of his attempt to kill himself and the Yeti, speeding through 'Snake Pass,' had spread throughout the college. The most foolhardy of students would not hand over their ignition keys or even get in a car with the lunatic. This had left him with only one option; to 'borrow' the cars of friends and acquaintances when they did not need them. That is to say, when they were in lectures or in bed. Thus, with the aid of a set of duplicate keys, he was free to tour the streets of the City and the roads of the surrounding countryside in the car of his choice. Needless to say, he usually picked the one with the most petrol in its tank.

For some months, the Boss was at a loss as to the poor performance of the Hillman. In vain, he tinkered with its carburettor. New points and plugs failed to solve the problem. A new air filter was fitted.

"It's O.K. on a run," he would complain.

"I get good mileage on long trips but around town, it guzzles the gas."

Promise of dinner had recruited the best mechanical minds in the college. There was much talk of main jets, pilot jets and blocked floats. Faulty valves were a favourite. It soon came to light that several cars had developed the same problem. Tristan even came forward to volunteer the information,

"Can't understand it. Alright on a run, don't you know?"

Things came to a head, the day that Gross 'borrowed' Big Dave's car. Ignorant of a faulty petrol gauge, he had sped into the countryside, tank almost empty. Lost in the backroads, the car had sputtered to a halt. With no money for petrol and even less inclination to buy any, Gross had abandoned the car and walked back into the City.

Soon, the stories of his misdeed were spread throughout the college.

CHAPTER EIGHTEEN:
AND PUNISHMENT (HEAVY ON THE HEAD)

The Boss paced the lead as they made their way through the long underpass that led to the football stadium. There, on the car park, the two cars sat in safety, steering wheels secured with padlocks and chains.

As they reached the exit of the tunnel and started down the hill, a voice echoed behind them. It was Big Dave.

"Right, Jones, you bastard. I've got you this time," he shouted triumphantly.

Gross looked back to see Big Dave's silhouette, huge shoulders swaying, come galloping out of the subway towards him. Gross was off and running like a greyhound out of the traps. He sprinted away down the hill, the gap between himself and his irate, lumbering pursuer growing with every stride. His would-be assailant was soon left far behind him. Laughing over his shoulder, he shouted out, taunting the despairing hunter,

"Hey, Englishman, you'll never catch a good Welshman in a million...."

The sentence was never finished. It was cut short by a loud, metallic 'dong.' There was a gasp of breath as the sprinter careered into one of the metal crash barriers that guarded the entrance to the football ground. Gross rebounded to the pavement.

Seeing his quarry's fate, Big Dave found a second wind. Running to where Gross lay, he lashed out at him with his heavy work boots.

"Yes, I have. I've got you, now, you bastard!"
Gross rolled away from the murderous kicks and struggled to his feet as the Boss, the Yeti and the Boy clung onto his attacker. Finally, all four collapsed onto the roadway, overwhelmed by fits of laughter.

The retired driver now sported a lump, the size of an egg, on the side of his head. Outlined in the streetlight, it seemed to be growing with every second that passed!

"It's not funny," he groaned, prodding gingerly at the ever-increasing growth.

But it was!

CHAPTER NINETEEN: GOOD ADVICE

It was time to leave. Once more, the Boy found himself at odds with his mentor.

"Listen. For the last time, use some common sense. Before you go, get your hair cut! Things are different in Spain." The Boy had already railed against the suggested haircut. Destroy the very symbol of Revolution?   Snip away the manifestation of his own, personal rebellion? Never!

"Definitely, not!" he said.

"Then at least, buy yourself some decent clothes." Now, the very 'uniform' of the Federation had come under attack.

"I've consulted with the rest of the staff. We are all of one mind. That is to say, we all are agreed that it would benefit you to study an aspect of Right Wing politics. It will broaden your outlook. You approach a problem from only one direction and never get the full picture. Who knows? You might even find some parallels with your own views."

"What do you mean? The two are opposite, absolutely opposite."

"I would argue the point. However, today, we haven't enough time. The topic for your dissertation will be 'The Life and Times of José Antonio."

"The fascist?"

"Leader of the Falange."

"Yes, the fascist!"

He had hoped to research the Republic, the Union of the Left, at least retrace his uncle's footsteps. It was not to be. Alan's resolve was unshakeable.

"What about your grant? Have you arranged your rail pass, yet?"

"I'm not going by rail."

"Not by air? You won't be able to afford it."

"No, I'm going to hitch-hike."

He was tired of fighting this constant battle with his student. As the Boy left the room, Alan held his head in his hands. As if the fingers, bars across his eyes, could protect him from the Boy's stubbornness and foolhardiness. He knew that logic and reason had lost the day.

The little car maintained a steady 25 m.p.h. as it chugged through the Fens. Big Dave at the wheel, nose almost pressed against the glass of the windscreen, checked and double-checked his every, uncertain manoeuvre. From the passenger seat, the Boy gazed out at the dark shadows that threatened to engulf the empty fields. It would be nightfall before they reached his father's house.

Dave's diligence had again doubled the time of a journey!

The bright, yellow light that flooded through the doorway dazzled the new arrivals. Nervous and stiffly formal in the presence of the Boy's father, Big Dave made his excuses for an immediate return.

"It's getting very dark. See?" He explained at the door.

"I shall have to take it very steady on the way home. See?"

He dropped the Boy's luggage on the doorstep and returned to the Morris.

"I'll see you, next year, Large."

After much crunching of gears, completion of a seven-point turn, the car disappeared into the night.

"Come on inside, Boy. You'll let all the heat out of the house."

Inside the house, father and son exchanged awkward handshakes. The Boy longed to hug his father but he was now considered an adult in his own right. To do so would have been unmanly. He disliked this cold formality thrust onto him by 'Manhood,' the distance it forced between himself and his father. They sat in front of the blazing fire, talking late into the night. The Boy told his father about the college, the City and his new friends. In his turn, the Man informed him of the latest births, deaths and marriages.

"They've got the Champ digging gardens for a living, three pounds a day. How soon they forget!"
The Man's voice bore no trace of triumph that his prophecy had come true, only bitterness at the predictability of the Town's population.

"If you want something to eat, there's plenty of food in the larder. Help yourself. I'm off to bed. It's been a long day. Switch off the lights and unplug the television set before you go to bed."
There was more pride than caution in the words. The Man paused at the bottom of the staircase,

"You know, everybody's proud of you, Son."

"I know. I won't let you down."
With a rare smile, the Man turned and climbed the stairs.

"I know, you won't, Son."

The Boy rolled onto the bed and looked around the room. In it, the Man had hoarded a catalogue of his childhood; toys, books and clothes. His old, school satchel and rugby boots were there. In pride of place, the set of encyclopaediae glistened in the electric light.

The memories of his childhood were now little more than dark shadows retreating before a shining future. As night chilled the bedroom, he was filled with a mixture of ardour and trepidation at the thought of the adventure to come.

He should not, he could not, let this chance escape.

PART FOUR

THE ADVENTURE OF A LIFETIME

"So I looked, and behold, a pale horse,

And the name of him

Who sat on it was Death.

And Hell followed with Him."

To the Victims of War.

CHAPTER ONE:

HITCH-HIKING FOR BEGINNERS: LESSON ONE.

Lurking in the evening mist, the monster of old awaited. Exhaust spewed its white breath into the encroaching darkness.

In the dim light of the cab, wire-framed spectacles half-way down his nose, Jack strained to read the crumpled newspaper. Tonight, in place of its usual, human cargo, the trailer of the lorry was piled high with bulging Hessian sacks; potatoes for market.

"Hello, Jack," the Boy shouted above the noise of the engine.

"Hello, Boy. Get you on in and shut the door."
Kitbag, sleeping-roll and his navy-blue duffel coat safely stowed, the Boy climbed up next to the old man behind the 'wheel. The engine revved loudly and the Dodge powered its way through the Town and out across the Fens.

The headlamps probed the banks of fog, turning the road ahead into yellow candyfloss. Undaunted by the lack of visibility, Jack sped onwards. He had driven those roads for over twenty years and knew by heart their every twist and turn. As the lorry weaved its way between the empty fields, he solicited stories of the City from the Boy. His shouted questions vied with the rattle of the engine, invisible road seemingly forgotten in conversation. By return, Jack repeated the gossip of the previous evening, informing of the same births, deaths and marriages as his father.

"Oh, yes, and the Champ is digging gardens for two pounds a day," he informed with a wry smile.

To the Boy's great relief, the lorry finally cleared Fen and fog. The headlamps fixed on the long ribbon of tarmac as they turned south, towards the Capital.

Brakes squealing, the lorry came to a halt. A white sheet of frost now covered the sacks of potatoes that shivered to the beat of the diesel. Jumping down from the cab, face upturned, he raised his arms to catch rucksack and sleeping-bag. The old man's face appeared above him. He leaned out of the cab, flat cap pushed to the back of his head, shouting down to the Boy,

"Keep on this road. You'll soon get a lift. You know, your dad's real proud of you, Boy. Don't let him down! I'll maybe see you, next year. Best of luck!"

Once the noise of the lorry's engine had faded into the distance, he found himself alone at the side of the road. It was very late and without the rattle of the engine, the night seemed strangely silent. He pulled on the duffel coat against the biting cold and waited.

Five minutes' later, the first set of headlights made its appearance. Thumb raised, the Boy watched as the car sped past. The next car and the next one passed without slowing.

"Bastards!" He called, patience eroded by the cold.
An hour later and no car had stopped. His feet and hands were numb from the cold. Rucksack and sleeping-bag over his shoulder, he began to walk.

"At least, it will keep me warm," he thought.

It seemed like he had been walking for hours. By then, he was shouting at the top of his voice like a madman; each set of tail-lights more vilified than the last. The wind had started to blow. Swirling flurries of sleet hung in the air. Illuminated by the passing headlights, the little clouds danced and dived in the slipstreams of the cars. The Boy let out a stream of abuse at the last car as it passed by him. To his surprise, it stopped some way down the road; brake lights blinding in the pitch darkness. Engine whining, it reversed to where he stood.

"Get in! You must be frozen," the driver said, passenger door now opened.

"I nearly ran over you. You're almost invisible in that dark coat! Especially with the hood up! Have you been trying to get a lift for very long?"

"About ten minutes," the Boy lied, embarrassed by his, most basic of mistakes.

"If I were you, I'd keep that hood down and face the traffic. Then, they might be able to see you!"

"Thanks for the advice."

"Where you heading?"

"Dover."

"Dover! You're going in the wrong direction! You've missed the road! The junction is about three miles back there!"

"Fool," he thought, "how could I have walked past it, even in the dark?"

With heavy heart, he abandoned the newly found warmth of the car and crossed to the other side of the road.

"Best of luck, mate," the driver called, breathing steam through the open window.

"Thanks."

Within minutes, another car stopped at the behest of the outstretched thumb. Several lifts later, he was clear of the Capital and hopelessly lost.

Exhausted, he unfurled the sleeping-bag and climbed inside. Shivering, he prayed for sleep; the hedgerow, his only shield against the weather.

CHAPTER TWO:

L'AUTOSTOP.   HITCH-HIKING   FOR   BEGINNERS: LESSON TWO

Sleep was but a short respite from his ordeal. Morning awoke him; its clear sunlight invading his dreamless refuge. He tried to move but his body was stiff with pain and cold. His hip and shoulder ached from their contact with the frosty ground. His spine shuddered, teeth chattered with the cold. He must move. He had to reach the coast, that day. He could not have endured another night outside in the open air. Confident of his visibility, he hitch-hiked to the nearest railway station.

On the night ferry and train, he snatched precious sleep; sprawled across the seats in the warm carriage, sleeping-bag for a pillow. The early hours of the morning found him outside the Gare du Nord. Alone, beneath the arches of the square, he stamped away the hours until dawn. Only then, would the Métro deliver him to the southern part of the city.

Neither pedestrian nor vehicle disturbed his vigil. Paris was deserted, closed for the night. Only the smell of baking bread betrayed any human presence. Drifting across the square, it cramped his stomach; painful reminder that he hadn't eaten since he began his journey. Parched lips yearned for water but every bar and shop was closed.

First light brought sudden and unexpected life. Heralded by the high-pitched note of their engines, an army of mopeds invaded the square. They emerged from a dozen separate entrances, criss-crossing the square at full throttle. Thirst and hunger forgotten, the Boy gazed in wonder at the ever-changing patterns of this motorized kaleidoscope. Paris was open!

Clutching a bottle of mineral water, remains of the warm loaf safe in his pocket, he walked down the stone steps into the Métro. There, he bought a ticket to the suburbs at the south of the city.

He took up position at the exit to the traffic island. As the first car came past him, he stuck out his thumb, confident in his newly acquired skill. Sure enough, the car stopped, past and clear of the island.

"Easy!" He chuckled to himself.

Grabbing up his luggage, he trotted to where his benefactor waited. As he reached for the door handle, the car suddenly raced off, the driver's mocking words trailing behind it.

"Salaud.* Hippy, Salaud," they taunted.

Biting his lip with anger, the Boy resumed his position by the traffic island.

Every car that passed seemed to have an insult or centime** to hurl at him. From time to time, one of the vehicles would stop; beyond the place where he stood. Although wise to the ploy, he could not risk the loss of a genuine lift. So, time after time, he trotted after a car. And time after time, the car accelerated away, just as he reached for the door handle. Again, the Boy was reduced to hurling verbal abuse and 'Victory' signs after the retreating vehicles.

"¿Hombre, qué haces?" ***

The unexpected voice from behind had startled him.

"El autostop, claro," **** he said, turning to face his inquisitress.

The two girls, standing behind him, could have been twins. Apart from the colours of their clothes, they were dressed in identical fashion. Both wore calf-length boots, heavy skirt and overcoat. Thick gloves matched their woollen jumpers. Wide-brimmed hats were pulled down tightly over cascades of jet-black hair.

"You speak Spanish?" The first girl asked, surprise on her face.

"Yes. I am studying it," he replied.

"We are also students but I repeat. What are you doing? You'll never get a lift on your own, especially with that hair. Come, we'll help you."

Removing her hat, she pulled it down over the Boy's head. Pushing his hair into the crown, she revealed a perfect 'short back and sides.'

"¡ Estupendo!" She said, stepping back to admire her handiwork.

"¡ Qué guapo eres!" *****
Embarrassed by the stranger's compliment, the Boy felt his cheeks redden in the chill air.

"Handsome, maybe, but cold, definitely," he said in a weak attempt to cover his discomfort.

"Now, stand back, away from the road, over there, next to the hedge. We'll soon get a lift."
A B.M.W. motorcar stopped for the girl's outstretched hand. She leaned inside to talk to the driver, pointing back towards the Boy, at the same time. She beckoned him.

"He's German but he speaks English. Come, you can translate," the girl said.
The driver said that he would take them as far as Orléans. So, the Boy travelled in style. Seated on the front seat of the luxury car, he translated Spanish to English for the benefit of the driver; English to Spanish for the two girls. At Orléans, Teresa and Maria bid him, farewell.

"You must take the train. From here onwards, you will make it difficult for us to get lifts. Nor will they stop for a man on his own. Even with short hair! Keep the hat. It suits you; my present. No, don't worry, I have my scarf. Until we meet again!"

They parted company, neither realizing how prophetic her words would prove.

CHAPTER THREE: JOURNEY'S END.

The train was filled with Andalusians; migrant workers, homeward bound from the factories and building sites of Germany's economic renaissance. All wore black berets, thick suits and heavy boots against the northerly climate. Ironically, warm sun hailed the train's approach to the border, filling the carriage with bright light.

Bread and wine passed from hand to hand. Strong fingers broke great chunks from the long loaves, squeezed red jets of wine from goatskin into gaping mouths. The Boy took some of the bread and ate, refusing wine in favour of his bottle of water. One of the workers grabbed the 'bota' from him, believing 'El Inglés' too shy or inept to participate in the ancient art.

"Look, it's easy," he laughed.

Head tilted back, he sprayed a great, sparkling arc of wine into the air. From forehead to nose to waiting tongue flowed the blood-red stream. This tremendous feat of skill and accuracy was greeted by much laughter and back-slapping from his companions. Each, in turn, tried to emulate this incredible manner of drinking, spraying wine into eyes and nostrils in their failed attempts. Each failed effort was followed by some transparent excuse;

"He hit my elbow."

"The sun was in my eyes."

Voices raised loudly with happiness; more jokes and laughter.

The miles had passed unnoticed, the hardships of the previous three days soon forgotten, lost in the warmth of the carriage, swept away by the camaraderie of his fellow travellers. As the train crossed the border, leaving behind the land of the flying centime, the Boy and Spaniards cheered as one. Somehow, it reminded him of his last day at school.

Like life-long friends, they said their goodbyes. The Boy left the train, carrying half a loaf of bread and one of the wineskins;

"So that you can practise."

"Don't worry, we have plenty more," they told him, by way of reassurance.

At last, he was in Spain. He crossed the bridge that spanned the river and walked towards the sea.

He had never before seen such a place. Nothing could have prepared him for such a sight. Lush, green mountains pressed the town towards the seafront, the only apparent escape inland; the river. The elegant façades of apartment blocks overlooked wide, tiled promenades and yellow sands. Gentle waves lapped against the island in the bay. Above, loomed the giant, stone statue, saintly guardian of the small, fishermen's harbour and its castle. He found a bench on the promenade and sat. His eyes wandered from the castle to the beach; beach to statue, from mountain to town. At the entrance to the bay, a small fishing boat came into view, the rest of the flotilla bobbing along behind it, like corks in the distance. After a short time, the smell of sardines, barbecued on the very quayside, drifted across the seafront.

His body gave a shiver as the chill breeze brought him from his reverie. It would soon be dusk and he had nowhere to stay. Once again, his lack of organization had won the day. It had been his plan to sleep on the beach; Californian style. It had not even occurred to him that the buildings of the town would be so close to the beaches. Besides, his night in the Kentish hedgerow had stifled any ambitions he might have to sleep beneath the stars… ever again.

"Hombre. ¿ Qué haces?"

He could not believe his ears or eyes. He turned to find two, small, well-insulated hitch-hikers standing behind him.

"¡ El autostop! ¡ Claro!" He said before a storm of playful punches rained down on him.

Once again, the two girls took charge of their apprentice hitch-hiker.

"Where are you staying?"

"I don't know. On the beach, probably."

"You can't. The Guardia will arrest you."

This was one aspect of the problem that the Boy had not considered.

"What should I do?"

"Wait. One moment," the girl said.

She hailed a young passer-by. A few words of conversation, arms waved to give pointed directions and the Boy was off, chasing after the two girls as they weaved a path through the maze of apartment blocks. Before long, they came to a small college hidden away in the backstreets.

From here, the small group emerged, its ranks swollen by a dozen or more students intent not only on helping 'El Inglés' but also on viewing his clandestine locks. The ranks of the procession had swollen even more, by the time they stopped outside the door of one of the blocks. Inquisitive friends now tagged along, forewarned of the trilby's contents.

The door was opened by an old lady. A very, very old lady, she seemed to the Boy. White hair, pinned back in an austere bun, contrasted sharply with the unadorned black of dress, shoes and stockings. The wrinkled face showed no surprise at the crowd that surrounded her door. The two girls pushed him through, into a large entrance hall, followed by the small army of students. Crowding in the doorway, they jostled to witness the strange scene.

The Boy faced the old lady across the foyer, his height and size exaggerated by her shrunken stature. With some hesitation, he took sleeping-bag and kitbag from his shoulder and placed them on the floor between his feet. He caught sight of himself in the large mirror that stood by the door. With the wide-brimmed hat and duffel coat, he looked like some, strange missionary. Every eye in the room was upon him. Compounded by the old lady's stern stare, this made him feel completely alien; like a fish in a bowl.

"Are there any spare places?" Maria asked.

"I don't know," the old woman replied.

Her hawk-like eyes remained fixed on the Boy.

"Are there or aren't there any?"

The old lady looked the Boy up and down, eyes now filled with suspicion.

"I don't know," she repeated.

In the crowded doorway, loud whispers informed a latecomer;

"¡ Tiene el pelo largo!"*

The old lady's hearing was as sharp as her eyesight.

"¿ Cómo? Take off your hat."

---

* "¡Tiene el pelo largo!" : "He's got long hair!"

"Yes, take off your hat. Let us see," the crowd chorused behind him.

Reluctantly, he removed the hat. Hair, now freed of the trilby, hung thick and greasy onto his shoulders. Behind him, all were silent. All talk had ceased in a single gasp. Chicken's claw of a hand raised to her face, the old woman uttered an involuntary,

"¡ Ay! ¡ Madre mía!"

"¡ No hay sitio!" She almost screamed.

It was as if she had been confronted by some barbarian, by the devil himself. She was even more outraged when the Boy pleaded to sleep on the floor,

"Anywhere, just to rest," he said.

"¡ No hay sitio! ¡ No hay sitio! ¡ Véte!"*

She drove them all from the flat, brandishing her walking stick like a cudgel behind them.

Ambitions to see the 'Hippy Hair' fulfilled, the group on the pavement dispersed quickly. Only one of the students remained.

"My name is Fernando. There is a spare room where I live. I know, they need the money."

"Now, we must go. It will be dark, soon. We have to be in Madrid by tomorrow night," Maria said.

* "¡ No hay sito! - ¡ Véte!": "There are no vacancies! Clear Off!"

For the second time that day, he parted company from his two guardian angels. With a wave, they had disappeared into the maze of streets. This time, he was sure that he would never see them again.

"Follow me," said Fernando, grabbing up the sleeping-bag.

"It's not far."

CHAPTER FOUR: A REFUGE

The Boy followed Fernando up the stone steps and into one of the buildings that lined the seafront. Ignoring the caged lift in the centre of the tiled foyer, they walked up the six, short flights of stairs.

"It's faster than taking the lift," Fernando explained.

On the third floor, they stopped at a door, the left of two. Fernando knocked on the door and it was opened by a squat, muscular woman. Her nose was large and flat, accentuated by cropped hair and small chin. Her figure and appearance were at odds with the chequered dress and white apron that she wore. Recruited from one of the many hill farms that surrounded the town, this was Pepe, the maid. She stood, hand frozen on the doorknob, staring at the Boy. Her eyes were wide with surprise.

"Fetch Rosita," Fernando ordered, "this lad is interested in renting the spare room."

The young woman disappeared inside the flat to return a few moments later with Rosita, mistress of the household. The Boy waited, braced himself for the inevitable rejection. If his appearance had the same effect on Rosita as the maid, she showed no sign of it.

"Come, enter," she smiled.

"Look, here is the room. It overlooks the beach. You are English, No?"

Rosita had none of the austere appearance of the women that the Boy had so far encountered in the town. Her hair was back-combed like a fan, framing a face still pretty for her years. Full lips pouted beneath aquiline nose and large, dark eyes. Her complexion was pure white. Although slightly plump, her figure was voluptuous in the pink housecoat that she wore. Fixed on the woman's dark eyes, the Boy fought to keep his gaze from straying downwards.

"The room is one thousand pesetas per week. Payable in advance. That's full board."
Her eyes smiled knowingly, as if to taunt his discomfort.

"I'll take it," he said, not knowing where to look; up, at the mocking eyes or down, at the incredible cleavage.

He slumped down onto the wide bed. Seconds later, he was asleep.

He was awakened by a bright flash. Illuminating the whole room in garish light, it lent the illusion of a black and white still; a photograph from the vampire's archives. Shadows, large with life, danced across the panelled walls. Then, came the thunder; a deafening crash that seemed to come from directly above him. Out on the balcony, he watched the great, dark clouds come rolling across the horizon.

On jagged legs of white light, they came striding, cloaking moon and stars. The seas frothed, glowed, incandescent beneath the strobes of lightning; pure wool on boiling tar. Soon, there was more light than darkness as thunder cracked; a hundred bullwhips all around him.

Then, the rain came. It swept across the bay in thick, heavy sheets. With a noise pounding like the very thunder, it moved from sea to beach, from beach to town. He only had time to run from the balcony before the deluge could swamp him. As he slammed shut the French windows, it struck, rattling the doors with its force. Raindrops hit at the glass with the same, urgent staccato as a machine gun. They hit so hard that he thought it must shatter.

As quickly as it had struck, the storm was gone. Thunder grumbled into the distance, rain sweeping in its wake through the strobe-lit mountains. When he opened the windows, the air was clean and fresh. So fresh that he could smell the wet grass on the hillside, half a mile away. With the sweet smell of Spring pervading the room, he resumed his sleep, happy to be on bed rather than on beach.

He was awoken by the maid knocking at the bedroom door and the delicious aroma of hot food drifting through the flat. When he entered the dining room, the family had already taken their seats at the table. They were arranged in strict order.

At the head of the table sat Don Isidro, a retired tailor from Guernica. He was dressed in suit and tie for the afternoon meal. His full head of hair was as white as the starched shirt that he wore. Care-worn face and thick-lensed spectacles gave him every appearance of a university professor. At his left elbow, like a large, black button, lay the mandatory 'Boina vasca.'* At his right, stood a large glass porrón ** filled with red wine. He never used a glass to drink, not even at the dinner table.

On his left-hand side sat Rosita, his daughter. On his right, opposite his daughter, sat her husband, Manolo, a dour, red-headed man from Galicia. Then came Fernando and the two small children of the family. To Rosita's left sat Mari-Helena, a girl of some twelve years of age. In between Rosita and Mari Helena, an extra place had been prepared. The old man at the head of the table stared grimly as Rosita introduced the Boy to her family.

Pepe carried in a tureen brimful of soup, bulbs of garlic floating on its surface like jellyfish. This they ate, supplementing spoons with slices of bread from the basket that passed from hand to hand around the table. Beans with chorizo *** followed, sweet rice for dessert.

---

* Boina vasca – Basque beret. ** Porrón: A spouted drinking vessel. *** Chorizo: A smoked, spiced, pork sausage.

It had been several days since he had last eaten a properly cooked meal. Yet, he took pains to disguise his hunger from the family. He ate slowly, joining in the conversation around the table. He relished every mouthful of the new and delicious cuisine. He devoured every morsel of the dinner-time 'tertulia.' **** Rosita asked him question after question. He answered as best he could, talking slowly and precisely. At the head of the table, 'El Abuelo' listened intently to his every word. When everybody had finished their meal, he pronounced his judgement;

"He speaks well, very correctly, like one from 'Las Valladolides: *****

The Boy glowed with pride at such praise. The dinner at an end, he made his excuses. He would spend the afternoon exploring the port.

After the bleak Fens and the polluted grime of the City, the town was like something from a dream. He had never seen anywhere so fresh and clean. The cold resorts of England's eastern coast could do nothing to compare with its glory. Unhindered by smog or fog, the sunshine beamed down upon him. It warmed his body and animated his mind, raised his

****Tertulia: A conversation or gathering for conversation. *****Las Valladolides: The area around Valladolid where true Castillian is spoken.

spirits. He walked the length of the promenade and out onto the cliffs.

Seated on the massive, stone blocks that guarded the beaches, aged fishermen kept watch over their long rods, lines lost in the distance. They forsook their daily chore to stare open-mouthed as he passed. Engrossed in his sightseeing, the Boy was totally unaware of their ignorant stares, insignificant in the presence of such beautiful scenery.

He strolled around the small harbour, through the crates of flapping fish and the ever-present smell of sardines on the barbecue. He wandered into the narrow streets of the 'Old Quarter.' Here, washing-lines with dripping clothes criss-crossed between wrought-iron balconies. Overhead, neighbour shouted to neighbour, informing of the latest scandal. Their voices floated down into the crowded shops and bars that lined the labyrinth of streets below them, compounding the brouhaha.

When he emerged from the shadows of the alley, the sun blinded him so he was forced to shade his eyes with his hand. As his eyes became accustomed to the light, he saw that he had entered a small, arched plaza. This square was dominated by a low, stone-built church. After the confines of the narrow streets, it loomed overhead like some grand cathedral, dwarfing the surrounding buildings. The Boy stood for some time, amazed by the illusion created by church and alley, unaware of the small crowd that had gathered around him. It was as if they mimicked him.

As he stared up at the looming church, the group around him also gazed up; jaws slack in grotesque amazement.

CHAPTER FIVE: THE DAILY GAUNTLET

Ignoring the bar of chocolate and bowl of coffee that Pepe had prepared for him, he left the flat. As he descended the staircase, he removed the sunglasses from the top pocket of his shirt. Ostensibly, they would protect him from the bright light that flooded through the doorway. In the foyer, the young daughter of the concierge awaited him. Waited with the same question that she had asked of him on every morning for the previous eight weeks.

"¿Eres chico u chica?" *

He marched through the foyer without acknowledging the child. Out in the street, he donned the sunglasses. He was ready for his daily ordeal.

He walked along, head held high, ignoring the exaggerated stares of the passers-by, his eyes safe behind the smoked lenses. He passed the old woman at the same place on the street as the day before and the day before that. Dressed in the compulsory, black uniform, she tottered along the pavement, back bent beneath the weight of the two bags that she carried. Batons of bread stood proud in the bags, evidence of her morning shopping expedition. The Boy walked onwards for a

* "¿ Eres chico u chica?" : "Are you a boy or a girl?"

dozen paces then stopped and turned. The scene was all, too familiar.

He took his stance on cue. Hands on hips, he confronted the old woman. The latter, having already adopted the same stance, stood ready; jaw slack with amazement.

"O.K., Annie Oakley," he drawled in his best John Wayne accent, "make your play!!"

"¿ Cómo?"

"Go for your gun, Shorty!"

"¡Joder!" The woman said, picking up the shopping-bags at her feet.

He stood facing her until she turned. Muttering to herself, she carried on her way.

Now, the tram passed him, crammed with shop and office workers. The same faces pressed against the glass as the day before and the day before that.

"¡ Oyé, Marica!" *

"¡ Maricona!"

The same voices with the same insults. To no avail, he gave the gawking passengers a vigorous sign of 'Victory'.

Next, he came to cross the river. The old man was in his usual place on the bridge. He wore the pensioner's uniform of

---

* Marica/Maricona: homosexual/queer

serge suit and black beret. Dark glasses and white stick gave notice of his disability. Strips of lottery tickets hung from the front of his jacket, secured to lapels and pockets by clothes' pegs. As the Boy reached the end of the bridge, the man's plaintive cry went out;

"¡Sorteo para hoy! ¡Sorteo para hoy!" **

He crossed the bridge to where the old man stood. The latter had ceased his calling. Head rigid, blind sunglasses stared straight in front of him.

"¡Marica!" He hissed as the Boy walked by him.

Safe behind his own sunglasses, the Boy carried on his way. As he left the bridge, the 'blind' man's cry went up, one more time,

"¡Sorteo para hoy!"

Yet, the worst was to come. Now, he must face the persecutors against whom he could find no recourse. There were very few people on the path that followed the river bank. As he approached the school, he knew that the children would be waiting. From its entrance, they came running and shrieking. Swarming around him, they pulled at his clothes, reached up to grab at his hair. Each had the same ridiculous question shouted at the top of his voice.

"¿Eres chico u chica?"

** "¡Sorteo para hoy!"; Today's lottery.

He walked faster, desperate to escape, afraid to topple one of the infants in his haste; gentle bear hounded by relentless jackals.

No sooner had he outpaced the children than he came to the next obstacle. Waiting to enter the station, the same train as yesterday stood, hissing steam. Inside its coaches, faces pressed against the thick glass. Mouths shouted, voices muffled in the closed carriages. Hands struggled frantically to open windows, release the captive insults. Without breaking stride, he marched onwards, safe behind the sunglasses. As he reached the bottom of the ramp that crossed the railway line, his final test appeared.

Laden with huge logs bound for the paper mills, a lorry came into view. As it passed, the driver's shouted insults were drowned by a deafening blast from the air-horn. One, last, frustrated effort, lest the sign of Victory have any effect, and he crossed the bridge to the safety of the college.

As ever, the prospect of the walk home for dinner and return for afternoon lectures filled him with trepidation and frustrated anger.

CHAPTER SIX;   AN ODD PAIR OF FRIENDS

The college was housed in new buildings dominated by a strange, three-spired church. The appearance of this, his latest seat of learning, was a stark contrast to its counterpart in England. Bright, red brickwork had replaced grimy stone, open lawns instead of dingy courtyards. Priests strolled in the warm, spring sunlight; no need to scurry from acid rain.

Within the red walls, there was no room for the freedom of self-expression. Lectures were conducted in strict form by the motionless, black figures that stood at the head of each class. They were to be addressed as 'Padre,' constant reminder of the religious origins of the instruction. Discussion was kept to a minimum. Lessons were for the propagation of facts alone; no time for questions.

Two of the students were already on the bridge. Although both of them were English, their looks did nothing to betray the fact. They were Josh and John, the only true friends that the Boy had made during his long months at the college.

Josh's broad, north-eastern accent belied the dark features that he had inherited from his Greek ancestors. To have described him as hirsute would have been an understatement, for he was covered from head to foot in thick, black hair. Even the tops of his feet and backs of his hands had been invaded by the dark mass. It seemed that light to his eyes was only guaranteed by a twice-daily shave! Sunbathing on a crowded beach, he could be seen from fifty yards' away, lurking in the lines of bare flesh like a plump tarantula.

John, his companion, was the opposite. His slim figure boasted none of Josh's hairy bulk. Pale, blue eyes, white skin and bright, red hair betrayed his Irish ancestry. He spoke with a strong, Liverpudlian accent that was virtually impossible to decipher. Josh would joke that his spoken Spanish was better than his English. So, how the indecipherable Liverpudlian and the incomprehensible Novacastrian understood each other, the Boy could only guess.

"What's the matter, Man?" Josh queried.

"I'm sick of them," the Boy answered.

"Take no notice, Man. Come on, have a night out with us."

"It's not worth it."

Josh began to argue but the memory of their only excursion together into the Old Quarter was all too fresh in his mind. He had witnessed the silenced bar-rooms; backs turned by barmen and waiters, the gaping incredulity of passers-by. He had ranted at the blank faces, angry to the point of violence. They had been forced to escape the narrow streets to seek food and drink elsewhere in the town.

"Why, Man. Just give them the fist!"

"What do you mean, the fist?"

"Like this, Man!"

Clamping the flat of his left hand into the crook of his right elbow, he fisted the air.

The Boy was not alone in his criticisms of the college. The majority of the students yawned their way through the lectures. Their attention would drift clandestinely towards the hands of the clock that hung above the droning voice at the front of the room. The noisy stampede at the end of the day bore true testimony to the popularity of the lessons.

At least, the other students could enjoy the nightlife of the town, untroubled by its populace. Exiled from both the town and the Old Quarter by the cold ignorance of the local population, the Boy spent his evenings in the flat. After supper, which usually consisted of soup followed by an egg swimming in oil and heaps of fresh bread, the family would watch television until bedtime. Invariably, the Boy would find himself alone at the table with 'El Abuelo.'

The old fellow would tell anecdotes of his time as a tailor in Guernica, slapping the table to punctuate every punchline. Then, a stream of red wine from the porrón would stir his long memory and he would begin another story. As the night wore on, the streams of wine would become more frequent; the stories more poignant. The Boy would soon come to learn of death, defeat and despair from the trembling lips of his new friend. On evenings when the old man was too tired or too drunk to talk, the Boy would retire to his bedroom and work on his project.

Shortly after his arrival, he had ventured into the town to find a bookshop. Under the suspicious glare of the shopkeeper, he had purchased as many books about the Party and its history as he could afford. In the quiet shadows of the bedroom, he read the dogmatic speeches of justification, the sermons of self-righteousness. They all filled him with distaste and loathing. Meanwhile, in his room down the hallway, the old man slept alone, alcohol impotent against his nightmares.

He had no mother, no father, no wife to wake him from his terror. There were no aunts or uncles for poor Rosita, his one, surviving child; only their memory. All trace of them had perished in the maelstrom of the firestorm; mere statistics in the destruction of Guernica.

How dare the Boy's studies ever delve so deeply? Victims were not the declared subjects of his assignment. He decided to dedicate his spare time, now so abundant, to the swift completion of this, most hated of tasks.

CHAPTER SEVEN:

LEARNING THE LANGUAGE (LESSON ONE)

The conversation around the table had ended with the arrival of the customary garlic soup. Only Rosita's voice sounded above the chinking cutlery as she described to her husband a dress that she wished to buy.

Mari-Helena passed the basket to the Boy. From within, he took one of the large slices of bread, then the basket from the girl. He turned to Rosita. The woman was too engrossed in her fashion lesson to notice the proffered basket. Seeing the smallest piece of bread remaining on the plate at her elbow,

"Excuse me, Rosita...."

Face and massive cleavage turned as one. Rosebud mouth parted in a shining smile. She seemed mockingly unaware of the straining silk that threatened to release her swinging flesh; oblivious to the Boy's efforts to fix his stare at eye level. Once more, the Boy presented the basket of bread slices.

"¿Rosita, tienes bastante?" (Have you got enough bread?) He asked.

Rosita's eyes dilated with surprised anger. Her face flushed, crimson as the red lips. All was quiet in the room; a moment frozen in time. Manolo sat motionless, spoon raised halfway to his mouth, eyes fixed on the Boy. Fernando and the three children sat in shocked silence. The only noise had come from 'El Abuelo' as he spluttered a mouthful of soup back into the dish in front of him.

The moment finally passed. The rest of the meal was completed in absolute silence. The last course consumed, the diners quickly left the table. The Boy found himself alone with 'El Abuelo'. After a few moments, the old man broke the silence.

"Boy, I'm going to tell you something."

"Yes, don Isidro? What is it?"

"When you say of a woman that 'Tiene Bastante', then, it means,

¡TIENE BASTANTE!"

A wink at the Boy and he juggled the weight of two, imaginary melons; gnarled hands cupped in front of his chest.

"And Rosita, ¿TIENE BASTANTE, NO?"

The old man's eyes filled with tears of laughter. This time, it was the Boy's turn to blush crimson!

As he approached the ramp that crossed the railway line, klaxon blaring, the lorry rounded the bend in the road. The Boy turned. Head high, he faced the oncoming vehicle, like bullfighter before charging bull. As the lorry came near, he delivered the 'estocada;' * a fisted salute.

* Estocada: Fatal strike on a bull (with a sword)

With great satisfaction, he watched as the lorry, seemingly out of control, weaved past him, almost plunging into the river. He crossed the bridge to the college, saluting the train as he passed. His heart filled with glee at the outrage that had been unleashed in the carriages below him.

NOW, they could understand!

CHAPTER EIGHT: A POP CONCERT

In a great display of enlightenment, the priests had prepared a 'going away' party for the students. A bandstand had been erected in the grounds of the college. This was faced by a dozen tables littered with drinks and snacks of every description. At the entrance to the college, the fathers waited in a stiff, formal line to greet the 'revellers.'

The Boy arrived in high spirits. He had rarely walked the streets at such a late hour so he had avoided many of his persecutors; no children, no shoppers, no tram, no train. Only the unrelenting stares of the few pedestrians followed him.

Sitting and standing in small groups, the students waited for the entertainment to begin. On stage, drumkit and electric guitars promised great things to come. Then, the band entered .

A deafening roll on the drums along with a disjointed series of shrill, guitar rifts and the singer began to murder the song. His accent was so heavy that it distorted the lyrics beyond all recognition.

"Hay Jou, where ya doin' wit dis gun in dat han..."
If the audience had any thoughts of vocal criticism, any attempts were immediately thwarted. No sooner had the torture of the song begun than there was a blinding flash. It was followed

immediately by a deafening thunderclap and sheets of heavy, pounding rain.

If it was the "music" or the weather that drove them, running, cursing and laughing across the bridge, no one could say. But nobody called for a repeat of the single-lined concert!

Water dripping from faces and clothes, they sheltered in the entrance to the infants' school. Josh said that they should organise their own, going-away party.

"Why Aye, Man! I'll give you a party to remember," he promised.

A second prophecy had been made.

CHAPTER NINE:
LEARNING THE LANGUAGE (LESSON TWO)

He gathered his courage for the daily gauntlet, sunglasses ready in his hand. Before he left the flat, Rosita stopped him by the front door. Eyes smiled, teeth shined, bright in the shadowy corridor.

"Boy, ven acá. * Soon, it will time for you to leave us, no? We will all be sorry to see you go, even 'El Abuelo'. You have behaved like a gentleman in our home. So we wish to do something for you before you go…. a farewell meal, an English meal. What do you eat in England? What is your national dish?"

"Pescado con patatas fritas," (fish and chips) the Boy replied without thinking.

"¿Pescado con patatas fritas?"
Rosita seemed hesitant, her dark eyes, quizzical.

"Yes, pescado con patatas fritas," the Boy confirmed.

"Then, tomorrow, we will eat fish and chips," Rosita said with determination.

The family was gathered for dinner, each seated in his respective place.

* Ven acá: Come here

"Today, we eat like the English," Rosita proudly announced.

"Pepe, ven acá."

Uniform freshly washed and pressed for the occasion, hair brushed back neatly beneath her cap, Pepe entered. Before her, she proudly carried a large, earthenware tureen, lid firmly in place.

"Put the dish here. Go fetch the patatas fritas," Rosita ordered.

Pepe returned to the kitchen while the family waited expectantly. She returned carrying a large basket. This, she placed with great ceremony on the table next to the tureen. However, its contents were not what the Boy had expected.

Rosita now served the meal. Glances passed back and forth between the diners but no words were spoken. The Boy, too embarrassed to admit his mistake, ate along with the rest of the family.

Potato crisps cracked beneath knives and forks, small, sharp fragments shooting across the table in every direction.

And the fish? Not battered, as expected, but boiled; its juices, the only antidote for the flying potato shrapnel!!!

"Boy, do you often eat this in England?" Rosita politely asked as a fugitive crisp exploded from her plate, narrowly missing 'El Abuelo.'

"Only on Fridays," the Boy answered as seriously as he could but there was no avoiding the laughter in her eyes.

'El Abuelo' concluded that the English' taste in food was …."very strange."

CHAPTER TEN: BIG MAN, SMALL VOICE.

To atone for the disastrous 'pop concert,' the priests endeavoured to make the final day of the course as entertaining as possible. The morning was dedicated to a series of word and parlour games; more suitable for children than the score of twenty-year olds that lounged and yawned in the lecture hall.

The afternoon's proceedings were conducted by el padre Estéfano. At first sight, nobody would have guessed that he was a Basque. For, this was a true giant of a man, who made all around him, even the Boy, seem small. Some sixty years old, his great height had not yet been bowed by time. A full head of red hair and clear, blue eyes that laughed with his every word, seemed to deny his age and nationality.

For an hour or so, el padre Estéfano dutifully followed the list of games furnished by the rest of the priests. Realising his students' apathy towards the proceedings, he finally called a halt.

"I think that we shall do something very different," he said.

Although his eyes still sparkled mischief, his tone of voice had become very serious. With comic subterfuge, he tiptoed to the door of the lecture hall. He opened it with great care. Ducking beneath the lintel, he poked his head outside, his great body filling the doorway. He surveyed the corridor outside, his head moving from side to side like some giant turtle. Seeing that the coast was clear, he quickly withdrew. Smiling and wiping imaginary sweat from his brow, he returned to the lector at the front of the room. From an inside pocket of his jacket, he produced a small book. It was lost in the palm of his huge fist. Fingers like giant sausages carefully turned the pages.

"Ladies and gentlemen, this story is called; '¿Por qué los perros se huelen los rabos?'* The last time that I read this book in public, they sent in a gunboat!"
There was sporadic laughter in the room at this lame attempt at levity.

El padre Estéfano read from the book; an allegorical tale that ridiculed the Spanish regime. It held nothing risqué for the students. It seemed innocuous, no more controversial than any political article in any English newspaper. This was not England.

None seemed to understand the great risk taken by the priest in reading the story. None seemed to understand that he risked his life. As for the allusion to the gunboat in the bay of San Sebastián, it was completely lost on them all.

All but the Boy; 'El Abuelo' had told him all about it.

* ¿Por qué los perros se huelen los rabos?" Why do dogs smell their own tails?

CHAPTER ELEVEN: THE BEACH PARTY

The full moon shined down from the star-studded sky. Its light played across the dark waters of the bay so they flashed and rippled like the scales of some giant fish. On the island, the statue of Saint Sebastian glowed eerily grey.

Josh and the rest of the students had brought bread, olives and several leather botas swollen with wine. The girls laid out this 'buffet' on a blanket on the sand while the boys scoured the beach for driftwood. A small fire kindled, they gathered around, sitting cross-legged on the fine sand. Wine and bread passed from hand to hand inside the small circle. Jokes and stories followed but despite the combined warmth of fire and alcohol, the atmosphere was hushed, the merriment forced. The very next day, they would take their leave for destinations new. Josh picked up his guitar and started to strum.

The music gathered pace as his nimble fingers, like fat, hairy insects, scurried up and down the strings. One of the girls, Helen, a slim, attractive brunette, jumped to her feet and started to dance. Stamping in the sand, she whirled, clapping her hands together over her head. It was not long before all the girls were dancing, goading the boys to join them in their stumbling efforts.

The Boy wandered away from the drunken dancers and sat down on the shoreline to watch the incoming waves. The sea breeze was cool but he ignored it, lost in thought. He felt guilty that he should be happy to leave this, the most beautiful place that he had ever seen. But he knew that beneath this vision of paradise there lurked bitterness, hate and prejudice. Otherwise, how could its inhabitants have treated him so cruelly?

Footsteps, muffled in the soft sand, raced down the beach behind him. A breathless Helen flopped down at his side.

"What are you doing down here, Boy?" She gasped.

"Watching the waves, thinking."

"What are you thinking?"

"Nothing much."

Josh started to play the guitar again, his tired fingers now, slow on the strings. Helen leaned close as the soulful strains of the 'Romance Sonámbulo' drifted across the sands. When she spoke, the sweet smell of wine brought doubt to her words.

"You know, I really like you, Boy," she said.

The muscles of shoulder and arm, against which she leaned, tensed tightly. The girl had taken him by surprise so only the puritan answered, suspicious and harsh in defence.

"Me, too."

The rebuttal had been involuntary. He laughed to turn his answer into jest. But, the girl did not laugh. The answer had been so unexpected, so severe. Her voice was now a whisper.

"Oh, but you're a strange one, Boy. You laugh but never smile. Tell me. Why do you never smile?"

Here, the conversation ended.

At the far end of the beach, a group of dark figures had appeared. At the double, they trotted towards the group of students, their three-cornered hats silhouetted in the moonlight. Without a word, they herded the revellers together then formed a crescent facing them, rifles at the ready. Legs apart, thumbs in pistol belt, only the officer spoke,

"Put out the fire! You will leave the beach. Immediately!"

Yes, he would be glad to leave that place.

CHAPTER TWELVE: NO ESCAPE

It was time to leave; stout handshakes from Manolo and Don Isidro, tearful kisses from Rosita and Pepe. For the last time, he descended the stone staircase, spiralling around the lift to the foyer where the child awaited him.   Ignoring the inevitable question, he emerged into the street to face the stares of the evening shoppers. For one last time, he ran the gauntlet through the town.

Across the bridge, he gained the sanctuary of the railway station. At the luggage office, he paid the price for shipment to England then handed the bag, containing books and precious research, to a uniformed official of the R.E.N.F.E.* The bag disappeared into a storeroom and then, presumably, into the Spanish postal system. Whether it travelled by train, 'plane or automobile, nobody will ever know. It was never seen again.

He walked the length of the station platform, peering into each carriage of the train, squinting to see through the gap left by the blinds. He found an empty carriage and climbed inside. Luggage safely stowed, he settled down for the long journey. At least, he would be able to sleep away the hours, stretched out across the seats. Any such hopes were dashed when the short,

---

* The R.E.N.F.E. The Spanish National Railway System.

dark figures climbed into the compartment. Silently, they took up their positions on the opposite seat.

His first thoughts were of panic, of escape, but it was too late. As the door slammed shut behind them, he heard the shrill whistle of the guard. The engine released a sudden gasp of steam and the carriages lurched into motion. Slowly, the train shunted out of the station and began its laborious climb into the darkening mountains.

The Boy resigned himself to his fate. Was there no escape from these sombre agents of Spanish womanhood? The next twelve hours, spent beneath the inscrutable stares of the women, seemed like an eternity. He felt like a guilty man before his judges. Not a single word was spoken throughout the journey. Only the unblinking eyes of his tormentors betrayed their slightest sign of life.

His only consolation was the rattle of the wheels beneath his feet; desperate reminder of the slowly passing miles.

CHAPTER THIRTEEN: A NEW HOME.

Before any of the other passengers could move, he had grabbed his bag. Throwing open the door of the carriage, he dropped down into the semi-darkness of the railway station.

His only knowledge of the geography and topography of the capital had been imparted by Alan,

"Argüelles is the student quarter. You'll find someplace there. It's fairly close to the university."

A kiosk in the cool foyer of the station promised rented accommodation. He selected a card from the window display and paid the fee.

"One duro*," the woman in the kiosk had demanded.

"And how do I find the pensión?"

"One duro more."

No sooner had he paid the extra money than an old man, loitering next to the kiosk, picked up his bag and marched towards the station exit. The Boy looked in confusion from the woman to the disappearing figure of the guide.

"Follow him! After him!" She urged.

He followed, struggling to stay apace of the black beret as it bobbed along through the sea of jostling passengers. The Boy was not so sure, he was not chasing a thief.

* One duro: A five peseta piece.

Out on the street, light and heat struck him with the power of a sledgehammer. A steel band seemed to tighten around his chest. He gasped for breath in the unaccustomed rarity of the atmosphere. The lack of oxygen cramped at his legs and chest so that he could hardly keep pace, not even with the old man.

His guide disappeared down the steps to the Metro, weaving his way through the throngs of pedestrians like an eel through grass. To the Boy's great relief, the old man was waiting for him at the ticket office. He had taken time to roll and light a cigarette.

"Buy two tickets for the Plaza de España, one return," the old man ordered.

"Follow me."

The railway platform was crowded with impatient passengers who fanned at the stale air with their rolled-up newspapers. The atmosphere remained clammy and stifling. The train's arrival was heralded by a great gush of burning air that assailed lungs and skin. Crammed into the carriage, the Boy prayed for the freedom of the oxygenless streets.

The square was massive. White, stone buildings rose on all sides, reflecting a myriad of glass in the sunlight. There was no time for him to appreciate such splendour because his guide had already breached the maze of shadow-filled streets that surrounded the square. Panting for breath, the Boy was forced to run to catch up with him.. As he reached the corner of the street, he was just in time to see his guide go through one of the large sets of wooden doors that guarded the central courtyard of each building.

The small, cobbled courtyard was cool and shady. The Boy leaned forwards. Hands on thighs, he fought to regain his breath. Sweat dripped from his face onto the smooth stones.

"Sir, one moment, please. I can't breathe."

"Are you ill?" The old man demanded.

"No. I'm just not used to this altitude."

"Altitude? What altitude? Come along, it's only on the first floor!!"

With a shrug of his shoulders, the old man entered the stairwell of the block of flats and sprinted up the first, two flights of stairs. The Boy trudged heavily behind him, up to the landing. The first of the two doors sported a polished, brass plaque.

"Hostal General Mola," it read in bold letters.
His guide rang the doorbell.

When the door opened, the Boy felt his heart sink. The woman that greeted him was dressed in the dreaded, black uniform.

"How could one of his persecutors have preceded him to his destination? Of course, it was impossible. Surely, it was impossible?"

When the woman's face broke into a beaming smile, he knew that it was.

"Come. Come inside," she said.

"You must pay the guide his tip."

"What should I give him?"

"Why, a duro, of course!"

The Boy gave the guide some coins from his pocket and the old man handed him his bag.

"Muchas gracias, señor," he said, tipping the brim of his beret with the forefingers of his free hand.

"Have a nice stay in Madrid," he said as he descended the staircase.

"Do you want a room only or full board?" The new landlady asked.

"Room only."

"That will be five hundred pesetas per week, payable weekly, in advance."

"I'll take it."

"For how long will you stay?"

"For several months."

"Good, good. Come, follow me. The room is down this corridor."

In the little room, he finally regained his breath. Suddenly, it dawned on him. He had just passed by a thousand people. Not one of them had given him a second glance!

CHAPTER FOURTEEN: A NEW FAMILY

The woman was the wife of Don Pedro, the owner of "Hostal Mola." The two had originally worked a farm to the south of the city. They had been successful enough to save the money for a deposit on the pensión. Their land was now worked by Don Pedro's parents. Every Saturday, the old couple would bring fruit and vegetables for market, provisions for the boarding house.

They were the very image of Don Pedro and his wife, only they seemed so much older. The harsh country life had weathered the old man's face and hands to the appearance of wrinkled parchment, bent his back like a bow, burned forearms black. The Boy recognized, only too well, the marks of his trade.

There it was; the pale line of skin across his forehead from the protective beret. Beret or flat cap, the story was the same. This, the Boy knew.

Don Pedro and his wife had been blessed with three children, all daughters. The eldest worked in service. Due to some presumed scandal, her name was seldom mentioned in the household. On the rare occasions that Don Pedro spoke of the girl, he referred to her as 'La Otra;' 'the Other One.' The two, remaining daughters were gorgeous.

The youngest of the two was Nati. A girl in her early teens, her appearance contrasted greatly with that of her parents. Her tan was light and even, acquired at poolside, not in the ferocious heat of the fields. Long, dark tresses hung loose, free from the steel pins that imprisoned her mother's hair. The slacks and brightly coloured blouses that she wore denied the traditional 'widow's weeds.' Her voice, high and sweet, would often be heard drifting through the flat as she sang away the household chores.

The word 'beauty' could not be justly applied to her sister. There was something more. Tall and slim, her skin was flawless, milk-white; testimony to a preference for library over swimming-pool. This complexion did nothing but enhance her looks, emphasize the jet of eyes and hair, the crimson of full lips. The Boy envisioned her with mantilla * of fine lace, graceful figure draped in pure silk; the queen of any 'Feria.' ** Instead, modestly, she preferred the drab fashion of her mother. When he first saw her, the Boy was amazed by her beauty. She was like a precious pearl, hidden away in the shadows of the pensión. When he first saw her, his heart and mind came to understand the true meaning of the word 'castiza.' ***

For Carmina was its true embodiment.

* Mantilla: Veil ** Feria; Bullfight/bullrun *** Castiza: Pure blood/caste.

The walls of the flat were whitewashed; doors, floors and furniture of light pine. There was no air-conditioning but these simple measures seemed adequate, enough to guarantee that the pension remained cool, even on the hottest of summer days. The foyer was large and so doubled as a lounge and television room.

Here, the Boy would spend many, happy hours, chatting with the two teenage girls. Here, his command of the language would bloom beyond the scope of any classroom.

He would take great delight in baiting the two sisters with tales of his derring-do. They, in turn, would protest his ridiculous claims. Carmina, hands on hips, would stamp her disbelief, tossing her head like some beautiful, wild mare.

"You? You, alone, could not have done that!"

"How many girlfriends do you say that you have? Ten?!! Because you are so handsome? Whoever told you such a lie?"

"You lifted a lorry? You lifted a lorry by its axle?"

"One-handed?!"

The conversations usually ended with the Boy punched into a laughing ball by the two, outraged girls.

The room was small and sparsely furnished with none of the grandeur of his accommodation in San Sebastián. The window opened above a central courtyard. During the daytime, the balconies that surrounded it resounded to the songs of a hundred caged birds. Directly below, a small bar backed onto the cobbles.

In the cool of the night, he would lie on his bed listening to the animated conversations of the patrons. Animated to the point of violence, it seemed. Then, there would be laughter and the slap of domino against tabletop would begin anew, the argument about the 'morrow's weather already forgotten.

At weekends, guitars would sound to the accompaniment of clapping hands and stamping feet. A woman would sing, her harsh lyrics interrupted only by soulful 'saetas' * from the audience. In the room above, the Boy once more enjoyed a free lesson in Spanish, a lesson that no amount of money could ever buy.

Here; he had found a new family and the friendship of two, lovely sisters. Here, there was happiness.

Stark contrast to his misery in the north of the country.

* Saetas: spontaneous chants or laments.

CHAPTER FIFTEEN: A GRIM REMINDER.

On his second day in the city, the Boy decided to explore. By the time that he had walked the short distance to the Calle de Princesa, he was already sweating profusely. The steel band reappeared around his chest, crushing the very air from his lungs. He slumped, breathless, onto one of the many benches that lined the sunny boulevard. As soon as he could catch his breath, he retreated to the pensión. It would be another three days before hunger forced him back into the cauldron of the city's streets.

From a small supermarket, he bought a loaf of bread, pat of butter and a bottle of undrinkable milk. The bread gave energy, enough to revive him. After his next expedition, he returned from the Plaza de España, armed with a map, lungs intact. He was ready to venture forth.

During the next, two weeks, he walked the streets of the city centre. He methodically explored every church, museum and palace shown on his map. With every step, he wondered at the grandeur of the buildings. Glorious stone statues lined their very rooftops; warriors that basked in the sunshine, chiselled reminders of a glorious age.

He toured the lush parks where wrinkled old men, their rubber boots incongruous in the shimmering heat, sprayed rainbows from their hosepipes. In the wide plazas he watched the sparkling fountains, lounged to the sounds of their dancing waters.

He entered the rooms and corridors of the Prado.* Here, kings and queens gazed down from their portraits of perfected beauty, flattered for their wealth and power. Vivid colours assailed his eyes from every corner. In one room after another, he found himself overawed by the talents of the great artist. His mastery of colour, light and form was all too obvious; magnificent corruption. But the Boy was not prepared for the contents of the last room at the end of the last corridor. Here, he discovered the dark heart of the gallery; the artist's lunatic truth.

On a plain, white background, Goya's charcoal Saturn, terrifying and satanic majesty, devoured his child. In stark, Gothic reality, merciless jaws ripped head from body. This was the artist's statement, born of hopeless and bitter frustration, liberated only in the safety of drunken solitude.

Within the walls of the museum, the Boy had unwittingly discovered the paradox that was Spain. With blind eyes, he had also seen depicted, a terror that could do nothing to match his own.

*Prado: Art gallery featuring many of Goya's paintings.

In the arched cloisters of the Plaza Mayor, he rested on a bench and absorbed the tranquillity, shielded from the afternoon sun. The square was deserted; shopkeepers and customers at home for siesta.

He did not recognize the first that he saw, nor the second and third; hollow shadows in the bright sunshine.

"Chips in the ancient stonework," he told himself.

Yet, the more that he looked, the more he saw; One Thousand Scars.

CHAPTER SIXTEEN: SUSAN.

It was time to resume his formal education. The walk to the university had been effortless now that he was accustomed to the heat and altitude. He had reached his destination within half an hour.

The Faculties stood, imperious in their isolation, each surrounded by its own grounds. Here, students went about their business, preoccupied by a second round of examinations. But for the bright sunlight, this could have been any university in England. It was not.

As he climbed the steps to the Faculty, his senses had heightened. The hairs on the back of his neck bristled. He shuddered, felt wary like prey on the sight of predator. The bullet holes in the plaza had awakened his subconscious so that his only thoughts were of Uncle Sidney.

The printed lists were pinned on a notice board in the foyer. He scanned them for a second time, once more in vain. There was no sign of his name.

"Webinassignedclasses?"

The voice was female, the accent, American. He turned to face his riddler, bemused by the breathless question.

"Webinassignedclasses?" The girl repeated, as frenetically and unintelligibly as the first time.

Eyes, large as saucers, blue as sky, stared up at him. Auburn hair, straight to the girl's waist, shone like fine thread; a frame for her golden complexion. She spoke again, this time very slowly, so that the gaping moron might understand.

"Have wee beeen assigned classes? Doo yoo speeek Eeengleesh?"

"I am Eeeenglish so I speeek Eeeenglish. Theee question eeez, dooo yoooo?" The Boy mocked.

There was a moment's pause, surprise in the girl's eyes before she spoke again.

He had just met Sooozan.

CHAPTER SEVENTEEN:
YOU CAN'T JUDGE A BOOK......

He balked at the lectures. The other students in the classroom were mainly Swiss and German, who seemed to look on education purely as a matter for dictation. Frantically, they would scribble the tutor's every word. After the first week, he could stand it no longer. The lectures seemed only to mirror the teachings of the priests. He decided that his time would be much better spent reading alone; by the side of the university swimming pool!!

There was a flaw in this plan. He was forced to attend Friday morning lectures because an 'attendance card' was to be signed by the course tutor. This was Conchita, a woman in her mid-thirties. Keen and intelligent, she vainly strived to breathe life into the staïd content of the lectures. The Boy's absences from the classroom had not gone unnoticed by Conchita. After a month of missed lectures, she decided to take action. When the Boy arrived for the ritual signing of the card, she was waiting for him.

"I have decided to do something different, a departure from the normal course work. Starting from today, every Friday, we will have an hour of discussion in Spanish. One of you will initiate the class with a five minute speech on a topic of my choosing. Now, who shall I pick to begin today's lesson? Let me see......"

She was grinning, mischief in her eyes, when she announced the Boy's name.

"Come to the front of the class. Yes, take my place. What subject shall we name for your speech? Ah yes, I know; Las Drogas."

The Boy walked to the front of the classroom to take the teacher's place but once he began his monologue, her smile faded. Her expression became intense.

"I presume that having asked me to talk about drugs, you are not referring to aspirin or penicillin? That you are referring to cannabis, L.S.D. and the like?"

The teacher did not react to his question.

"That you expect me to speak in defence of these illicit drugs? All this because of my long hair, because my appearance is different, purely because my appearance is different?"

The class sat, pens poised, ready for action.

"I will begin my speech by telling you that I am completely against the use of drugs for anything other than medical purposes. I refuse to condone the use of any drugs and I do not merely refer to hashish and the like. I refer to all drugs. Nicotine, caffeine and alcohol, I include in this prohibition. Drugs that have received society's sanction. These are all replacements for religion in the western world, palliatives for the oppressed, the People's new 'opium'........"

The Boy continued his tirade until the teacher finally interrupted him.

"I will ask the first question," she said.

"So, you drink no coffee or alcohol. What about your famous, English tea?"

"No."

"No? Truthfully, no? An Englishman who does not drink tea?"

"No," the Boy repeated.

"Any questions, class?"

The pens remained poised, students mute, shocked at the unexpected content of the speech. Seated at the rear of the classroom, Susan stared in admiration.

"No questions? Then I have one more," the teacher continued, a smile tugging at her lips.

"What about women, girls?"

"A mere distraction from the Cause," the Boy said without thinking.

He sat in the grounds of the Faculty and watched as the small group of American girls gathered for whispers, looks and glances. Then, she was standing over him, hair glistening like gold; a halo in the bright sunshine.

"Yawannaplayfrizbeeee?"

CHAPTER EIGHTEEN: A NIGHT TO REMEMBER.

He met Susan outside the Prado. Together, they walked the short distance to the night club.

The club was small. A score of tables were crowded together in front of a low stage. The patrons chatted and drank wine while they waited. Smoke from their cigarettes hung like a heavy fog in the room. The Boy had reserved a table at the front. It was so close to the stage that he could have reached over and touched it. He drank mineral water while they waited. Susan sipped red wine from a long-stemmed glass.

The troupe of gypsies took to the stage; old to sing and play guitar, young to dance with tambourine and castanets. One of the old women sang, her harsh voice rising higher and higher to the shouted encouragement of her fellows. Hands clapped, lending rhythm to the strumming guitars, backing to the woman's soulful 'saeta.'

Then, the young danced. Bejewelled combs, pinned in raven hair, flashed in the spotlights. As the women whirled, thick, lace petticoats opened like wild flowers, an explosion of pink and white beneath the blood-red satin of their dresses. The heady smell of perfume fanned across the audience. Fat fingers, mere blurs on the strings of the guitar, urged the posturing women to ever-greater efforts.

One of the dancers broke away from the troupe and stamped her way to the front of the stage. Castanets and wooden heels punctuated the clack-clack-clack of her flying feet. Faster, she stamped, head thrown back in proud ecstasy, heels pounding like a thousand heartbeats.

Just when it seemed that she could go no faster, her partner was at her side, his feet a blur of motion on the bare boards of the stage. Black ringlets and white teeth flashed as he circled in the harsh spotlight. Tight, red sash and short, black waistcoat accentuated his narrow hips and waist. Dark trousers covered taut thighs and buttocks, contrast to the white frills of his shirt cuffs and collar.

His back arched as he followed the castanets that chattered above their heads. Faster and faster he stamped, circling closer and closer to his statuesque partner. Then, he stopped.

With a single leap he was on their table; feet once more a blur of motion, glasses falling to escape the flying leather shoes; Susan like a child, her face raised in wonder and surprise.

Outside the club, the streets were deserted. The moon shone down from star-laden skies, reflecting its pale light onto the stonework of the city. Susan took off her shoes. Hand in hand, the couple slowly walked along the green grass of the

Paseo del Prado, their footprints, two trails in the diamond dew. They stopped at the entrance to a new block of flats.

"This is it, Boy. Home," she said, staring up at him.

Then, eyes closed, lips pursed, she awaited his first embrace. Mind in turmoil, heart against reason, Boy kissed girl.

In a second, she was gone, running into the foyer to take the lift, hair flowing behind her.

"Seeyatomorrowatthepool," she called.

His brain was swimming with confusion as he walked home. The girl was so lovely. He could not believe that she found him attractive. His heart pounded at the thought of her. There was no mistaking the warmth in her eyes, the honesty of her words when she spoke to him. This was no mere temptress. How could she have such impact on his resolve?

"This is more than a 'mere distraction' from the Cause," he told himself with irony.

Don Pedro had left a letter on the table at his bed-side. It was from his father. It held bad news and good tidings.

There was no sign of his bag; books and research lost forever to the R.E.N.F.E.! Also, the Champ was dead.

"He finally managed to drink himself to death. There weren't many people at the funeral. How soon, they forget," the Man wrote.

The good tidings came in the form of a clipping from the local newspaper.

"Pupil Assaults Headmaster," the headline read. In the margin, his father had written "one punch!" in large, capital letters. Obviously, Josh had not been able to show the same restraint as his brother, Big Jake, or the Boy!

These stories now seemed of little importance to him. They came from another world, from a different life. In the bar below him, the guitar softly played. As he drifted into sleep, his thoughts were only of Susan.

CHAPTER NINETEEN:
A TASTE OF PURE INNOCENCE.

Despite the number of students swimming or lazing by the pool, the day was strangely quiet. Only the sound of splashing water broke the silence. The heat of the afternoon stifled any inclination to move, to even speak.

The Boy lounged on the cool grass. Susan lay on her back at his side, eyes closed tightly against the strong sunlight. His skin was now deeply tanned, product of many hours' study by the 'pool. Its dark colour contrasted heavily with the golden skin of the girl. To pass the time, he read, sweat dripping from his face and hands onto the printed pages.

A young man hauled himself out of the water. Feet burning on the hot tiles, he padded over to where the couple lay. He stood over them, dripping water. Gold glistened from neck and fingers. His skin was dark, body slight and lean. The Boy turned away from his book, twisting around to look up at the newcomer.

"Hello, Susan."

He had completely ignored the Boy. Susan looked up, smiling at the dark shadow, squinting into the sun to distinguish his features.

"Hi, Abdul."

"Would you like to go to a party, tonight?"

Before Susan could answer, the Boy had interrupted the conversation, cutting it short.

"She's with me. We can't go. We've got something already planned."

The girl looked over at him. A flash of anger had crossed her eyes.

"I wasn't talking to you. I was talking to the young lady," the intruder answered coldly.

"Well, I'm talking to you. Clear off!"

The Boy had jumped to his feet. Looming over the interloper, he intimidated him with his height and size. Smiling, Abdul retreated.

"I was only being friendly," he explained but when he turned away from his antagonist, the smile had become a sneer. The girl looked up at him. Her lips pouted, cheeks reddened.

"Whatever's the matter with you, Boy? I would have loved to go to a party."

"Forget it."

"We're not doing anything, tonight."

"He didn't invite me."

"No, but you could have come with me, all the same," the girl pressed the point.

"Forget it."

"Why can't we go?"

"Because we can't."

"Don't be so jealous, Boy."

"I'm not being jealous and we're not going. We're not going because we won't be safe."

"What do you mean?"

"Who will be at this party?"

"Abdul and his friends."

"Who are….?"

The girl looked at him, bemused.

"Who are all men and all Palestinians," the Boy continued.

"So what?"

"Listen. Abdul and his friends are no friends of mine. But neither are they your friends."

"Why not?"

"For God's sake, Susan. It's only three years' since the war."

"WAR? WHAT WAR?"

He could not believe her naïvety, her innocence of the world.

"But that," he told himself, "forms part of her attraction."

CHAPTER TWENTY: THE VICTORS?

From a distance, he could see the group of men gathered in front of the metal gates. Talking and smoking cigarettes, some lounged on the grassy bank outside the high, stone walls. Others sought shade beneath the sparse trees that lined the approaches to Party Headquarters.

As he drew closer, sunlight flashed at him from the medals on their chests. Closer still, he was able to distinguish the individuals that composed this rag-tag army. Not one of the men was intact. Empty sleeves were pinned to shoulders. Patches covered sightless eyes. Pathetic, three-legged sentries stood guard before the ornate metalwork.

The automatic gates began to open and the rabble sprang to attention as a black limousine swept past. From the back seat, the official casually acknowledged the pointed salutes of this unofficial guard; his sharp suit at odds with their worn, patched uniforms. Once the car had passed through, gates swung shut, the group of veterans slumped back into their lassitude.

With exaggerated care, the Boy picked his way through the lounging men. Their eyes were dead, hopeless. At the gate, he rang the bell.

"I have an appointment to see señor Blanco," he announced into the intercom.

The gates swung open and he entered.

Señor Blanco was small and fat; dwarfed by the highly polished desk behind which he sat. Dark shirt and tie matched his three-piece suit. His grey hair was cropped short, in an American style 'crew' cut. His spectacles, tie-pin and wristwatch were all of gold. A single ribbon was pinned to the breast pocket of his jacket; an affected understatement of the man's rank within the Falange. Papers and books were piled neatly in front of him. Three telephones stood ready at his elbow. Behind him on the wall, the Spanish standard hung alongside the despised, black arrows.* Señor Blanco stood to shake his hand.

"Good afternoon, sir. How can I be of assistance to you?"

His tone was soft, face, bland. The Boy explained his quest; the topic of his research, loss of books and paperwork. The official nodded sympathetically at the mention of the R.E.N.F.E.

"Let me see what we can do to rectify this, most unfortunate situation. One moment."

He picked up one of the telephones. His face grew stern, the soft tone evaporated as he barked a few, clipped commands into the mouthpiece. When he turned to address the Boy, the oily

---

* Black arrows: symbol of the Falange.

smile had returned.

"Please, one moment more."

While they waited, señor Blanco engaged the Boy in conversation; extolling the virtues of the Party, propounding the martyrdom of José Antonio.

"José Antonio was a great man, a light in our darkness, no?"

"Certainly," the Boy replied.

"His ideas on agrarian reform were innovative and far-reaching. Truly brilliant, no?"

"Certainly."

The Boy replied to the questions as ably as he could. He sensed that his knowledge was being tested, the sincerity of his research and his political allegiances, covertly monitored. He used all the diplomacy that he could muster; answering questions of fact and history, agreeing with the other's rhetoric. The conversation continued until there was a knock at the panelled door. A woman entered, carrying an armful of books and pamphlets.

"Here, take these," señor Blanco said.

"If you have any more problems, do not hesitate to get in touch with me. I am at your disposal."

He stood to say 'goodbye,' his limp, damp handshake serving only to augment the disgust of the departing student.

As the Boy walked towards the gates, his heart rate finally slowed. Strangely, he felt both relief and elation at the completion of the 'interview.' It had been Alan's intention that he be the interviewer but to his relief, señor Blanco's barrage of questions had precluded this. The Boy knew that he would only have betrayed his personal allegiances, had he been the interrogator. He felt elated that he had entered the lion's den and escaped, not only unscathed but also with several thousand pesetas' worth of books!!

He knew the gift had not been made as an act of generosity, only to propagate the 'Word' of the Falange. However, the newly acquired books would save a fair proportion of his meagre resources from the cash registers of Argüelles' shops. Given the option, he would have rather missed a few more meals than endure another hour of señor Blanco's company.

As the Boy reached the wrought-iron gates, the ragged squadron of veterans came to attention, hands arrowed to the sky. This time, the occupant of the car ignored their tired salutes.

CHAPTER TWENTY-ONE: GLIMPSES OF TERROR.

In the shade of the trees that circled the perimeter walls of the swimming pool, a small, canvas-backed camioneta was parked. It was rare to see a vehicle of any description on the Campo. The Boy thought that perhaps it belonged to workmen, there to maintain or clean the 'pool. So, as he passed the rear of the vehicle, inquisitively, he stuck his head inside the canvas flap.

Within, sat four, bareheaded Guardia; uniforms unbuttoned in the heat, steel helmets at their feet. Sub-machine guns rested across their thighs. For an instant, the four men glared out at him, dazzled by the sunlight.

"Clear off," the nearest growled, waving his gun in the Boy's face.

As he donned his bathing shorts in the sanctuary of the changing rooms, he saw that his hands were still shaking with fear. The 'click' of the safety catch had chilled him to the bone.

That evening, as usual, he sat and talked with the two sisters while they watched the television. After the news broadcast, he would walk to the 'Comedores,' the university canteen, to eat his only meal of the day. Normally, the programmes were of North American origin, dubbed in the south of the continent. Only sport, game shows and the news broadcasts seemed to be truly Spanish. The girls would chatter to each other, usually oblivious to the content of the programmes. They were more interested in their own gossip than in watching the detectives that struggled for American justice. However, tonight, their favourite programme, a quiz show, had been cancelled.

On the newsreel, 'el Caudillo' reviewed his troops. Mounted on a white charger, the diminutive figure sported full dress uniform. Row upon row of medals glinted in the sun, evidence of the rider's bravery and omnipotence. The pallor of his skin contrasted with the dark features and tunics of the legionnaires that formed his honour guard. Eyes forward, head high, he rode back and forth between the files of soldiers; object of their adulation. It was as if he paraded, not they. Behind the ranks of the Guardia Civil that lined his route, the crowd shouted with orchestrated unanimity, prompted by the Falangists in their midst,

"¡Viva Franco! ¡Viva España! ¡Viva! ¡Viva!"
The sudden din made his mount step high with fright. It arched its neck and pulled to toss its head. But the tight reins and cruel bit held it firm. Without pause, el Generalísimo carried on his way, down the bright boulevard towards the cathedral.

Then, came the news of the day.

In the arched splendour of the building, the pillars of state had assembled; Bishops on one side, Generals on the other.

Flanked by an aide de camp, el Caudillo slowly walked the flagstones to where the white ribbon stretched. He reached towards the tape, scissors open and ready in his trembling hand. The two blades snipped together, short of their target, leaving the ribbon intact. Unobtrusively, a uniformed arm reached out to guide the blind scissors. At the second attempt, two ribbons floated to the ground. There then followed the rapturous applause of assembled Church and Military.

When the applause had relented, el Caudillo took up his position behind the bank of microphones. He paused for a moment. With weak eyes, he scanned the blurred ranks of his acolytes. Then, with both hands raised, he began,

"Hemos tenido treinta años de paz...." (Appendix 1)

The two sisters sat silently in front of the small screen, the dark files of soldiers reflected in their beautiful eyes.

The Calle de Princesa seemed unusually quiet. All the bars and restaurants were empty. On the Moncloa, the usual crowd of courting couples was missing. The Campo Universitario was deserted.

Brittle trees stood, stark silhouettes in the bright moonlight. Scrubland between glowed ghostly white. This monochrome landscape appeared sinister and menacing. The full moon, high above him, seemed to have washed away its very colour. As he walked towards the Comedores, the Boy's thoughts once more turned to Uncle Sidney and the ghosts of thousands killed in the defence of Madrid.

Behind the trees to his right, an animal snorted. The noise of its heavy breath was amplified by the deathly silence on the Campo. Its sudden sound had startled him, made him quicken his pace. Then, he heard the muffled sound of hooves on turf.

Around the trees came a squadron of horsemen. They formed up in a perfect line, sabres to shoulders. Faceless in the shadows of their steel helmets, they sat poised in the bright moonlight; surrealistic figures on an ancient field of battle.

A sharp command from their officer and they were off and away, charging across the Campo; grim riders from Hell.

That evening, he ate alone in the Comedores.

CHAPTER TWENTY-TWO:
THE NATURE OF THE BEAST.

On a Saturday, he would forsake the crowded swimming pool to wander the streets of the city. It was quite early when he emerged from the narrow streets of Argüelles to follow the road down to the Plaza de España. Strangely, there was no traffic along the Calle de Princesa.

As he crossed the first intersection, he noticed one of the ominous camionetas parked in the side street. In the next, another lurked. Next, a dozen horsemen waited and in the next, twenty Guardia rested in the shade, dogs panting at their sides.

When he reached the Plaza, he saw that it was empty, completely empty. There were no people to disturb its tranquillity. Madrid was a ghost town. But, what he saw in the Plaza de España made him stop dead in his tracks.

What he saw in the Plaza de España turned legs to jelly, dried mouth like sand. What he saw in the sunlit plaza filled his heart with horror. He could not believe his eyes. He turned away and, too afraid, too weak to run, hastened back to the pensión.

Safely inside, he took his place with a nation in waiting.

CHAPTER TWENTY-THREE: FELLOW RESIDENTS.

The majority of the clientele of the pensión were foreign students; vacationing or taking a 'gap' year before the start of their new careers.   There were, however, more interesting lodgers that inhabited the rooms beyond the cool corridors of the hostel.

An Argentinian with wife and baby son lived in the room opposite that of the Boy. He was a lecturer in civil engineering at the university. He would accost the Boy outside his door with tales of his beloved Buenos Aires. He would tell of his passion for soccer, of the crowds that packed into the many stadia of the city on match day. One afternoon, he turned his attention to the Boy.

"You do like football, don't you?"

"Yes, of course," the Boy replied.

"Where is your home?"

"England. I'm not American."

"Of course not.   I mean to ask from which city in England do you come?"

"You will not have heard of it. It's not London."

"Tell me the name. Ah, yes. It's very famous!"

"You've heard of the football team? They are first division."

"The football team? No, I'm sorry. I've never heard of them. It's the City, itself, that is famous. It's famous throughout the world!"

"Because of the Industrial Revolution?"

"No, it's famous because it's the only place in the world where the ring road runs through the middle of the City. The only place where they demolished the City centre to build a ring road!"

Before the Boy could answer, his neighbour had entered his room. He could hear the man laughing behind the closed door.

Another of the guests was to afford the Boy even greater embarrassment.

This was Pilar, a woman in her early forties. She had arrived at the pensión, one Saturday morning, accompanied by her teenaged daughter and a mountain of suitcases. She wore western dress; blouse, skirt and high-heeled shoes. Her hair was dyed red, expensively styled. Diamonds sparkled on fingers and wrists. She was obviously a very wealthy woman.

The Boy could not fathom, why such a woman should be content with such basic accommodation. That night, on his return from the Comedores and evening tour of the city centre, he took his seat at the kitchen table to chat with La Señora. While they talked, the woman prepared vegetables for the next day's meals.

"¡Ay! Such scandal!" She reported, her knife, a blur on the chopping board.

"She has left her husband!"
However, Pilar and her daughter quickly befriended the Boy and the two sisters, bringing levity and good humour to their evening 'tertulia.'

"Next week, I will move into my new apartment," Pilar announced.

"Boy, when we are settled, you must come and visit us. I will cook for you the most fabulous of meals. I will cook for you a meal that you will never forget!!"

And a third prophecy was made.

CHAPTER TWENTY-FOUR: THE SPANISH WAY.

No-one on the Campo could explain the presence of the shock troops in the city centre.

There were rumours of 'Strikes in Granada,' 'Five Shot Dead in Asturias.' Of course, none of these could be substantiated. Whatever the truth of the matter, the Boy would never forget the day that he had wandered down to the Plaza de España.

He walked along the Gran Vía, enjoying the sights and sounds of the city. It was difficult to believe that, only a week before, this had been the stage for such a show of military might. The bright sun charmed and beguiled as if to distract from the cold heart that ruled this land, that pitted brother against brother. He paused to rest on the Puerta del Sol. Here, he listened to the hubbub of the city, watched a hundred dramas unfold on pavement and roadway.

Above the noise of the traffic, an American voice was raised; loud and plaintive.

"HELP!" And then, again,

"HELP! Does anybody here speak English?"

Standing next to a white Pontiac at kerbside, a tall, heavily muscled, young man frantically waved his arms at the passers-by.

"What's the matter?"

"Oh, thank God! You speak English!! I've locked my ignition key in the car. Do you know where I might find a garage?"

"You won't find one here in the centre. Hold on a minute. There are two Guardia over there. I'll ask them."

The Guardia were standing next to the entrance of the Metro. Stone faced, they watched the passing cars and pedestrians. As the Boy neared them, one of the two giants came to attention, hand raised in a sharp salute.

"At your service, sir. How can I be of assistance to you?"

Oh, how differently from the student was the English tourist received!!

"Excuse me, señor Guardia. This American has locked himself out of his 'car. Are there any...."

Before he could finish his question, the policeman had walked over to where the American stood helplessly waving his arms. He bent to look into the car, at the bunch of keys that dangled from the ignition lock. With lip curled in disdain, he gave his 'customer' a sidelong glance, casually pulling the truncheon from his belt. Before the American could utter a word of protest, he had smashed the window with a single blow from the hard, wooden baton. With his free hand, he reached through the broken window to retrieve the keys from the lock. Shaking his head from side to side, he handed them to their dumbfounded owner. Head still shaking, he walked back to where his unsmiling comrade waited.

"¡Estŭpido!" He muttered.

The two policemen resumed their patrol. Open-mouthed, the young American stood rooted to the spot, precious keys held in the palm of his outstretched hand. Glass from the shattered window lay scattered around his feet.

He said that his name was Harry. He said that he was taking 'time out' to tour Europe before enrolling on a course at the L.S.E.*

"I'd like to thank you for your help, buddy. Do you know where I could get a room for a couple of nights?" He asked.

The Boy gave him directions to the pensión and watched as the car disappeared, swallowed up by the heavy traffic circulating the Puerta del Sol.

Harry was already settled and waiting for him when he returned to the pensión.

"Hi, buddy," he said, "if you'll show me the sights of the city, this evening, the drinks are on me! I'd like to really thank you for helping me out, this afternoon."

* L.S.E.: London School of Economics

"I don't drink."

"Don't drink! You don't drink?! Then I'll pay for dinner."

There was no escaping the American's generosity. That night he acted as guide, touring the Mesones ** with his new friend. Money seemed to be of no object. They dined, sitting outside the most expensive restaurant on the Plaza de Cibeles; the well-dressed American and his 'hippy' scout.

As the night wore on, Harry became more and more intoxicated. The more alcohol that he drank, the less inclined he was to return to the pensión. It was far into the early hours of the morning before they made their way back to their beds. Harry staggered along, all sense of direction and balance forgotten. When they finally arrived home, they found that the high, wooden doors to the courtyard were locked.

"Darn it," Harry slurred.

"Locked out, again! It'll need more than a truncheon to break into here!"

"Don't worry," the Boy said.

"Sereno! *** Sereno!" He called at the top of his voice. In a matter of seconds, an old man appeared sporting the light blue hat and uniform of the sereno. Producing a large bunch of

. ** Mesones: Quarter between the Plaza Mayor and Atocha, famed for its bars. *** Sereno: A nightwatchman

keys, he unlocked the outer doors to the courtyard. With great ceremony, he led the two, young men through the doors and up the steps to "Hostal General Mola." On the landing, he waited.

"What should I give him?" Harry asked, pulling a handful of coins from his pocket.

"Why, a duro, of course!"

CHAPTER TWENTY-FIVE: BETRAYAL.

He awoke with a start. He had overslept! Pulling on his clothes, he rushed out of the pensión and down into the street. He was running by the time he reached the Plaza de España. Of Susan, there was no sign.

Instead of going on foot, which would have wasted too much time, he decided to take the Metro. The ticket, bought from his meagre resources, would mean no food for him that night. He did not care. He had to find Susan. Nothing in life was more important to him at that moment. At Atocha, he left the train and sprinted up the steps into the Rastro.*

It was hopeless. Even if Susan were there, he could never have found her. The flea market was crammed with people, a human tide that surged around the countless stalls. He searched for hours, all in vain. With heavy heart, he walked through the city. He cursed himself for his kindness, for his weakness before Harry's midnight meanderings. He must find Susan at the university, the very next day. He had to explain his absence to her. How must she feel? He had promised that he would be there to meet her at "their place" in the Plaza de España.

* Rastro: Madrid's flea market

How could this girl have come to mean so much to him?

The lecturer smiled when he entered the room.

"Good morning, Boy. It's not Friday, already, is it?" She inquired sarcastically. "The swimming-pool not open?" The class looked on, pens poised, confused by the speed of her words. The Boy had no time for the woman's questions. Instead, his attention wandered along the lines of eager faces. Seated at the back of the classroom, Susan pretended to read, avoided his gaze.

He took a seat at the front, among the apprentice linguists. He longed to turn and face the girl, try to catch her eye, disarm the situation with one, loving smile. Instead, for the umpteenth time, he was forced to relive the adventures of El Cid. After an eternity, the lesson ended.

He waited for her outside the lecture room. She emerged, five minutes after the last of the other students had departed. Seeing the Boy, she turned away, hastened her step. He chased after her.

"Susan, please wait. Please, listen. Let me explain." The girl stopped walking and turned around. Her face had flushed red with anger.

"Explain? Explain what? There's nothing to explain."

"Come on, Susan. I'm sorry about yesterday morning but I overslept. I really wanted to take you around the market. I only missed you by a few minutes. Look! I bought you a present."

He produced a package from the inside of his shirt. It contained a black, lace 'mantilla' bought from one of the market stalls of the Rastro; a peace offering that had cost him the price of several more days' food. The girl ignored the package.

"I waited for half an hour," she said.

"Yes, but this crazy Californian kept me out until four o'clock in the morning."

"I know."

"What do you mean, 'you know'?"

"I just know, that's all."

Susan's lips were now trembling. Tears welled in her lovely eyes.

"You know what? What do you know?" The Boy demanded.

"The two of you were seen getting drunk and staggering around the Plaza de Cibeles."

"It's not true! I was drinking orange juice, all night. I ate a meal, that's all. It was Harry, who was drunk. I had to carry him, most of the way home!"

He wanted to take her in his arms, prove to her that it was all a mistake. Tell her that he could never break his word to her, that he loved her. But anger and fear of rejection choked his words. She was crying.

"Oh, how could you?"

In murderous rage, he stalked the Campo; the rejected present now a lace garrotte in his hands. Abdul was nowhere to be found.

CHAPTER TWENTY-SIX: GOODBYE TO LOVE.

The course had come to an end. His last appearance at the Faculty would be for the traditional, end-of-year-party. No sooner had he walked into the room than Conchita cornered him.

"Are you alone, today, Boy? Where is Miss Greenberg? I thought that the two of you were inseparable?"

"I think, I saw her with her friends in the grounds. She'll probably be here in a minute or two," the Boy replied.

He had felt his throat tighten at the mention of Susan's name. But his past liaison with the girl was not the point of Conchita's interest. She was still intrigued by the content of his speech in her classroom. She shifted the subject of their conversation to politics; discussing the British 'system,' subtly prompting the Boy to repeat his previous tirade, until;

"Are you a communist, Boy?"

"Definitely not!" He replied, horror in his voice.

"Then, what is your, shall we say, political affiliation?"

"I have none, really. You would probably say Left Wing, a dissenter, a free thinker."

"An anarchist?"

"Some have said that."

"So, you are not actively involved in politics, back home?"

"Within the student movement, yes, I am. I attend meetings and demonstrations when I feel that the cause is just."

"This is important to you?"

"To voice my dissent? Yes, of course it is."

"You know that such organisations and gatherings are prohibited in my country? That trades' unions and opposition parties are outlawed We are not allowed to broadcast any opinion without official sanction. Hence my boring lectures!" Her voice seemed sad.

"I know. I have ears and eyes."

"My husband lives in exile, in Biarritz."

"Why? Is he a revolutionary?"

"Goodness, no. He is only a writer. Perhaps you have heard of him or his work? His most famous treatise is a parody of our political regime. For that, he had to flee for his life! It's called 'Why do dogs smell their own tails?' It is very cleverly written."

"I know it. I have heard it before, in San Sebastián, but he is unknown in England."

"You do?"

Once again, the Boy had surprised her, aroused her interest in him.

"It's as if nobody cares about Spain and her people....."

Conchita tried to prolong their conversation but the Boy excused himself. Across the room, the small group of American girls had gathered together; whispers, looks and glances. As he approached, the other girls wandered off, leaving him alone with Susan. The hurt and anger were gone from her eyes but when she spoke, there was still a slight tremble in her voice. Her words were formal.

"Well, this is it, Boy. Good-bye. Tomorrow, we return to New York. I have your address. I promise, I'll write you. I wish....."

She did not finish the sentence. Reaching up, she brushed her lips against the side of his face. She was running when she left the room. He knew that he would never see her again.

Her love and trust had been stolen from him. Broken, forever, by a lie.

CHAPTER TWENTY-SEVEN:
A VERY STRANGE AFFAIR.

The university was deserted, the Comedores closed for the rest of the year. Now, there was no need to brave the Campo by night.

During the daytime, only a few students were scattered around the lawns and terraces of the swimming pool. Even the Guardia Civil were absent from their stations in and around the grounds. So, the Boy's daily entrance to the 'pool was no longer a daunting experience.

The splendour of the city had been diminished with Susan's departure, with no-one to share the wonders of its discovery or the memories of its streets. His heart ached, emotions swung back and forth between anger and frustration. By way of escape, he immersed himself in his studies. As if, such a cold discipline might quell his emotions.

By night, he roamed the barrios in search of cheap restaurants. He avoided the shadowy arches of the Plaza de Toros where the gangs of gypsies lurked, the bright lights of the Mesones where drunken, American airmen shouted their national supremacy. In the Calle de la Pez, he ate paella; boiled rice with peas and chickens' feet, on the Puerta del Sol, arroz a la cubana; rice with egg and tomato. The restaurants were dull and dingy, their patrons subdued and morose; no cause for merriment in those dark streets.

The departure of the students meant that the brightly lit bars and restaurants along the Calle de Princesa were half-empty, unanimated. Gone, the bustling crowds that only weeks before had jostled to take the cool, evening air. Dinner at an end, he would hurry back to the sanctuary of the pensión, to the warmth and friendship of La Señora and the two sisters. One night, on his return, a surprise was waiting for him. It was a note from Pilar;

"I do not forget you, Boy. This Saturday, I invite you to come dine at my new home. Two o'clock, do not be late. We talk English Time! The address is written below,

Your friend, Pilar.

That Saturday afternoon, the Boy duly boarded the Metro.

The block of flats was in a fashionable area, close to the Avenida Calvo Sotelo. The foyer was manned, not by the usual concierge, but by a uniformed attendant who telephoned his arrival.

The door to the flat was opened by Lola, Pilar's teenaged daughter. The delicious aromas of food,cooking, drifted into the hallway from the kitchen. He took a seat in the dining room and chatted with the girl while he waited. After a short time, Pilar emerged from the kitchen. If she had spent the morning preparing the meal, she showed no sign of it. Her clothes, hair and make-up were as perfect as the room that she graced.

The Boy had never seen such a home. The flat was expensively furnished. Its décor was immaculate. Gold ornaments festooned the teak and mahogany furniture. Hand-woven carpets covered the highly-polished floors. Matching curtains and covers were all of rich velvet. The ceilings and walls sported moulded plaster figurines and coloured patterns of every description, interspersed with several, bright, oil paintings. Never before, had the Boy experienced such opulence.

"Hello, Boy. Welcome to my humble home. Would you like a drink? Some wine, perhaps? A glass of water? One moment. Dinner will soon be ready."
So, the Boy dined like royalty; the mother and daughter, his graceful attendants.

After the meal, the three sat around the table and talked; the woman in Castillian, her daughter in faltering English, testing the success of her efforts in the classroom. They bombarded him with questions.

"Tell us about England. Where do you live?"

"You have never been to Carnaby Street?"

"Have you been to the Cavern?"

"Are you a hippy?"

"How long have you been in Spain?"

"What places have you visited?"

"You mean to say that you have been in Madrid for all this time and you haven't been to Toledo?"

"You must promise me that you will go. It's so beautiful there."

More to stem the torrent of questions than from any true interest, he gave his promise.

"You truly, truly promise?"

"I promise."

After a time, Lola said that she would take a siesta and disappeared through one of the doors that opened into the dining-room. Pilar and the Boy continued the tertulia, time forgotten. Then, the doorbell rang.

Across the table, Pilar's eyes grew wide with surprise, wide with terror. In a matter of moments, she had been transformed from a self-assured, erudite woman into a frightened, babbling wretch. She almost ran about the room in her panic, like some trapped animal frantic to escape.

"¡Ay! ¡Los padres! Aquí, tóma," she half-shouted, half-whispered.

Grabbing the Boy's plate, glass and utensils from the table, she thrust them into his hands. Almost roughly, she bundled him into the room where her daughter lay sleeping. She closed the door behind him. Half a second latter, the door was reopened and the Boy's napkin fluttered into the bedroom. Only then, did he finally realise the seriousness of his predicament.

Which was worse, to be found alone with the woman at the dinner table or alone with her young daughter in the bedroom? Fortunately, the young girl had not been awakened by his untimely entrance and lay, lost in her dreams. But, he would rather have explained his presence at the dinner table than give reason for this intrusion. For there was none.

Little did he realise, the one was as dangerous as the other. All the same, he felt ridiculous, standing behind the bedroom door like a common thief; cutlery, glass and plate carefully balanced to prevent the slightest sound.

From the doorway of the flat came the muffled sounds of a man's voice, Pilar's indistinguishable answers to his questions. Then, there was silence.

A few, long minutes passed before Pilar slowly opened the bedroom door. Her eyes were still wide with terror.

"You must go. You must leave at once," she said.

That night, safe in the pensión, he told La Señora of the day's adventure.

"They will both finish their days in the convent," she said without looking up from her ironing-board.

CHAPTER TWENTY-EIGHT: TOLEDO

Toledo rose high above the arid plains of New Castille; picture from a fairy-tale.   Whitewashed buildings, ancient enemies of the sun, reflected its scorching rays from the hillside. Towering above, the Alcazar loomed in unchallenged domination.   The Boy left the 'bus and started his climb, upwards through the narrow streets of the town.

Lines of smithies and souvenir shops filled the alleys. Outside, their workmanship was displayed.   Row upon row of swords, knives and hammered metal ornaments of every description cluttered the cobbled pavements.   The town was deserted, people driven to siesta by the oppressive heat.   By way of escape from the fierce sun, the Boy paid a duro and entered the cool shadows of El Greco's house.

Candles fluttered as the door opened, scattering light across the oil painting that covered an entire wall of the small room.   Two benches, like pews in a chapel, faced the giant canvas where lay the image of Count Orgaz.   Around him flew the faces of the rich and famous; cherubs and angels intent on recognition, careless of the dead man below them.   The Boy remained seated for some time, his eyes fixed on the canvas. The faces were anonymous.   They meant nothing to him.   This, one time at least, their bribery had failed them in their selfish quest for immortality.

Cooled and refreshed from his rest, he left the little house and carried on his way. As he climbed, the Alcazar grew ever larger; symbol of power, of loyal and obdurate resistance. Here stood proof of El Caudillo's commitment to his men; mere excuse for prolonged and unnecessary butchery. (Appendix 2)

As he drew closer, the Boy could see that the stonework was like new. It was as if it had been scrubbed clean of the scars and wounds of its destruction. Inside, the building was completely empty; the smooth stone, unadorned.

There was no sign of God nor Man within its naked walls. It was nothing more than a sterile monument to an empty gesture.

CHAPTER TWENTY-NINE: THE RETURN.

It was time for him to leave; handshakes from Don Pedro and La Señora, hugs and sly pinches from the two sisters. He would leave this city with very mixed feelings. Here, he had enjoyed the friendship of the family in the pensión; another family that had embraced him with true warmth and feeling. Here, he had again witnessed a darker side of Spain, a side on which the sun did not shine. Here, he had found Susan. Here, he had lost her.

The carriages of the train had been quickly filled by students; Spanish travellers and English returning to their studies. Beyond the border, French, destined for university or farmland, joined the train. For these, the journey spelled adventures new. For the Boy, it meant a return to dull skies and dark City.

"Penury," he told himself, "is so much easier to cope with, when the sun is shining!"

From the seat opposite, Pierre and Angélique engaged him in conversation. They told him that they had three months' work on the fruit farms to finance and further their education. He gave them his father's address and promised them 'a night to remember,' should they pass that way. The melancholy that he felt about his return was only deepened when Pierre told him that there would be no more live music "Along the Watchtower." (Appendix 3)   As the train rumbled onwards through the night, he feigned sleep to avoid further conversation.

From the deck of the ferry, he watched the swell of the English Channel's grey waters. The breeze sent a chill creeping through his body, flapped the loose clothing about him. The sight of the sea made him think of his father. He knew how proud he would be on the return of his son; transformed, slim and tanned, educated abroad with the richest of the rich.

That education had brought a change in him, lent him resolve and a true purpose in life. How could he ever explain the political nature of his new being, that he did not share his father's ambitions for career and family, that the approbation of the Town's gossips meant nothing to him? His return would bring only bitter memories. Escape was all that he had ever craved.

Even the beautiful hues of the Kentish countryside failed to revive his spirits. Nightfall was fast approaching so he would not reach his father's house, that evening. Thanks to Dr. Beeching's 'axe,' (Appendix 4) the railway system had not served the Town for some years. He would have to wait until the next morning to finish his journey by 'bus.

The only, other occupant of the railway carriage was a woman in her early thirties. She wore a dress-suit and delicate jewellery. A black bow in her blond hair emphasized the cream-like texture of her skin; an English rose.

How strange she seemed, compared to the sun-burned faces and olive skin to which he was accustomed. Seated in the corner of the carriage, she pretended to study documents from the attaché case on her lap. The Boy realised that she was secretly staring at him.

He was puzzled for a moment. Despite his long hair, he could never remember coming under such scrutiny in England. Then, he caught sight of his reflection in the mirror of the carriage window. Long hair flanked a gaunt face almost blackened by the sun. He hardly recognised himself! It was he who seemed strange!

As the train shuddered into the deserted station, he pulled down his rucksack, sleeping-bag and trusty duffel coat from the rack.

Along with the few, remaining passengers, he hurried through the unmanned barriers and into the night.

Just as he suspected, the last 'bus had long since departed. In the lee of one of the stone walls that skirted the cathedral, he unrolled his sleeping-bag.

"This will be the very last time that I do this," he promised himself.

With duffel coat rolled into a pillow and soft, green moss for a mattress, he fell into a deep, dreamless sleep.

The Adventure of a Lifetime was truly at an end.

PART FIVE

THE SHADOWS OF PREJUDICE.

"Prejudice brings Honour to no Man,

Race or Creed; Dishonour only,

to us all."

CHAPTER ONE: 'WELCOME'

He awoke to a bright, autumn morning, warm on the soft, green mattress. Whether it was the sun, low in the sky, or the voice from high above his head that had disturbed his slumber, he could not tell.

"Did you see, who left this, 'ere boyke?"

He looked up at the fat, red face beaming down at him. The blue helmet perched atop seemed far too small for the very large head.

"No, I'm sorry. It was there when I got here," the Boy replied from the confines of the sleeping bag.

"O.KEY.DOKEY!" The policeman said.

Reaching over the wall, he grabbed the bicycle that leaned only feet from the Boy's head. With one giant paw on the crossbar, he lifted it over to his side of the wall.

"Hoy'll catch the bloyters, one day," he said.

With studied care, the police constable examined the wheels, tyres and brakes of the battered machine. Bicycle clips clamped firmly in place about his ankles, he mounted the bicycle.

"Happy Hitch-Hoyken," he aspirated.

He pedalled off, obviously hot on the trail of his 'boyke' thief.

"And Have a Noyce Holiday Hin Hengland!"

The Boy had no intention of 'hitch-hoyken' and so took the first, available 'bus.

He walked the short distance from the 'bus-stop to his father's house. Isaac, the next-door neighbour, was leaning against the wall of the small, front garden, enjoying the afternoon sunshine. He puffed on a hand-rolled cigarette while he watched the infrequent comings and goings along Canal Street. Although long since retired, he still sported the worker's uniform of flat cap and grey, serge suit.

"Afternoon, Issac," the Boy said as he bent to open the garden gate.

"You can't go in there! He's not at home. He's at work," the old man said.

"Isaac, it's me!"

"I don't care, who you are! You're not going in there!" Isaac insisted.

"But it is, it's me!"

The old man adamantly refused to recognise the Boy, despite his continued protestations.

"You stay there. He'll be home from work, soon. Then we'll see who you are!"

So, he waited silently under the watchful eye of the retired farmworker until his father's return.

The Dodge came to a halt by the 'bus stop. Four figures emerged from the canvas hood that covered the tailboard of the lorry. One by one, they dropped down over the tailgate and onto the roadway.

"See you, Johnny."

"See you."

"See you, Lefty."

"Certainly!"

Hessian sacks slung over their shoulders, two of the men began the short walk along Canal Street to their homes. As they walked along, they chatted about that day's work and the next day's weather. From a distance, the two men looked like twins. Both sported grey curls above the apple-red of faces weathered by wind and sun. If the summers had left their marks, so had the winters. They rolled from side to side like two drunken sailors when they walked, balance betrayed by arthritic joints. Their conversation continued until they came to the garden gate, where the Boy stood, waiting.

"Hi, Dad! I'm home!" He said.

His father had not recognised him until he spoke.

"I don't believe it, Herb. It's the Boy, back from Spain! Look, they've shrunken him!"

He grabbed his son, shaking him by the hand. Next, Herb then Isaac frantically shook his hand, each, in his turn, crushing it with a grip like a vice. Flexing the fingers of his right hand, he followed his father into the house.

"Hold on, Boy. I'll light a fire. The evenings are getting cooler. You're bound to feel the cold."

They sat before the blazing fire; the proud father and his prodigal son.

"Now then, Boy, tell me all about it."

But of course, he could not.

CHAPTER TWO: NOTHING NEW.

Surreptitiously informed by Isaac, the gossips soon spread the news of the Boy's return. He found himself inundated with invitations to this house or that party. Teenagers, who had once shunned his presence and derided his appearance, now opened their doors to him. He was sought after; the prized guest. He could not understand their pique at his refusals. Ostensibly, he was the same person that they had once rejected. It was his looks only, that had changed...... not their attitudes. Yes, their attitudes remained the same, he was still the outsider. He could not wait to get away from there, even though it meant a return to the grime of the City.

He lay on the bed, his eyes fixed on the ceiling of the small room.   Around him, the reminders of his childhood remained, untouched since his departure. The rat-a-tat-tat on the front door of the house roused him from his day-dreaming.

"Boy, there are some people here to see you. I think, they're FRENCH!" The Man shouted from downstairs.

Pierre and Angélique sat, uncomfortably perched on the seats of the two, ancient armchairs. The Man stood over them, beaming down at the captive proof of his son's truly international status. Pierre leaped to his feet, happy to escape his smiling captor. He spoke French; second escape.

"Hello, Boy. We are here to party like you promised. We can only come today, which is our day of rest."

"It's dinner-time. We could go to one of the locals pubs. They are typically English," the Boy scoffed.

"It sounds good. Let's go!"

"I'll see you in a few hours," the Man said to his son, proud that he had not understood a single word of the conversation.

They entered the pub' and walked through to the lounge. Behind the bar, Mary, the barmaid, eyed them with suspicion. The Boy turned to the French couple standing behind him.

"Qu'est-ce que vous voulez boire?" * He asked before turning back to Mary.

"A pint of orange juice, a glass of white wine and a glass of lager, please, Mary."
The suspicion in the barmaid's eyes intensified at the mention of her own name. Although she had known the Boy through his childhood and into adolescence, she did not recognise him.

"I'm sorry. Could you go through to the bar?"

"What for?"

"I'm afraid, I can't serve you in the lounge."

---

*"Qu'est-ce que vous voulez boire?": "What would you like to drink?"

"We have a young lady with us. She shouldn't drink in the bar."

"Then, I'm going to have to ask you to leave the premises!"

As the door to the lounge closed behind him, the Boy heard Mary's voice exclaim,

"Bloody foreigners!"

Outside, in the street, Angélique stopped, confused, her confusion expressed in a torrent of questions;

"I do not understand. What did that woman say? Why are we leaving? Why could we not remain and party?"

"She refused to serve us."

"Why? What did we do?"

"It's too difficult to explain," the Boy lied.

Of course, it was not.

That night, he sat by the fire with his father.

"I saw Mrs. Scott in the butcher's shop, today. She asked about you."

"That's very thoughtful of her," the Boy said sarcastically.

"She said that Jane is doing very well. She has a job at the bank."

"That's nice for her."

"It's her twenty-first birthday in a couple of weeks.' She's a very pretty girl."

His father gave him a knowing look.

"Good for her."

"Her mother gave me this."

He passed an envelope to the Boy. His name was hand-written on the front of it, in large, copper-plate lettering. The Boy took the envelope from his father but did not open it.

He felt more than suspicious that Jane should still seek his company. After all, the last time that she had seen him, he had been led away in handcuffs by the Sergeant!

"I won't be there, Dad. I'll be back in the City by then." The date of the girl's birthday was etched into his mind.

"You could come back if I gave you the train fare. Only for the week-end?"

The Boy gave his father a puzzled look.

"I'm sorry, Dad. I have loads of college work. I'll maybe go, next year. IF I get another invitation."

"She won't be twenty-one, forever," his father said.

CHAPTER THREE:
NO ROOM FOR FORGIVENESS?

It was Saturday. The Man had already departed for his morning's toil. No school, that day, meant the 'bus-stop was deserted. No screaming girls, either.

The 'bus service was unpredictable. Yet, he waited, determined to be away from the Town. The incident in the public house had not only embarrassed him, it had sickened him, reminded him of his treatment in the distant bars of San Sebastián.

He was concerned about his father's eagerness for his early return to the Town, especially after so many years of being told that he had to 'get away from there.' He was perplexed because he knew that his father could ill-afford to finance the proposed week-end excursion.

There was no denying that Jane was the belle of the Town. From that very spot, day after day, he had watched her grow towards womanhood. Framed in the window of the school 'bus, the redhead had slowly transformed into eighteen-year old perfection. Try as he might, look where he may to avoid her gaze, his every schoolday had begun with a smile from the girl's dark eyes.

The memory of his humiliation at the birthday party had ever left a cold spot in his heart, lent him an excuse that he had now used to avoid her latest invitation.

There was one thing more. She belonged there, in the Town with family and friends, secure in her position at the bank. He did not.

Eventually, the 'bus arrived and he climbed on board, paying the driver as he entered. There were no other passengers to witness the old, familiar route across the Fens.

He alighted in the small, market-square. Ignoring the dark entrance that led to the school, the blank stares of shoppers and shopkeepers, he began the long walk. Past the school sports' grounds, he carried on to the railway station.

CHAPTER FOUR: A CHANCE ENCOUNTER.

The dishevelled railway guard yawned the information that the train had been 'delayed.' The next was not due for another two hours.

Seated inside the waiting-room, he removed a book from his rucksack and began to read. Soon, he was transported back to the days of the 'Guerra Civil,' all consciousness of time and place lost within the pages.

The noise of squealing brakes tore him away from the siege of Granada. The train had arrived almost unnoticed! He grabbed up his bag and rushed out of the waiting-room.

The station was all but deserted. Only a handful of passengers waited to board the train. On his left, two, well-dressed women stood at the edge of the platform. The farthest, younger of the pair, was shielded from his view by her more corpulent companion. The Boy walked towards them, intent on verifying the final destination of the train.

When he was some twenty paces from the nearest woman, she turned, wary of his approach. She did nothing to hide her fear and disgust at the sight of the gaunt, long-haired foreigner who walked towards her. Without taking her stare from him, she unceremoniously hustled her companion up the steps and into the sanctuary of the nearest railway carriage. The loud noise of the door, slammed shut, echoed around the small station.

The Boy stood, rooted to the spot. He had finally recognized her. It had been ten, long years since he had last seen Mrs. Scott. Then, he had fled from her house. It was definitely her. There was no mistaking her beautiful, red-headed escort.

A whistle sounded and the train began to pull, slowly, away from the platform.

Under the scandalized directions of her mother, Jane turned to see the 'foreign tramp,' their would-be 'assailant.' As their eyes met, she sat bolt upright, startled by her recognition of the forlorn figure on the windswept platform.

Two hours later, the Boy boarded the next train.

CHAPTER FIVE: ALONE IN THE CITY.

He gazed from the carriage window as the train rumbled through the bleak landscape. On the rack above his head, the rucksack danced to the rhythm of the wheels.

The countryside seemed more desolate than ever. The furrows in the black soil reached out to the very horizon. Gone, the pastures where the great shire horses once grazed. Gone, the few hedgerows and trees that once dotted the edges of the fields, disappeared in the name of agricultural efficiency; one more step towards a Fenland dust bowl.

The City lay beneath its usual, grey shroud. However, many things had changed. If nothing changes in the countryside then things are well. But in a city this means only stagnation and decline. The famous ring road had grown rapidly, cutting its swathe through the lines of Edwardian terraces that skirted the shopping centre.

The college, itself, had been extended; new sports hall and two Union Bars for the students, new classroom blocks and halls for the lecturers. On the opposite side of the dual carriageway, an Art College had been built; a giant, grey monstrosity that belied its function, a symbolic segregation of Art from Science.

The City centre showed great signs of improvement. Black grime had been blasted from the walls of the buildings, their stonework now protected by 'smokeless' zones and creeping industrial recession. Still, the anonymous crowds hurried about their business; still, no time for 'hellos' or 'goodbyes.'

The room was cold and damp. It was in a large, dilapidated house, part of one of the remaining terraces threatened by the expanding ring road. Testimony to the condition of the house was that the Boy was its only tenant. The landlord had charged him a week's rent in advance, leaving him almost penniless. He spent the next week, a financial prisoner of the dingy room, the 'Complete Works' of José Antonio, his only company.

He hesitated on the pavement outside the 'corner shop.' The silver half-a-crown was clutched firmly in his hand. He could not come to a decision. In the bed-sitting room, half a loaf of bread remained. He had money enough for butter. He had money enough for jam. However, he did not have money for both butter AND jam. Buttered toast or butterless jam sandwiches, he could not make up his mind. Finally, he entered the shop.

"A pot of jam, please," he said and handed his last coin to the shopkeeper.

Pot of jam safely wrapped in a brown, paper bag, paper bag clutched firmly in his hand, he left the shop.

As he stopped at the kerbside, glass shattered on hard stone! The bottom of the bag, wet and weakened by water on the shop counter, had given way!!

He stood for some time, looking down into the gutter. Here, a constellation of glass shards reflected its strawberry stars in the streetlight.

As he finished eating the last of his dry toast, he came to another decision.   The next day at college, he would seek out the Boss.

CHAPTER SIX: CHEZ BOSS

The Boss's greeting was less than formal, less than flattering.

"Whatever's happened to you, you great buffoon? Have you acquired intestinal worms?"

"No, Boss. I'm starving, Boss. Are there any spare rooms in your house?"

"There's not much space but I'm sure that we'll be able to squeeze you in. Especially, now you look like a bean-pole!"

"You can wash the dishes. Big Dave keeps breaking them, the clumsy oaf! He drops more plates than passes!!"

So, it was settled. The Boy moved in with the Boss and his lodgers. He was duly appointed official dishwasher and Big Dave demoted to dusting and sweeping.

"Provided he can keep a grip on the brush!" The Boss had dryly remarked.

The house had two bedrooms. The first and largest room was occupied by the Boss, Big Dave and the Boy. The three slept in strict order of their status within the household. The Boss, of course, occupied the large, double bed that almost filled the room. His two lodgers slept in the gap between the foot of the bed and the window. Big Dave, now a mere sweeper and duster, had been relegated from the camp-bed to the floor. This, he relished.

"It'll keep me tough. See? I'll be able to sleep by the window, now. See?"
Sleep by the window, he did. Come sun, wind, rain or snow, it was always open!

"You two have always got colds. It's because you're not fit. See? And you've got to be fit. See? I don't want to catch your germs! See?"

The Boy wondered if he would survive the freezing bedroom. It did seem true that he and the Boss had permanent colds. Whether it was due to their 'lack of fitness' or the permanently opened bedroom window, was anybody's guess.

The second bedroom had been taken by Mr. Ormskirk; bearded biologist and doughty owner of a rusty, 90c.c. motorcycle. Although there was space enough for another in the room; open window, camp-bed and floor were preferred to the company of the irascible scientist.

Mr. Ormskirk was in charge of shopping. This, Mr. Ormskirk would collect in his rucksack. Mr. Ormskirk's rucksack was the biggest rucksack in the whole world; the biggest rucksack that the Boy had ever seen. It was more suited for an assault on Everest than a shopping expedition. So he thought.

One day, despite the Boss's warnings, the Boy accepted a ride from the cantankerous Yorkshireman. Seated on the luggage rack of the little motorcycle, he clung desperately to the giant rucksack as they hurtled through the back streets of the City. Tighter, he clung as lamp-posts and pillar boxes flashed past, ever closer to his unprotected head. Footrests scraped at every bend in the road. Mr. Ormskirk knew only one rate of speed, 'flat out!,' when riding his motorcycle. He applied the same principle to his shopping.

Through the centre of the City, he marched, head down, chin thrust into his chest like some bristling badger. The heavy rucksack knew no friends. Male and female, young and old, all found themselves swept aside by the swinging canvas bag. The unwary found themselves crushed against walls and windows, pushed into shops that they had no intention of patronizing. Heedless, the rampant shopper surged forward like an icebreaker through pack ice.

The Boy followed behind him, astounded and gleeful witness to the devastation left in his wake.

The fourth and final lodger was "the Read." The Read lived in the cupboard under the stairs. At first, the Boy thought that he was nicknamed "the Reed" for his slender build. There, the comparison had ended because there was nothing less like a reed that the Read. He rarely seemed to move and was never seen upright. All he ever seemed to do was ....to read.

His cupboard was large enough to accommodate a mattress and his copious collection of books. The truth is, had there been a light in the cupboard under the stairs, no-one would have ever seen the Read. It did not matter, day or night, whenever the Boy left or returned to the house, he would discover the Read; elbows and torso on the living-room floor, legs lost in his cupboard...reading. He never seemed to leave his sanctuary, not for lectures, not even for food or drink. His whole world revolved around the latest tome to come under his scrutiny. His lifestyle was like that of some strange, scholarly terrapin.

Last, but not least, there was the Boss himself, aptly cast as 'Chef'!

CHAPTER SEVEN: A NEWS UPDATE.

The Boss brought him abreast of the situation at the college.

During the Boy's absence, the Federation had reached the zenith of its power; college occupied by a 'sit-in,' lecturers and administrators driven out into the streets. The police had become involved and after a three-day siege, the demonstration had ended peacefully, order restored. By way of a swan song, the Leader had launched an attack within the Union, forcing the resignations of president and executive. Only the urbane Tristan had survived the 'coup.' A tradition was begun.

Many of the 'old guard' had departed for pastures new, their education completed. Their gaps in the ranks of the Federation had not been filled. The latest batch of 'freshers' contained very few children of the working classes so the Federation held little attraction for them. Consequently, its membership and therefore, its influence, had been much diminished.

Gone, too, were the Welsh, returned to their beloved Valleys; no more mechanized mayhem on the City's streets.

"There is much to be done," the Boss had concluded.

"And I don't just mean the washing-up!"

CHAPTER EIGHT:
THE HILLMAN IMP ATTACK BRIGADE

The Boy's emaciated condition was the cause of much conjecture in the college. He greeted the rumours of his incarceration in a Spanish jail with a wry smile. His must have been the darkest 'prison pallor' in the world! As usual, the gossips preferred the 'truth' of their imaginations to the reality of the facts.

Times had changed. The romanticism of the 'Sixties' was fast yielding to the pragmatism of the 'Seventies'. The motives of the student body seemed more self-serving and much less idealistic. The War had ceased to be the 'flavour' of the day. However, it was not long before the Federation found another 'cause' worthy of its support.

News of the proposed demonstration was greeted with dismay, not only by 'activists' within the Union. Even Tristan and his Conservative group voiced their disquiet that the ogres of the Right planned to stage a rally at the very entrance to the college. Now, the Federation was given another chance to champion the student body. Its members campaigned for direct action; barricade the streets, a counter-demonstration, at least a 'sit-in'.

In the absence of Big Dave, deference given to the 'first fifteen,' the Boss winkled out the Read from his refuge under the stairs. For the first time, the Boy saw that the twenty-four hour scholar actually owned a pair of legs! Thus, the foursome was completed.

Earlier, that day, they had collected the posters, clandestinely hidden in the Federation's 'drop zone;' the college toilets. The Boss had 'liberated' two buckets from the caretaker's cupboard, brushes from the new Art College. Mr. Ormskirk had been dispatched to buy flour. They mixed flour and water to a paste in the buckets and waited until nightfall.

In greatcoat and gauntlets, face and head hidden by college scarf and crash helmet, Mr. Ormskirk mounted his trusty motorcycle. He headed for the City centre, closely followed by the Hillman. On the back seat of the car, the Boy and the Read clutched buckets and brushes. The pile of posters was heaped ready between them.

For the next, three hours, they toured the City; the two passengers bundling out to give every virgin wall, door, pillar and post a dollop of paste and its very own message. Mr. Ormskirk acted as outrider, scouting the movements of police and traffic. He would make an appearance, every fifteen minutes, to present his shouted report. Without dismounting from the motorcycle, he would wave his arms wildly in the direction of their hunters, signalling the safest route for them to follow. Then, he would disappear into the night. At last, the supply of posters was exhausted and the Boss turned the Hillman 'back to base.'

As they passed the police station, they saw the uniformed figure come sprinting from its floodlit entrance. Minutes' later, the flashing, blue light of the panda car brought them to a halt. Slowly and triumphantly, the desk sergeant walked towards the headlights of the Hillman. Leaning into the driver's window, he shined his torch full in the Boss's face.

"My men have been chasing you clowns halfway around the City for the last two hours!"

"What for?" The Boy protested.

The torch played over the two figures seated on the back seat of the car. The passengers glowed, white in the bright light, covered from head to toe in thick paste.

"Come on! Out!" The sergeant ordered, ignoring the protestations of innocence.

"This is a very serious offence!"

The Boy squinted at the sergeant in the harsh light of the interview room.

"What? Flyerposting?

"Yes. You could go to prison for this!"

"You must be joking!" The Boy said, staring with disbelief at his interrogator.

The sergeant carried on quickly, as if to disguise the transparency of his ploy.

"Where did you get those posters?"

"Who finances the Organisation?"

"Is there a cellar where you live?"

The questions blurred into one, long sentence as the policeman unfolded his fantasy of the anarchists plotting the downfall of society, printing posters by the thousand on a 'press hidden in the bowels of the Earth. Until, finally;

"We will have to search the premises."

As the Boss, his two, ghostly companions and their police escorts entered the house, the exaggerated sound of Mr. Ormskirk's snores echoed from above. Of course, in the cellar of the house, there was nothing to be found.

Much to the exasperation of the Federation, the Union finally decided to take no direct action, only to boycott the rally.

As if, to ignore its presence would deny the existence of its threat.

CHAPTER NINE: THE SEEDS OF DOUBT.

Another 'Cause' had been recognised. Apartheid had to be fought.

Even so, on that day, there were only two coaches travelling south to the Capital. A different set of fresh faces, band of innocents to confront the cynical forces of Law and Order, had crowded onto the 'buses with the 'Veterans' of the Federation. The journey was all too familiar. Anecdotes and stories of former 'victories' were told, anthems sung to keep high spirits.

When they arrived, the demonstration was in full swing. This time, there were few, black banners and no 'little, red books' to be seen. The crowd, although animated, allowed itself to be controlled and shepherded by the police lines. Reserves dressed in riot gear waited, hidden in vans in the side streets at the approaches to the Square. Chants and shouts raised in complaint as the lines squeezed tighter. Only a few dared resist the advancing cordons of police. Not until the crush became too great, did the crowd finally retaliate against the lines of linked arms. Pushes became shoves; shoves, punches and kicks. Anger and panic grew within the blue stranglehold.

Suddenly, the chain of linked arms was broken. Three hundred demonstrators burst through the police lines like water gushing from a ruptured main. Reinforcements rushed to plug the gap, too late to contain the escaping phalanx of demonstrators. The small army surged unopposed, through the Square. The Boy ran with the lead; black flag flying overhead. As they neared the Embassy, he saw that its windows were empty, unlit. The building was completely deserted. It was at their mercy!

A lone policeman, his motorcycle broadside across the road, was their only obstacle, only barrier to their goal. Frantically, he shouted into the handset of his radio as the mob surged towards him. Elated, the Boy sprinted onwards, flag flying, eyes fixed on his target. It was several seconds before he realised that he ran alone.

He stopped, stranded between the police motorcyclist and the now, hesitant mob. The black flag flopped lifelessly around him.

He felt confused, almost embarrassed as he trotted back to rejoin the shuffling ranks of demonstrators. Why had they stopped?

The answer came, seconds later, when a score of police vans emerged from the side streets. Their doors flew open and the officers poured out, linking arms to form a chain, the breadth of the road. Only then, did the crowd advance, pushing and jostling against the newly formed cordon. The Boy walked away.

Alone, on the back seat of the empty 'bus, he sat; the black flag furled at his side.

CHAPTER TEN: THE RETURN OF THE MADMAN.

The Boy opened the door of the small, terraced house as the tune of 'Colonel Bogey' sounded, ever louder, outside in the street.

At kerbside, Gross beamed up at him from the open window of the little Morgan sports car. Denim jacket had been replaced by expensive sheepskin coat, denim shirt by white collar and tie. Dark sunglasses hid the bright, blue eyes. A chequered, flat cap and moleskin gloves provided the finishing touches to the mad Welshman's new image.

"What do you think, Large?"

Climbing out from behind the steering wheel, he pumped the Boy's hand.

"Where's the Boss? See? I've brought somebody to see him!"

"He's not here. He's at college. There's only me..... and the Read, of course."

"Give me a hand, then," Gross said, walking around to the far side of the car where his silent passenger waited.

"We've spent all morning, riding around Swansea, window shopping. He's a much better passenger that the Yeti. See? None of that screaming and wrestling when I'm trying to drive!! He never made a sound, coming through the Valleys!

The passenger was dressed in identical fashion to the driver; sheepskin, flat cap, white collar and tie. Dark sunglasses hid the bright, blue eyes. But they were dead!

"Don't stand there gawking!" The Welsh lunatic laughed.

"Lend me a hand. See?"
Together, they pulled the passenger's corpse from the car and dragged it into the house.

"Seems a shame to eat him! We're almost friends. See? Aren't we, Percy? I've got a job in this research laboratory. See?" The madman explained.

"The meat's alright. See? Take my word for it. You can see, it's fresh!"

"I bet!! You can have the first chop!" The Boy laughed.
The meat was 'alright' and for the next month, the Boss and his lodgers ate pork at every meal; bacon for breakfast, chops for lunch and loin for dinner!

"Come on, I'll give you a lift to the college. See? We'll find the Boss. See?"
However, the Boss's cooking had already taken its toll on the Boy's waistline. As the 'car pulled away from the kerb, the exhaust pipe rattled and scraped, sending sparks shooting across the tarmac.

"You're too heavy. You'll have to get out. She won't carry the both of us. See? I'll meet you in the bar. See?"

As the car roared down the street, stray children, cats and dogs ran for their lives. Gratefully, the Boy began the long walk into the City.

In the new, union bar the Boss and Gross talked of old times while they sipped beer from pint glasses. Eventually, the Boy arrived and joined them at their table, drinking lemonade from the bottle.

"Still not drinking, Large?" Gross quizzed.

"Yeah. No alcohol."

"I don't know. What's the matter with you? See? Have you turned Methodist?!"

"Something like that," the Boy laughed.

The conversation was interrupted when another student, wearing jeans and striped rugby shirt, stopped at their table.

"Hello, Gross. What are you doing here? I thought that you had left college? See?"

"I'm up here, working. See?"

"We're a man short for the second fifteen. See? Do you fancy a game?"

"Wouldn't say no."

"I've got some spare kit that you can borrow. See? The 'bus leaves in half an hour."

Half an hour later, the Boss, the Boy and their Welsh friend boarded the 'bus.

They waited while Gross changed his clothes for the borrowed rugby strip. Together, they followed as the teams click-clacked their way towards the rugby pitches. Soon, the large group of players, officials and spectators was strung out along the country lane.

In a field opposite the rugby pitches, a large marquee had been erected. It was surrounded by a number of lorries and Land Rovers. Strung between the poles of the tent was a white banner. In bold, red letters, it proclaimed;

"EURO-PIG SHOW."

As the three friends came in sight of the rugby posts and the improbable advertisement, Gross let out a gasp of surprise.

"Oh, no!" He said.

Crouching over, with the Boy and the Boss for a shield, he scurried past the tent.

"Don't let them see me!" He pleaded.

"If they do, I'm a dead man. I should be over there. See? They've got a stand especially for me and poor, old Percy. He's one of the stars of the show!!"

All was forgotten when the speeding Welshman sprinted across the try-line for the third time.

CHAPTER ELEVEN: FAIR WARNING.

Alan's response to the Boy's arrest had been one of criticism.

"What do you think, you're playing at? You could have been thrown out of college. Luckily for you, the police aren't pursuing the matter. The Principal is furious but has decided to take no further action."

"That seems to be the norm, around here."

"I sympathize with your motives but you can't go around, breaking the law."

"Flyerposting is nothing compared to what these people do."

"Two wrongs don't make a right."

"Don't they?"

"You know that they don't, Boy."

"There's one thing more," Alan said.

"What's that?"

"It's about Mick."

"Mick?"

The Boy could not hide his surprise at the mention of the name.

"Yes, Mick. You know that he's going to fail his final examinations, this year?"

"I don't know anything about it. What's that to do with me?"

"I was hoping that you'd have a word with him. He's in a pretty bad way."

"Why me? I haven't spoken to him for nearly three years!"

"For some reason, he seems to think that you're his best friend, his only friend in the college!"

"Alan, he hasn't a single friend in the college, least of all, me. Nobody likes him. I can't stand the sight of him. He's an arrogant, tight-fisted….."

"O.K., O.K. I get the picture. Let's get back to your case. For the last time, listen. Keep out of trouble. You've had a great opportunity handed to you. Don't blow it!"

"I'm listening," the Boy said, Again.

CHAPTER TWELVE:
THE RETURN OF THE POLITICIAN.

The news of the Politician's return was greeted with cheers from Tristan and entourage, dismay from the depleted membership of the Federation. As usual, they campaigned for action from the Union; a sit-in, demonstration, at least a boycott of the official opening of the new Art College. Tristan and his Conservative group held sway and once again, the Union decided to take no action.

The Politician's notoriety had been little diminished so the Federation decided to mount a demonstration without the support of the Union. Two hundred students had rallied to the call. They crowded into the bar for its unobstructed view, across the dual carriageway, of the Art College.

Rugby songs and socialist anthems merged into one with every round of drinks that they consumed. Meanwhile, the Boss and the Boy waited, sitting apart from the revelling 'revolutionaries.' As the time ticked by, the reasons for their gathering seemed almost forgotten by the half-drunken students. Then, the cry went up,

"Here he comes!"

A black limousine came to a halt on the opposite side of the infamous ring road. Two men emerged from the rear doors of the 'car. The first, a police officer of high rank, wore blue hat and uniform, their colour, deep contrast with the wealth of gold braid and ribbons at his shoulder and breast. Behind him, the Politician, dark and immaculate, wore a suit and overcoat. His hair and moustache were their normal, groomed perfection. The two men began to climb the steps that led into the entrance of the Art College.

"After him!"

The small army of students streamed out of the bar, onto the ring road, bringing the traffic to a screeching stop. Chanting at the top of their voices, they vaulted the crash barriers in the central reservation, now bringing the traffic on the other side of the dual carriageway to a halt.

As he reached the entrance to the Art College, their quarry turned. Ice-grey eyes swept slowly over the faces of the mob, as if to fix each individual in his mind. His cold stare had brought silence to their lips as surely as the steel blade of a guillotine.

The leading students stood, rooted at the foot of the stone steps, their progress halted by some invisible barrier. There was one, final look of utter disdain. Then, like a bullfighter in the face of a beaten bull, he turned his back on the crowd. Slowly and proudly, he followed his escort into the Art College.

From the comfort of the Union Bar, the Boss and the Boy watched as the dissolute band of students made their way back, across the ring road. This time, the traffic failed to slow down, splitting them into small, disconsolate groups, like a defeated army in flight from the battlefield. But there had been no battle fought. It had been nought but a sham.

The game was up, exposed for what it was; only a game. The Boy determined that such weakness would never prevent the pursuit of his Truth, never shake his faith in the Cause, even though, at the college, the Cause was lost.

He little knew that his 'Truth' did not lie within the Cause. The Cause was merely a symbol of something deep inside him.

THE A.G.M.

He waited to wreak his vengeance on the meeting.
In the tradition of the Federation, he berated the Union executive at every possible opportunity. He contested their every statement, their very word. 'Point of order!' was followed by 'Point of order!', votes of 'No confidence' by resignations. None could stand against his cold logic and wicked wit. The President and Executive were forced to step down from the stage, victims of the very rules that they had sought to uphold.

Testimony to their rout were the eight, empty chairs lined behind the table in the centre of the stage.

Subtle and servile subversive, Tristan, alone, remained in the spotlights.

CHAPTER THIRTEEN: RAG WEEK.

The lunatic Welshman was to make one, final appearance at the house. Intent on alcoholic chaos, he had arrived for the beginning of the annual 'Rag Week.'

Apart from a few, minor bumps and scrapes, the little sports car seemed remarkably unscathed. Gross, himself, had dressed for the occasion, reverting to the old denim uniform of his student days. It now bulged tight with muscles bloated from his mother's cooking and his full-time commitment to the rugby pitch. Only, the flat cap remained, perverse reminder of its owner's former status in the world of employment!

The Boss hurried to open the front door as the notes of 'Colonel Bogey' blasted, outside in the street.

"Stop that infernal noise, you great buffoon," he called, voice drowned by the deafening sound from the car horn.

"What's that? I can't hear you!" was Gross's shouted reply.

Sitting next to him, his passenger stared straight ahead, eyes fixed on an invisible road. His face had drained of all colour. His hands, knuckles white, clutched at the armrests of the car seat. Despite the car heater and his uniform of purple fur, he was shivering. Beads of cold sweat drained from beneath the purple hat that he wore. Slowly, lest his legs betray him, the

Yeti hauled himself from the passenger seat. Turning to the driver, he shouted into the car, his words drowned by the noise of the horn.

"You rotten, rotten bastard!" His silent lips mouthed.

"I won't tell you, again. Stop that confounded noise," the Boss screamed at the smiling miscreant.

Reaching in through the car window, he grabbed Gross by the ear and twisted. The sound of the horn ceased in an instant.

"What have you done to the Yeti, you great ape?"

"We had a little incident coming through the Valleys. See?" The madman laughed as the Boss's finger and thumb pinched even tighter.

"Little incident?!!" The Yeti screamed over the noise of the now silenced horn.

"One of the wheels went over the edge!!"

"Come, lunatic," the Boss said.

Without further ceremony, the little mahout pulled the delinquent driver from the car and with a firm grip on his ear, marched him into the house.

Inside the house, the Boss, the Boy and the two Welshmen gathered around the Read's cupboard. After prolonged and intense discussion, the five friends hatched their plot.

"I've got a spare kit in the car," the Welsh madman had volunteered.

The Union Bar was full. Most of the students wore shorts and running shoes, vests or 'T' shirts. They had formed up in pairs; right leg tied to partner's left, ready for the three-legged race. In a corner of the bar, Tristan and entourage sipped from their glasses of lager. They laughed loudly at their own facile jokes as they watched the antics of their perceived inferiors.

"Alright, Boyo!"

Gross had marched straight up to the group of suited spectators. Tristan turned, glass in hand.

"Oh, hello, er…..I thought that you had left college."

"I have, Boyo," Gross leered.

"But now, I'm back! See?"

The giant Welshman eyed his quarry, up and down.

"Aren't you going in the race? What's the matter with you, Boyo? You're the entertainments' officer, aren't you? You should set an example. See?"

"I hadn't planned on entering….."

"No sweat. See? We'll soon sort that out, Boyo!"

"But I haven't got a tracksuit or any other kit to……"

"You can borrow my kit. See? I've got it here with me, Boyo. Here, take it!"

Gross thrust the bundle of clothing into Tristan's chest.

"But I haven't got a partner to run with….."

"I'll go with you! See?"

"Now, you haven't got any kit."

"I don't need any, Boyo. I can run O.K. in denim. Especially, when there's free beer! See?"

Thus, Tristan was shamed and cajoled into entering the three-legged pub crawl; half a pint of beer to be drunk in each of a dozen public houses on a three-mile run around the City centre. Strictly no vomiting allowed!!

Tristan reappeared in the bar, dressed in the borrowed sports kit. The only items that fitted him were the plimsoles. Shorts and shirt, three sizes too large, hung from his body like the clothes of a scarecrow. As the Yeti bound his ankle to Gross' with the Welsh equivalent of the Gordian knot, Tristan's forced, jolly laughter vied with the shouted jokes of the other competitors. Here, the proof that he, too, could be a 'Man of the People.'

They all lined up, hands on knees, on their marks. One blast from a whistle and they were away, off and running to the first public house. Gross and Tristan were the first pair to reach the corner of the college building. Gross had powered away from the 'start' line like an olympic sprinter, his victim flapping at his side like a broken marionette. As they rounded the corner,

Tristan looked back, terror on his face. He made one, last, desperate grab at the brickwork before he was dragged out of sight, mouth working wildly, words lost in the distance.

"What did he say, Boyo?" The Yeti asked.

"Something like; 'Please, God, save me!'" The Boss conjectured dryly.

After three quarters of an hour, the first of the runners returned. Two at a time, they rounded the corner. Bloodied knees and elbows bore painful testimony to the hazards of drinking beer and running at the same time. Staggering along, they crossed the 'finish' line in exhausted disorder. Much to the shouted delight and encouragement of the spectators, several disgorged both beer and breakfast as they crossed the line. However, of the Welsh lunatic and his prey, there was no sign.

"If he thinks I'm waiting for one minute longer, he's got another think coming!" The Boss grumbled as he paced up and down on the pavement at the 'finish' line.

"It's half an hour since the race ended and it's getting dark. I want my dinner!"
Just then, the last, two competitors appeared around the corner.

Gross staggered along, his face flushed crimson from the combined effects of effort and alcohol. Head down, the corpse-like figure clutched to his hip followed his every step; unfettered leg trailing behind on the pavement.

"He couldn't run if his arse was on fire!" The madman gasped as they came within earshot.

"So, we took our time and had a pint in every pub! See? Slow but sure. See? Wins the race. See? We could have still won, too. If only he hadn't thrown his guts up, in the bar of the Red Lion!!"

Gross stood before them, his face bathed in sweat. Steam rose from his head and shoulders, drifting up into the yellow light from the street lamps. The semi-conscious body of the entertainments' officer hung, slumped at his side. He smiled victoriously, his teeth white in the semi-darkness,

"Got him!!"

He looked down at the knot that had guaranteed Tristan's completion of the race.

"Who's got a knife?"

But his three friends had run off, screaming and laughing into the college, leaving him alone with his victim.

Mr. Ormskirk was absent for the next few days; cold, Yorkshire moors preferred to the unbridled exuberance of 'Rag Week.' The Welsh had therefore commandeered his bedroom. As the Boy opened the door and stepped inside the darkened room, tin cans cracked beneath his feet.

"Just like old times," he thought.

"Come on, you lot. Breakfast's ready. Rise and shine!"

"Leave us alone. We're dying!!"

"Yes, just like old times!" The Boy thought as he poured the dregs from one of the discarded beer cans into the bed.

"Bastard! I'll get you for this, Large", the Yeti spluttered under the stream of cold, stale beer.

"Take it back!" The Boy said, the can in his hand poised above the Yeti's head.

"Come on! The walk starts soon. Boss has entered the both of you! For your sins!" The Boy laughed.

In the kitchen, Gross and the Yeti sipped gingerly from their mugs of hot, black coffee and watched as Big Dave wolfed down his breakfast.

"Do you want that sausage, Gross?" He asked.

"Noooo!! Take it, Boyo!"

Big Dave reached over with his fork and daintily speared the sausage from the untouched breakfast on Gross's plate.

"Aren't you hungry, Yeti? You haven't eaten a thing! Do you want that egg?"

As Big Dave speared the fried egg from the Yeti's plate, yellow yolk spurted across the table. The Yeti sprang to his feet, chair clattering down behind him. He ran from the room, hand clamped across his mouth.

"Guess not!" Big Dave said as he pulled the Yeti's plate across the table.

"How about you, Gross? Can I have yours, too?"
The question was moot. Gross was already on his way through the back yard, to elbow the wretching Yeti away from the outside toilet.

"Yes. Just like old times!" The Boy thought.

"See you, gentlemen," the Read said from the entrance to his cupboard as the five friends trooped out of the house. As they made their way towards the parked cars, the reluctant charity walkers lagged behind them.

"Come along! Keep up, you two, useless, drunken fools! You'll have to walk faster than that!" The Boss chided.

"I'll come in the car with you and Large. It'll save petrol! See? " Big Dave said, giving Gross a prolonged and meaningful stare.

In stately fashion, the Hillman and the Morgan paraded through the City streets to the college; 'Colonel Bogey' announcing every belle that they passed.

The Boss, the Boy and Big Dave watched the large crowd of charity walkers disappear into the distance.

"They're not fit! See? They'll never make it! See?" Big Dave said gleefully.

He was wrong.

At first, Gross and the Yeti had kept apace of the leading walkers, the brisk exercise and cool, spring air clearing their throbbing headaches, enervating tired bodies. After an hour of walking, Gross began to slow the pace. The pub' race and the previous four miles' walking had finally taken their toll on the giant Welshman's physique. Not, however, in a way that one might expect.

"What's the matter, Boyo?" The Yeti asked.

"I'm not wearing any underpants. See? These jeans are too tight for me, now. They're chaffing the skin off me! See? I'll have to stop walking. I'm that sore! See? I can't go any further, Boyo!!"

The crowd tarried, even though the winners had long since passed the 'finish' line. For the second time in a week, the lunatic Welshman would be last in a race!

Whispered confirmation had been given by the stragglers in the field as they completed the course. Each, latest report was greeted with peals of laughter and shouts of glee from the waiting students. In the distance, they could see that the larger of the two figures was limping.

As Gross and the Yeti crossed the 'finish' line, Gross held his arms aloft in triumph. The waiting crowd of students cheered and wolf-whistled.   Some even rolled about on the pavement, overcome by their own laughter.   Because, from the flies of Gross's jeans hung an improvised 'jock strap'.....

One of the Yeti's purple gloves!

CHAPTER FOURTEEN: MORE 'GOOD ADVICE.'

Alan's tone was more critical than ever.

"I want you to listen to me, Boy. Just this one time, listen to me! This is the chance of a lifetime, a great opportunity. Don't blow it!"

"I've no intention of 'blowing it,' Alan," the Boy said.

"Do yourself a favour. Smarten up your appearance. When you're in the interview, toe the line! Lose the Left-Wing rhetoric. Once you've been accepted on the course, you'll be able to dress as you like, do and say what you want. Please, listen to me, Boy. I have your best interests at heart. You'll find that, in life, sometimes you have to compromise."

"I refuse to compromise my ideals."

"I'm not asking you to do that. I'm only saying that, sometimes in life, you have to be pragmatic to get what you want. Live to fight another day, as it were. Are you listening?"

"I'm listening, Alan," the Boy answered.

Alan stood from behind his desk to shake the Boy's hand.

"I have enjoyed our time together. I have found our 'little debates' very stimulating, very challenging. I wish you, the very best of luck for the future."

The Boy shook his mentor by the hand.

He had just been given the greatest accolade of his entire life.

CHAPTER FIFTEEN: CLOTHES MAKETH THE MAN.

The college was empty. Students, friends and colleagues had departed in search of employment or adventure. The only lodger to remain "chez Boss" was the Boy, now the proud doyen of his very own bedroom. It would be several months' before the interview so he had found work on one of the many building sites that now flanked the ring road.

The site was manned by past masters of the art of the shovel. On the shovel, they cooked breakfast; eggs and bacon sizzling on its bright blade above a flaming brazier. On the shovel, they leaned while they debated the likely result of the 3.30 at Newmarket. On two shovels, mini stilts beneath their Wellington boots, they would race the length of the building site, hopping and striding through the bricks and steelwork. The shovel was used for everything but shovelling. There was one exception to this rule. That was when the foreman made a rare appearance. Then, backs would bend, shovels become a blur of movement as the liquid concrete flowed around the steel skeleton of the building.

His muscles, long unused to physical labour, stiffened and ached, but the work was as nothing compared to the backbreaking fields of his childhood and adolescence. Still, his strength returned with the labour. Bored with his failed attempts at 'shovel walking,' he threw himself into the work, searching out extra tasks while the other labourers stood idle. Fired by the vitality of his youth, he chomped on the bit of this physical exertion, like a racehorse in full flight. It did not matter, how hard he worked. He treated every day as a mere physical workout. For his fellows, the job was a life sentence, not a game. They had another summer and two more winters to endure before the building would be completed. Then, they would take up their shovels and move on, to the next 'site. It came as no surprise to him when, one morning, the foreman called him into his office to 'give him his cards.'

It did not matter. He had already saved more money than he needed.

He could hardly recognize his own image reflected in the full-length mirror of the 'gentlemen's outfitters,'

His hair was cropped short, face and neck shaved of all stubble. He was dressed after the fashion of the day. Button-down collar with tie peeked from between the lapels of the three-quarter length, dark-blue overcoat. Light-grey trousers reflected in the high gloss polish of his black brogues. A neatly folded, red handkerchief protruded from the breast pocket of the 'Crombie;'last vestige of the rebel and the finishing touch to his second-ever, new set of clothes.

"What do you think?" He asked the Boss, turning, this way then that way, in front of the mirror.

"You look like a bloody skinhead," the Boss groused.

"Don't be so daft, Boss," he said, once more turning to inspect the new clothes.

"Like a bloody skinhead," the Boss repeated as they walked out through the shop doorway.

CHAPTER SIXTEEN: THE QUESTION.

The Boy sat, passenger in the Hillman, while the Boss drove southwards. After a few miles, the dark skies of the industrial heartland gave way to clear blue, the factories and blackened chimney stacks to lush green. Trees and hedgerows lined the twists and turns of the road.

On the university car park, the Boss shook him by the hand.

"Well, off you go, you great buffoon. I suppose that 'good luck!' is the order of the day?"

"Good luck? What's that?"

"I'll see you, back here at six o'clock. I'm going to grab a bite and a beer."

"See you, later, Boss."

He walked through the glass doors that opened into the giant, red-bricked building. The hall porter directed him to a waiting-room away from the main lobby. He was early. He sat and waited. The smell of floor polish, mingled with that of his new clothes, was stifling in the small room. Muffled voices came from behind a door in the far corner. It opened and a youth with long hair and rimless spectacles emerged. Shortly afterwards, a middle-aged woman in grey dress-suit and frilled blouse came to the door and bid him enter, calling him by name.

The size of the room was surprising, almost intimidating. He had expected something not quite so large, something more intimate. At the far end of the room, five, middle-aged men sat behind a table. Sunlight from the large, plate-glass window at their backs outlined them in dark silhouette. Files and folders were piled, open in front of them on the polished tabletop. A single, high-backed chair had been placed opposite them. It seemed as if it were a mile away in the distance.

The leather soles of the brogues echoed loudly as he walked towards the table. He had not felt so intimidated since the time, he made that long walk to the headmaster's table. As he drew closer, he could see the faces of the professors. One, he recognized from his picture on the dust jacket of a reference book; definitive work in its field. There was a long pause while he stood under the scrutiny of the five-man board. Only the tick-tock of a clock, hidden somewhere in the far corners of the room, broke the deathly silence. At long last; one of the professors spoke.

"Please, sit down," he said.

The interview proceeded. Its content had been covered many times by his studies at home and abroad. Then, the Professor, himself, acknowledged guru of modern, Spanish history, spoke.

"I read your work with great interest. I would like to ask only one more question. What resistance is there to Franco?"

CHAPTER SEVENTEEN: THE RIGHT ANSWER.

The clock tick-tocked loudly the long seconds while he considered his answer.

The question had been totally unexpected. It was beyond the scope of his past and projected studies. It was vague and imprecise, at odds with the detailed interview that had preceded it. What had the Professor meant, exactly, by the word 'resistance?'

Did he refer to the terrorists of the north? Their futile campaign with bomb and bullet brought only premature replacement of general by colonel; Guardia by new recruit. Again, they sought to repeat the mistakes of the past, divided the people.

And the measure of their success? A public word, spoken in Basque, would cost a life.

What use, the miners who bared their chests to the bullets of the Guardia? Theirs was no clarion call to arms, only censored, whispered martyrdom.

What use, a People alone, unaided against such monstrous tyranny? There would be no more 'support' from communist Russia, least of all from the United States, there, in N.A.T.O.'s backyard.   Gone, the age of the International Brigades.

He thought of those who HAD resisted; of Don Isidro, the old tailor, screaming the terror of his nightmares, of Uncle Sidney, alone in the cold waters of the canal.

He thought of the two beautiful sisters and the relentless goose-step of El Caudillo's dark legions.

But, his memory of the solitary battle-tank; grim, metallic symbol of Franco's power, unchallenged doyen of a deserted Plaza de España, dominated all others. The shock of its appearance, steel blasphemy in the beautiful, sun-lit square, had never left him.

Would that he could leap from his chair, punch the air with clenched fist. Proclaim the imminent Revolution, the Rise of the Spanish People. Lend to them an ambition that no longer existed.

He knew that they only waited; victims of Franco's Past, prisoners of his Present.

Alas, in Spain there was no 'resistance' lurking, simmering beneath the surface of everyday life, ready to oust the hated dictator, wrest the reins of power from his evil grasp.

All that lurked was cold, deliberate, institutionalized terror.

What use, resistance with no hope of victory? That had already cost the flower of one generation. Only Death could finally release Franco's grip on that betrayed and abandoned Nation. Franco's Death was their only hope for the future.

So, the Boy answered, not from the heart but from the mind. When he spoke, his words were free of all rhetoric, his thoughts pragmatic; Alan's proud and honest student at last.

"While Franco lives, there can be no resistance."

In the silence of the room, the clock tick-tocked loudly the long seconds into the rest of his life.

CHAPTER EIGHTEEN: THE WRONG ANSWER.

The sound of the envelope, dropping through the letter box onto the bare floorboards, resounded through the house.

The Boy rushed from the breakfast table to gather up the brown envelope. Feverishly, he ripped at the thin paper, pulling the typed sheet from within. He read.

"Dear Sir,

With regards our interview of the fifteenth of August.

We are sorry to inform you that at this moment in time we are unable to offer you.........."

He crumpled the letter into a little ball in his hand, crushing it until his fingernails bit into his palm. He threw the paper and envelope to the floor. His head was throbbing, his heart, thumping. All his plans were ruined. His only ambition, to teach like Alan, had evaporated into nothing; dust in the wind.

Failure was a bitter pill for him to swallow. He had worked so hard for so long. How could he have done more? What would he tell his father? He would be devastated.

"Your breakfast's getting cold. What are you up to, in there?" The Boss's voice called from the adjoining room.

When he rejoined the little fellow at the table, he had finally managed to compose himself.

"I got my answer, Boss. They turned me down."

"Bloody nincompoops," the Boss said without pausing from his eating.

"That's their loss," he continued, talking through a mouthful of baked beans.

"Yeah, bloody nincompoops. That's their loss," the Boy repeated bitterly.

He felt lost, devastated by this, his latest rejection.

CHAPTER NINETEEN: FRIENDS IN HIGH PLACES.

His hard-earned savings were gone; wasted on the new clothes, depleted by the demands of food and lodgings. He had lost his job on the building site. Now, a strike by the threatened construction union ensured that there would be no more work. He found himself penniless, living off the Boss's charity. He would have to register as unemployed.

He entered the new glass and concrete building; spawn of the ring road. After a short telephone conversation, the woman at the reception desk directed him towards one of the many doors that lined the interior of the building. On its front, a plastic sign announced "Manager" in plain, black lettering. He knocked the door and entered.

On the other side of the paper-laden desk, the manager peered up at him from behind his heavy, plastic-framed spectacles. His hair was styled, cut short; gone, long hair and mutton chop whiskers, gone, combat jacket and football scarf; all replaced by the dark, three-piece uniform of the Civil Service. Of course, this new disguise had not fooled the Boy.

"How are you getting on? Take a seat. How can I help you, Boy?" The Leader smiled.

He walked out of the unemployment centre and up the hill towards the City square. He had arranged to meet the Boss there for a 'lift' back to the house.

For once, the sun seemed to have broken through the blanket of cloud. Its watery disc shined down in a pale imitation of summer. It could do nothing to diminish the feelings of hopelessness and exasperation that he felt.

Ahead of him, a voice called out from the crowd of bustling pedestrians. He looked out across the square but could see nobody that he recognized. He carried on his way.

"Boy! Boy! Wait!" The voice repeated.

He turned to see Henry, one of the college lecturers, come striding, breathlessly, towards him. Tall and gangly, he was well-liked by his students for his liberal attitudes and respected by all for his dedication to teaching. His long, black beard and equally long face gave him every appearance of a soulful rabbi.

"How are you doing, Boy?"

"I've just been to see about a job."

"Good! That's great! What did you get?"

"Roadsweeper," the Boy said, showing Henry the white card in his hand.

He saw Henry's face sag, jaw half open. He seemed shocked and saddened by the news.

"Listen," he said, "if it's of any consolation, all the staff at the college think that you got a raw deal. I'd like to say, personally, how sorry I am."

"What do you mean? Raw deal? Sorry? What are you talking about, Henry?"

"Didn't you know? Alan was so upset at your being turned down, that he wrote to the university and asked the reasons for your rejection."

"What? I wasn't good enough. I didn't make the grade."

"That's not what Alan thinks," Henry said.

"They wrote in answer to his letter. The consensus of the interview board was that you are too Right Wing for their University! It's a Socialist stronghold in both staff-room and Students' Union. They said that you would not 'fit in' with the course.

"What?!!"

"Calm down, Boy. It's not your fault."

"What?!!!"

He felt the anger rising in his voice, his father's red rage boiling in his veins. He turned away, lest it explode upon somebody who cared. On legs like jelly, he turned and walked from the square; forgotten, his rendez-vous with the Boss, forgotten, the work application in his hand.

Safely contained inside the house, his frustration erupted with animal power

After a while the anger abated. The turmoil in his mind calmed. He collected his thoughts. These, his thoughts, were clear and logical.

"Who were these men to so judge him? Could he have been happy, accepted by such closed minds? What did his political persuasions have to do with his standards of education? Had he been the 'skinhead', the 'Fascist' of their libel, could he have only brought further dimension to their thought, hated as it might be?"

"Morally and intellectually, they could not equal Alan's guidance. He could never have subscribed to the circle of these Armchair Socialists."

Oh, how easily are the sacrifices of others expected from those without danger, are wistful fantasies born of dogmatic daydreamers safe in their protected world. Yet again, he had been judged for his appearance. Yet again, had the Shadows of Prejudice tainted his life.

"Where have you been, you great buffoon? I waited for nearly an hour!"

"Whatever have you done to the door? It's matchwood!!"

The Boss's voice had brought him back to reality.

"I lost my temper but I'm alright , now," he said quietly, looking down at his bloodied hands.

His mind felt cold, his heart, empty.

EPILOGUE

VINDICATION, FOOD FOR THOUGHT, OR MERE IRONY?

Following the conclusion of my third sortie into the world of literature, my wife and I decided to take a well-earned break and a holiday in the Canary Islands.

Rested and refreshed by a fortnight of sun, sea and sand, we idled in the airport at Fuerteventura, whilst we awaited the departure of our homeward flight. In one of the many shops within the airport, I perused the shelves with their rows upon rows of books. I had thought to choose one to read on board the aircraft; something in Spanish to continue my renewed interest in the language. I stood for some time, amazed, rooted to the spot, almost paralysed on sight of one of the paperbacks. It was not its title that had caught my attention, but the name of its author. There, in bold type was printed the name of the professor of history: mistaken and misinformed inquisitor from my interview at the university!

Forty, long years had passed since a day when his perverse and biased resolution had served to affect such a radical change in the direction that my life would take.

I stood for some time more, staring at that name emblazoned on the spine of the book. With shaking hand, I pulled book from shelf. I turned the first page, intent on verifying the timely death of my nemesis. I guessed him to be a long time passed from this earth. Much to my disappointment, I found that the book was in fact a first edition, only recently printed.

"Look at this!" I almost shouted, holding the book aloft for my wife to see. "That bastard is still alive!"
I returned the tome to its place on the bookshelf with a vigour that was of more force than necessary, and a stream of profanity that was not.

"Well, that's one book that I won't be buying," was more or less the gist of my outburst.

The completion of this, MY first book, had prompted me to renew the acquaintance of Henry, my former lecturer. Now a professor in his own right, he had recently retired from his position as a Head of Department. His time spent in the education system had seen the former technical college and polytechnic of my era blossom into one of the largest of our "new" universities. I found him to be as considered and erudite as ever before. As former student and lecturer, we established a friendship of which I am duly proud. We have reinforced this friendship by a series of gastronomic adventures (dinners!), accompanied by our respective wives.

Recently returned from the aforementioned holiday, we met Henry and wife at a local restaurant for one of these periodic encounters. By this time, the anger evoked by my visit to the bookshop had subsided. Maturity from one's passing years allows a calmer consideration and an acceptance of life's vagaries. Seated around the dinner table, we four engaged in idle conversation, while we waited to be served.

"When we were on holiday, I came across an old acquaintance of mine," I casually informed Henry.

"Who would that be?" he asked.

I recounted the episode at the airport.

"I would have thought him to be dead by now. He should be well into his eighties," Henry said.

"The book was published eighteen months ago. He seems to be very much alive."

"Let's see," Henry said, producing a mobile telephone from his jacket pocket.

The waiter appeared, carrying the first courses of our meals. Ignoring the plate set before him, Henry began to work at his handset, while the rest of us began to eat our food.

"Ah, here's his bibliography. Yes, you're right. Now, let's have a look at his biography."

Henry's fingers moved rapidly across the touchscreen. Attention fixed on my eating, I ignored him for a few moments, expecting him to read out loud. Yet, it was a few minutes before he finally spoke.

"Oh dear," he said.

I looked up to see him staring fixedly at the screen.

"What does it say, Henry?"

"Nothing, really."

"Come on. What does it say?"

Almost reluctantly, Henry read "aloud" from the screen.

"1972, that was the year of your interview, wasn't it?"

"Yes, Henry."

"1972, he was appointed special advisor to the Tory government!"

"What!"

"Yes, and get this. Eighteen years later, ennobled by Baroness Thatcher, when she retired!"

Returned home, after the end of the evening, I forsook that calmer consideration and acceptance of life's vagaries lent me by the passing years!

"I was right. Bunch of hypocrites! bunch of arseholes!" I ranted.

"You didn't see Henry's face," my wife rejoined. "When he first read that screen, his mouth sagged wide open. His eyes, for a split second, turned black with anger."

My brain overflowed in a torrent of emotion and anger. It raced with conjecture. Had there been a hidden conspiracy to scupper the progress of a prominent activist? I thought of my arrests, of the battles in Grosvenor Square and Manchester. I remembered the ubiquitous cameramen in Trafalgar Square; hounds of the status quo, eyes of the security services. I remembered my many provocative and dissident speeches to the students' union. The staff of that southern university were obviously not as left wing or as radical as they had claimed. Were they?

Had the swing to the right already begun to permeate that seat of learning? Or had their left wing pretensions been no more than that – a mere façade? Or were they truly socialists, alarmed and alienated by the appearance of my "skinhead" persona, wary of fascist incursion? Truly unaware of my political pedigree? I think not. Let posterity be their judge; witness the Shadows of their Prejudice.

Either way, once more I have caught a whiff of society's hypocrisy, have been reminded that to deny knowledge is to deny power.

I feel vindicated for the path that I have followed through life; justified at last for my rebellion, all doubt dispelled.

So, let posterity also be my judge. Hear the Scream.

APPENDIX

(1) P. 80   "Hemos tenido trcinta años de paz........

"We have had thirty year of peace."

Franco's customary opening words to his speeches; a
reminder of the 'stability' brought to Spain by the
overthrow of the Republic and her 'neutral' status.

(2) P. 104   During the Spanish Civil War, Franco
diverted his march on Madrid to relieve the garrison at
Toledo. Loyal to Franco, the defenders had retreated to
the cellars of the Alcazar as the Republican forces
bombarded the building. Franco's propagandists were
quick to hail this as a great victory, final example of his
loyalty to his men.

It was, in fact, just another example of 'el Caudillo's'
overly cautious handling of his rebellion. The besieging
forces of the Alcazar were a much easier target than the
army that manned Madrid's barricades. It was also an
example of a darker side of his strategy.

The delay in his advance on the Capital allowed its
defenders to consolidate their fortifications. This only

served to prolong the fighting during Franco's final assault, ensuring optimum Republican casualties, maximum bloodshed. Notice of his true intent; not only the defeat of his enemies but their total eradication. The Alcazar was reconstructed after the war.

(3) P. 106   Allusion to the death of Jim Hendrix.

(4) P. 106   Dr. Beeching's 'Axe:' Refers to the closure of multiple branch lines by Dr. Beeching, minister of transport, which left many country areas isolated from the English railway network.